Two Wrongs Don't Make a Right

Two Wrongs Don't Make a Right

by
Brenda Hampton

www.urbanbooks.net

Urban Books
1199 Straight Path
West Babylon, NY 11707

ISBN 13: 978-1-60162-028-6
ISBN 10: 1-60162-028-4

First Printing December 2007
Printed in the United States of America

10 9 8 7 6 5 4 3 2 1

Submit Wholesale Orders to:
Kensington Publishing Corp.
C/O Penguin Group (USA) Inc.
Attention: Order Processing
405 Murray Hill Parkway
East Rutherford, NJ 07073-2316
Phone: 1-800-526-0275
Fax: 1-800-227-9604

Acknowledgments

Wow, nine books later, just where do I begin? Of course, I must thank my Heavenly Father for this journey He has chosen for me. It's been more than good and never in my wildest dreams did I expect for my writing career to become what it is today. At times, it's been rough, but I know that my everlasting faith has allowed, and will allow, me to overcome my obstacles and challenges. So, thank you Lord for all that you've done and will continue to do.

Carl Weber, for rescuing me in my time of need, no words can express how grateful I am to you. You've taught me a lot about this business, and even though I struggled with making the right choices with my career, let's just say that I'm glad to be home. Truly, you are an inspiration to me and your kindness will never be forgotten. Too, I must show love to the Urban Books Family who assisted me with bringing this novel alive: Roy Glenn, Arvita Glenn, Martha Weber, the Kensington staff . . . thank you.

Always, to my family: Aaron & Aaron J., Cleveland, Monica Marie, Monique Marie, Joyce Marie, Regina Marie and Jarina Marie, much love and thanks to you all. You've taken this journey with me and I am forever grateful for your support. To my mother and father, Phyllis Marie and Clyde Hampton Jr., even though you've moved on to a better place, I hear those words expressing how proud you are. But in return, I am proud of both of you for being all that you could be as parents, and mom, for raising three daughters as a single parent . . . I commend you for a job well done! Nobody could have done it better than you!

Finally, a more extended thanks to all of my readers. Your support means everything to me, and to the best of my ability, I will continue to release novels that provide you with any and everything you may request from an author . . . bring the heat, I love the passion, a well written story, characters that remind me of myself, sexy men and women, thugs that show love, etc. With that being said, LET THE DRAMA BEGIN . . .

ISAAC

Simply put, I was tremendously discouraged with my wife, and she felt the same way about me. We'd been married for fifteen years, and the last five years had been like living in hell. It wasn't as if we disrespected each other, but I could tell there wasn't much love left between us. Basically, Cydney had gone her way and I'd gone mine. She was doing her thing with whoever she chose to do it with, and I surely was doing mine.

To this day, I don't know where we went wrong, but I didn't have the guts to ask her for a divorce. And, I guess, neither did she. Neither one of us wanted to let down the people in our lives who had so much faith that we'd someday celebrate our silver and gold anniversaries. My parents were still together and so were hers. Yes, they were the perfect examples for us to live by, but it was more than obvious to me that we weren't willing to do what it took to make things work.

At first, marriage was a breeze. We got married right after college, had several good years thereafter, and then, it was downhill from there. Cydney got a job as a senior executive for a major health insurance company and her head swelled. Shortly after, she picked up about ten pounds, and months later, ten more was added to that. Still, she was a beautiful woman, but since I was a man who kept himself in shape, I expected my wife to do the same. Being a police officer, I had to stay fit and trim. Whenever I'd ask Cyd to go to the gym with me, she always made excuses. But when I talked about going to get something to eat, she'd be geared to go. It was little shit like that, that pissed me off.

Surely, I could overlook her weight, but it didn't make much sense to be as thick as she was, especially since we didn't have any kids. For her, kids were out of the question. Not now, not never. After marriage, her whole damn tune changed, but before then, I could have anything I wanted. How many kids, was the question.

Her decision didn't matter to me anyway. My life was fulfilled in so many other ways. As a matter of fact, I had a two-year-old kid that Cyd didn't even know about. I wasn't one hundred percent sure if she was mine; actually I had serious doubts.

My good piece of ass, for the time being was named Laquinta. She was what many would call a "ghetto queen," but at times, that's what I desired to have. A deep, dark sista with mega attitude. Attitude that went well with mine.

I couldn't go one week without seeing Laquinta, and she very well knew it. She also knew that making my wife aware of our relationship would cause much havoc between us. I told Laquinta that as long as she kept her mouth shut, she could basically have anything she wanted. And for a chick that was sucking up the welfare system, my proposal didn't sound too bad. At times, she said that she couldn't handle our "on-my-time" relationship, and if she ever decided to end it, frankly, I couldn't blame her. I liked her a lot, but not enough to give up my wife.

Every time I'd ask Laquinta for a blood test, she'd get all bent out of shape. Aside from screwing me, I'd caught her with another motherfucker before. I walked right in on the two of them, and she had the nerve to try to throw up my wife in my face. The first day we met, she very well knew what she was getting herself into. After walking in on her and her companion, I straightened her up a bit and kicked her companion right out the door. I told him if he ever came back again, I'd kill him. Laquinta got a kick out of the whole thing because through her eyes, a li'l ass-kicking from me showed that I must have cared.

Realistically, she was a piece of good ass for me, and it was no more than that. Of course, she continued to use my wife against me, but I never, ever lied about having a wife to any woman I'd met. I always gave them the choice of continuing the relationship or not. Maybe surprising to some people, but surely not to me, it didn't matter if I was married. Most women didn't even care, and it was a thrill to be with a man in uniform who knew how to use his stick.

As I got ready to hit the busy streets of St. Louis, I stood in the bathroom's doorway with my white T-shirt and blue police officer pants on. I looked at Cyd in bed, snoring loudly, and cleared my throat. The alarm clock went off more than an hour ago, but I guess she was too tired to get out of bed. She'd been out all night long, and I'd gotten to the point of not asking where she was or who she was with, especially since I already knew she was seeing someone else. I didn't know his name, and I really didn't care to know.

"Cyd," I yelled. "Wake up! You gon' be late for work."

She slowly turned around and rubbed her fingers around her closed eyes. "What time is it?"

"Almost seven." I turned and headed back into the bathroom to brush my teeth. As I turned on the water,

Cyd walked up to the other sink and widened her eyes. She looked in the mirror.

"I don't think I can do this," she said, slowly brushing her long hair back into a ponytail. "I am so, so tired, and I don't feel like putting up with this uncoordinated staff today."

I looked over at her in the mirror while scrubbing my teeth. I wanted to tell her she basically had no choice because we had bills to pay, but she already knew that. Money for damn sure wasn't growing on trees around here, and it took both of us working to make ends meet. Since she was the one who wanted to live in such a lavish home, then it was up to her to make sure we kept it.

After getting no response from me, Cyd cut her eyes and went back into the bedroom. Looking through the mirror, I saw her get back in bed. She wore a flower print long robe with a solid pink short negligee underneath it. The flower print made her appear bigger than she really was, and it frustrated me a bit that she'd let herself gain the extra weight. As for the pink gown underneath—it was okay, but it wasn't like her to wear anything sexy to turn me on.

Once I finished brushing my teeth, I washed my face and patted it down with aftershave. I brushed my waves with a wave brush and adjusted my police hat on my head. I tucked my T-shirt inside of my pants and reached for my shirt that hung on the doorknob. Cyd was on her way back to sleep, so I went over to the bed and stood in front of her.

"Are you going to lay in bed and do nothing all day?"

Her eyes popped open. "Didn't I tell you I was tired?" she griped. "I had a long night and I don't feel like going to work today."

"Look, we got bills to pay. You need to tell that Negro you messing with not to keep you out so late."

She quickly sat up in bed. "Please don't tell me what I need to do. If anything, you need to get your skeezas in order. Yesterday was Lea's birthday, and I wasn't in no rush to get home to a husband who turns his back on me every single night. Just in case you haven't noticed, I haven't had a day off in almost six months. One darn day without work isn't going to hurt anyone."

I ignored her sassiness and sat on the edge of the bed to put on my socks. "One day is fine, Cydney. Just don't make it two days. We can't afford to—"

"Isaac, if we can't afford for me to take off one day, then I suggest you start looking for another job. Besides, the police department ain't paying much these days anyway, and I'm the one who's been swinging all of the weight around here."

"You got that right, my dear. You are swinging extra weight around here. But you still look good, though. I—"

Before I could say another word, Cydney kicked me hard in my back. When she pulled back to kick me again, I quickly stood up and grabbed her foot.

"You need to watch what you say to me," she said. "You act as if I'm some type of whale or something."

"I only said that because you insulted me first. I'm well aware of what my job pays, and I don't need you to keep throwing it up in my face."

I dropped her leg, but not before looking between them. And as much as I complained about her weight, I only did so to make her angry. Through my eyes, she was still a sexy woman who could easily turn me on, if only she wanted to.

She quickly closed her legs and got out of bed. "Don't be looking at me like you want something," she said.

"And why shouldn't I? You're my wife, aren't you?"

"What a joke," she said, going back into the bathroom. She turned on the shower, pulled the rubber band from her hair and dropped her robe and negligee on the floor. When she stepped into the shower, I stood in the doorway and watched her. Knowing that I didn't have a damn thing coming, I pulled my shirt together and buttoned it.

"I'll be home late," I said. "Me and Miguel got some paperwork we need to get caught up on at the office."

Cydney turned and looked over her shoulder at me. She tooted her lips and rolled her eyes. She said not one word and turned back around. I looked down at her soapy and wet behind and could only think dirty things. Her dark, naked body was enough to stiffen me, and when she bent over to tease me, I walked away from the door. I reached for my holster and placed it around my waist, removed my shades from the dresser and placed them over my eyes. I stood for a moment and watched the news, but before leaving, I went back into the bathroom and told Cyd I'd see her later. She turned off the water, grabbed a towel and held it around her body.

"I'm not sure if I'll be here later. I have plans, too, and it's a shame that I have to spend my wedding anniversary with my only true friend, my boss."

I looked puzzled, as I'd seriously forgotten that today was our anniversary. "Are you serious?" I asked, and then paused. "Today . . . it's not."

She cut her eyes and walked past me. I followed.

"Hey, look, I forgot. Would you like to have dinner later, or wait until the weekend?"

Cydney ignored me and dried herself with the towel. She reached for some lotion and sat on the bed.

"Would you like for me to help you with that?" I asked.

"No, I would not. Now, if you don't mind, I'd like to have just a little bit of peace today. I won't be able to get it if you're standing around thinking of an excuse as to why you forgot about our anniversary."

"I didn't really forget, Cydney. I just had other things

on my mind this morning, and it kind of slipped. Besides, what's the big deal? You act like you're not happy, and you haven't made love to me in God knows when. But you want me to be excited about our anniversary? What sense does that make?"

"None," she said, giving me a wink. "Now, have a wonderful day, honey. I'll see you *whenever* you make it home tonight."

"Same here," I said, turning to leave. I could hear her mumbling something, but I didn't have time to encourage her thoughts. Bottom line, Cydney was crazy. She expected for me to be hyped about an anniversary that didn't mean anything to either one of us. If it did, she never would've been out all night long last night—or the weekend before, or the Tuesday before last. I wasn't trying to keep up with her late nights, but it was so hard for me not to, especially when she had no shame in her game. Last night, she walked in, made much noise so I could hear her, and moved around in bed to make sure I knew what time it was. I could tell she'd been drinking, and the men's cologne didn't help much either. I guess if she didn't care, then why should I? I wasn't giving up my forms of entertainment for nothing or for nobody.

I started my police car and placed a piece of Juicy Fruit gum in my mouth. Geared up to start my day, I backed out of the driveway and headed to work. As I drove down Grand Avenue, I stopped at Martin Luther King Avenue, and waited for the light to turn green. Suddenly, a red Corvette pulled up beside me, and the driver was the prettiest chocolate delight I'd seen in a long time. Her layered hair was cut short and swerved to the side. Her buttered brown lips were thick and full and were laced with shiny lip gloss. When she turned to look at me, she lowered her long eyelashes and smiled. I eased down my shades, got a better glimpse and smiled back. The light turned green, and she pushed on the accelerator and sped off. This, of course, was one of the best parts of my job. I turned on my flashing lights and drove up behind her. She pulled over to the curb.

I got out of my vehicle and slowly walked up to the driver's side of her car. I bent down and looked inside. "I guess you already know why I pulled you over," I said.

"No, I really don't," she flirted. "Unless you liked what you saw at the light back there."

"Oh, I loved what I saw at the light, but that didn't prompt me to stop you. Are you aware that you were speeding?"

"A little. But I did it purposely. I was hoping that you'd pull me over."

"Well, your wish is my command," I said, and then asked for her license and registration. She handed the items over to me and I looked at them. "Avena J. Richardson, huh? Twenty-nine years old and don't know any better."

"And what's that supposed to mean?" she snapped.

"It means, that even though I might like what I see, I still got a job to do. Stay here and I'll be right back."

I headed back to my car, and I knew Avena's eyes were all over me. While I was in my car, she kept looking in her rearview and driver's side mirrors. I pretended to be occupied with the information she'd given me, but I wasn't going to write her a ticket for going eight miles over the limit. Instead, I wrote my cell phone number on a piece of paper and placed it on top of a blank ticket. I got out of the car and went up to hers.

"Here you go," I said, handing her the ticket. "I need for you to sign on the bottom line."

With attitude, she reached for the ticket and looked at it. She flipped it over and saw that both sides were blank.

"I'm not signing anything that doesn't—"

"And that's your right," I said, leaning further down.

"Actually, I changed my mind about giving you a ticket. You seem like a nice young lady, and there's a time and a place for you to ride . . . drive fast. Not on Grand Ave., though. So, slow it down. And the next time I see you, I might not be so nice."

"What makes you think you'll see me again? I don't live around here."

I reached out my hand and gave her my number, along with her license and registration. "Oh, trust me. I'll see you again. I'm predicting that I'll see you real soon."

She looked at my number and the name I'd written on the paper. "Isaac Feelgood? Is that really your last name?"

"Call me later and you'll see."

She grinned and started her car. After taking one last look at me, she put the car in gear and drove off. I watched her drive away, and smiled. As my day had already started to look up.

I arrived at the station a little after eight o'clock. Before I could even check in, Miguel had his hand out and held the phone in it.

"Man, she's been calling you like crazy. I've been here since five o'clock and she's already called three damn times."

"Who is it?" I asked. "Laquinta?"

Miguel gave me a crazy look because he already knew what time it was. I snatched the phone and placed it on my ear.

"What is it?" I said.

"Well, good morning to you too, handsome. Yesterday I called you all day, and this morning too. You didn't answer your phone. Is that how a sista gets played?"

"Laquinta, I got work to do. Some people have jobs, unlike you. I can't sit around and chit-chat all day, so what is it that you want with me?"

"First, I was wondering if I could borrow a hundred dollars. My food stamps ain't coming until—"

"No problem, but I want it back. Now, I assume you might have second and third requests too."

"And I would say you're right. I'm requesting that you come over here and give me some pleasure . . . soon. It's been almost a week, boo, and you've been depriving me. You know how anxious I get for you, don't you?"

After seeing Cydney's naked thick body this morning, I was kind of horny. Also, I thought about Laquinta's awesome blowjobs and couldn't turn her down. "It'll be late, but I'll get there, all right?"

"Since you didn't ask, your baby girl is with her grandmother all week. You can stay for as long as you'd like."

"Laquinta, don't go getting any ideas. I have a bed to go home to, and once our business is finished, I plan to make my way home. Now, I gotta go. I'll see ya later."

I hung up and Miguel looked at me while sitting at his desk.

"You need to let that skeeza go," he said. "She is a pain in the ass, and I don't see how or why you keep dealing with her."

I took off my shades and put them on my desk. "Miguel, stay out of my business. I don't interfere with yours, so don't interfere with mines."

He stood up and placed his hat on his head. "Can't help it, partna. I ride with you all day, and when she works your nerves, she works mine too. Now, I'm hungry. Before hitting the streets, can we get some breakfast, or do you want to stop at Krispy Kreme?"

"Fuck a donut, man. I need some for-real breakfast. Cyd ain't cooking shit for me at home, and a brotha getting real sick and tired of not having home-cooked meals."

Miguel chuckled, and we headed for my police car. He'd been my partner for less than a year, but he was pretty cool to work with. Not only that, but we had a lot in common. He was thirty-four, and so was I. He loved his job, and so did I. We both loved to work out, and pretty women were our weakness. Miguel wasn't married, though. He flirted a lot and never talked about settling down with anyone. Wherever we rode together, the women were crazy about us. He'd been mistaken for Terrence Howard, and I had the looks of Blair Underwood. Of course, men hated to see us coming, but that's because we were two good looking brothas with street power and authority—authority that could be used any way we wanted it to be.

Breakfast at Denny's wasn't bad. Once we got a domestic violence call that was only a few blocks away, Miguel and I rushed to finish. We'd been to the apartment complex before and knew exactly where the problem was coming from. Truthfully, the last time Miguel and I had to go and settle things down, he wound up kicking it with the chick later on that night. I told him to be careful, but he assured me that it was only a slam, bam, thank-you-ma'am deal.

The moment we pulled up, we could hear much chaos going on inside. Jackie was yelling out loudly, and it sounded as if glass hit the floor. Miguel knocked hard on the door and yelled for someone to open it. When she did, Jackie stepped away from the door so we could come in.

"What's the problem here?" Miguel asked, as he could see Jackie tearfully standing by the door. She had a bruise underneath her right eye.

"I want him out of here, Miguel. I'm so sick and tired of him putting his hands on me," she cried.

We looked at her roughneck boyfriend as he stood in the kitchen's doorway out of breath.

"Man, why you can't keep your hands off women?" Miguel asked. He slowly walked up to him.

"She . . . she's the one who started it!" The boyfriend turned to his side and pointed at his arm. "Look, she cut me right here on my arm. I have every right to defend myself, don't I?"

"Let me see your arm," Miguel said calmly, and then reached for it. He held Jackie's boyfriend's arm, looked at the cut, then twisted his arm behind his back.

"Ouch," the boyfriend yelled, and dropped to his knees. "You hurting my arm!"

"Good," Miguel replied. He kneed him in the stomach, and Jackie's boyfriend fell to the floor. Since he got a bit out of control, squirming around on the floor and yelling obscenities, I walked over to help. I placed my hand on the back of his neck and pressed his head hard on the floor to keep it still. Miguel handcuffed him and read him his rights. After he lifted him from the floor, Miguel searched his pockets and shoved him in my direction.

"Isaac, take this bastard to the police car. I'm gon' stay and talk to the young lady to see what happened."

I escorted him out to the car and waited on Miguel as he stood near the doorway and talked to Jackie. They both smiled, and when she reached out to give him a hug, the brotha in the back got a li'l anxious.

"Ain't this about a bitch! What the fuck she hugging on him fo'?"

I reached for my Juicy Fruit gum and observed Miguel slightly close the door so we couldn't see. I assumed some lip action might have been going on.

"Bro, I guess this is what happens when you use your woman for a punching bag. When you don't handle your business the correct way, there is always another motherfucker who will handle it for you."

Soon, Miguel opened the door and jogged down the

steps. Jackie closed the door, and happy-go-lucky Miguel got into the car. As I drove off, he removed his silver-framed glasses, turned and looked at the brotha in the back seat.

"This time, I will make sure that you stay in jail for a long time. I got other shit to handle, and my partner and me ain't got time to keep running to your house 'cause you can't control your woman without hitting on her."

"Man, fuck you! I told you that the bitch hit me first! If I go to jail for defending myself, then so be it! I ain't got nothing to lose."

"Then good," Miguel said. " 'Cause every night that you stay in jail, I'm gon' go over to your house and fuck her for you. So, when you lying on that hard-ass cot, staring up at the ceiling, thinking about what you should or should not have done to her, please think of me handling my business and doing it well."

The brotha didn't have much else to say. He turned his head and looked out of the window, as if Miguel's words weren't eating him up on the inside.

We were almost at the station, and we pulled up to the traffic light on Washington and Tucker. I looked over at a black Cadillac Escalade with two brothas inside. The loud system in the car had nearly the whole block vibrating, including our police vehicle and the other cars around it.

"Man, yell for them to turn that shit down," Miguel said. "It don't make no sense for mothefuckers to be riding around with music up that loud."

I lowered my window and yelled out of it. Of course, they didn't hear me, so I blew the horn. When the light turned green, they sped off, but we all had to stop at the next light because it was red. I drove up as close as I could to them, nearly swiping the side of the Escalade. Obviously, they didn't have a problem seeing me this time.

The man on the passenger's side snapped his head to the side, and his forehead was lined with wrinkles. He lowered the window and looked at me.

"What's up?" he said angrily.

"What's up is you need to turn that loud-ass music down."

He reached for the knob and lowered the volume. "Is that cool enough for ya, off-i-sah?" he asked sarcastically.

I nodded. "Yeah, I think so. But I'm gon' follow y'all for a little while, and if the music goes back up, I'll arrest the both of you for disturbing the peace. And you and I both know that if I have to pull your vehicle over, disturbing the peace might not be the only charges against you."

He smiled and showed his grill. "Are you insinuating something, off-i-sah? Me and my friend here are hard-working citizens who—"

"Negro, save the drama for your mama. Get that piece of shit out of here and don't let me creep up on you again."

The passenger gave me a hard stare before rolling up the window, then the driver drove off. For us, pulling up on brothas like that was an all-day thing. We caught gripe every now and then, but many of them did what we said because they didn't want to go to jail.

After Miguel booked Jackie's boyfriend, we hit the streets again. I'd thought about calling to see how Cydney's special day was going, and when Miguel went inside of the liquor store to get us some sodas, gum and chips, I called her at home. She didn't answer, so I tried her at work. Her secretary answered, and after conversing with her about a favor I wanted her to take care of for me, she transferred me to Cydney.

"I thought you wasn't going in today," I said.

"Oh, I had so many other options, but since we're so broke, making money was the priority."

"It always is the priority, but by the sound of your voice, I guess you're still angry with me for forgetting about our anniversary."

"What anniversary, Isaac? Whose anniversary are you talking about? I don't know—"

"Alright, Cyd. I got your point, but I just called to see how you were doing today. Like I said earlier, I thought you'd maybe like to have dinner, catch a movie, and indulge in some of that hot and heavy sex we used to have."

She snickered. "Oh, that sounds so lovely, Isaac. Honestly, before I open up my legs to you, I'd rather go somewhere and walk . . . walk a dog. Save the sex for your whores you've been giving it to. I'm not interested anymore."

"Damn, I guess you're right. But what I don't understand, Cydney, is if you hate me that much, then why don't you just divorce me? Lately, your choices of words have been kind of harsh—wouldn't you say?"

"And they're going to get harsher if you continue to criticize me about my weight. I weigh one hundred and seventy-five pounds, and you act as if I weigh a ton."

"You're breaking my heart, Cydney. Not only that, but you'll break my back if you continue to pick up more weight. You know darn well that you need to add five or ten more pounds to your calculations. "

She hung up on me. I called back, and her secretary told me to hold again. When Cydney picked up, I could tell she was fuming.

"What are you so angry about?" I said. "I was only playing with you. What . . . I can't play with you anymore?"

"Not about my weight, Isaac. I don't think your jokes are funny, and you need to appreciate the woman that you have."

"And I do appreciate her," I said, taking the soda from Miguel's hand as he got in the car. "I appreciate you a lot, but I warned you. Whenever you disrespect me, you'll get the same in return."

"Why must you always go there with the weight thing? You know how much it hurts my feelings, but you continue to throw it up in my face."

"Look, I'm sorry. Yes, you've picked up weight, but you still look good. I never said that you didn't look good, did I?" Cydney didn't answer. "Fine, but I gotta get back to work. Can we spend some time together later, or will you be walking your dog?"

"If I could walk you, I would. However, I think I'll pass on your invitation. Maybe some other time, all right?"

"Maybe so," I said, and then hung up.

Miguel was working his chips while mumbling something.

"What are you saying?" I asked.

He swallowed. "I asked who you were talking to. Your wifey?"

"Yeah, that was my wifey. I was trying to get some time with her today, since it's our anniversary."

"Well, congrats, man. Why you ain't say nothing earlier? I would have gotten you a present or something."

"No need," I said, driving off. "You know just as well as I do that my marriage stinks. Cyd's been doing her thing and I've been doing mine."

"If that's the case, then why don't y'all just get a divorce? From what I see, y'all both act like y'all don't even like each other."

"I know, man. It's crazy. At times, I hate her, but then I hate to love her. I've thought about divorcing her, but I've also imagined my life without her. It's a scary feeling, and I don't think I'm ready to be alone."

"No offense, but all these women you've been dealing with and you're afraid of being alone? Shit, they wouldn't let your ass be alone, Isaac."

"Being with Cydney and being with them is a different feeling, Miguel. None of them can measure up. She has a decent job, she's smart, sex is off the chain, and . . . and I still haven't found a woman who can throw down in the kitchen like she does. And even though she hasn't cooked for me in quite some time, I miss the days of being served breakfast in bed."

Thinking of Cyd, I smiled, in deep thought. When my phone rang, I didn't recognize the number, but answered.

"Officer Conley speaking," I said.

"I knew your last name wasn't Feelgood," she said. "But I still hope you'll be able to live up to my expectations."

"Avena, right?"

"Of course. Were you expecting someone else to call you?"

"Not really, but I was waiting for your call. So, when we gon' hook up?"

"I'm not sure. You tell me. I saw the ring on your finger, not on mine."

I looked at my wedding ring. Cydney didn't want to spend any time with me, so Avena had to do.

"Where do you live?" I asked.

As she gave me her address and directions to her place, I said them out loud so Miguel could write them down for me. After I got Avena's information, I told her I'd see her around nine. We ended the call, and Miguel held the paper in front of his face.

"I know this chick," he said. "These directions, her name and . . . let me see her phone number."

I handed Miguel my phone, and he looked at her num-

ber. "Avena . . . Avena," he said while in deep thought.
"Dark-skinned, pretty, seductive eyes, short hair and fine
as hell!"

"So, you know her?"

"You damn right I do. I boned her about three months
ago. She was at the nightclub where I work security at. I
followed her home and got the shock of my life."

"What . . . what happened?"

"Have you seen her ass . . . her body? Damn, her body!"

"I saw some of it. From what I could see, it looked
pretty damn good."

"Aw, man, baby girl body got it going on."

"Then why were you shocked?"

Miguel shook his head and pounded his fist on the
dashboard. "All that, and she wasn't worth two cents in
the bedroom. I left that day and wanted to kick my own
ass for wasting my time." He spoke loudly and counted
down on his fingers. "She was stiff, she couldn't kiss, she
knew nothing about foreplay, and the dick-sucking was
pathetic! Please, don't say that I didn't warn you. It was
one of the worst experiences in my life, and the tragedy
of that night still haunts me!"

"Damn, man, calm down. Maybe you were her first or
something."

"No way. I could tell she'd been tampered with, but
she hadn't learned a damn thing from the motherfuckers
who hit it before me."

"I just can't believe it was that bad, Miguel. I've been
with very few women who didn't know how to use what
they had, and if they didn't, I had no problem showing
them how to. Maybe you didn't put in work on your part
either."

Miguel reached for his chips. "Isaac, handle your business. Again, don't say that I didn't warn you."

* * *

Around eight o'clock, Miguel and I headed back to the office to shut down for the evening. It had been a busy and chaotic day, as we made seven arrests in the city of St. Louis. I changed clothes, and since I didn't want to drive my police car to Avena's house, I drove my white Dodge Ram truck with major horsepower that was already parked on the lot. Miguel kept warning me about Avena, and I started to change my mind and go see Laquinta like I was supposed to do. Since she kept bugging the hell out of me, I decided to leave Laquinta alone. Earlier, I'd already caught gripe from Cydney, and I didn't feel like hearing it from no one else.

It was five minutes to nine, and since I was low on condoms, I stopped at Walgreen's to purchase some. While inside, I got more condoms, some bottled water and a pack of Juicy Fruit gum. I then stopped to chat with a security guard on duty that I knew. Not wanting to appear anxious to see Avena, I talked to him for about thirty minutes before I made my way over to her place.

I was nearly forty minutes late, and my conscience was bugging the hell out of me. It was my anniversary and I wanted to be with my wife, but lately, we'd been arguing and disagreeing so much that a part of me seriously needed some peace. With Avena, I figured I could probably get it. No arguing, no disrespect, no questions, and straight to business. I purposely ignored Avena's two previous phone calls, which implied she was waiting for me. Casually dressed in my loose-fitting white pants that tied around my waist, leather sandals and a sleeveless white T-shirt, I went to her door and knocked. Without asking who I was, she pulled open the door and smiled.

"I thought you'd never get here," she said. I stepped inside and closed the door behind me. She walked into the living room and I followed. As I listened to her end a phone call, I thought about what Miguel had said. No doubt, her body was intact. She wore a loud yellow strapless halter that stretched across her breasts and showed her nicely cut midriff. Her blue jeans were low, held up by a belt with her name across it. She saw me admiring her, and quickly put the phone down on the receiver.

"Sorry about that," she said, moving her short bangs away from her face. "Can I get you anything to drink?"

I held up the brown bag in my hand. "No, thanks. I have bottled water in here. I got you one too."

She walked up to me and took the bag from my hand. She placed it on the coffee table and stood in front of me. Her hands went up my shirt, and she rubbed them against my abs, looking up at me.

"Oooo, solid as a rock, but smooth. I have nothing but good things to say about a man who takes care of his body in such a way."

I placed my hand on her back and pulled down her halter. It rolled down in the back, and then in the front. Her perky chocolate breasts stood at attention, and I reached around and squeezed them in my hands. My thumbs rubbed her hardened nipples, and I quickly brought the tip of my wet tongue to them. I held her closer to me and licked around both of them. She put an arch in her back, dropped her head back and moaned. I stopped my motion and felt for the belt buckle around the hoops of her jeans.

"Avena, I have nothing but good things to say about a woman who's capable of making me as hard as I am now. I hope you plan on taking good care of me tonight."

She reached for the strings on my pants and untied it, reaching down inside. She gathered my ass in her hands and squeezed it. Soon, she eased her hands around to my hardness and stroked it.

"Nice," she said as it grew. "Very, very nice."

I reached down inside of her panties, touched her hairless slit and sunk my index finger inside.

"No . . . not too bad either."

She brought her lips to mine, and well . . . her kiss . . . it was just a kiss.

CYDNEY

I swear, that husband of mine wasn't worth a darn. Little did he know, a while ago he could have had any and everything he wanted from me. Our marriage started out fine, until he started using his job as an excuse to stay out late. I knew something was up with him, but it wasn't confirmed until I actually saw, with my own eyes, him screwing another woman in the back seat of his truck. I did the norm and confronted him and her on the spot. He was shocked to see me, and all he could say was, "I'm sorry."

Well, "I'm sorry" wasn't and still isn't good enough. And it proved not to be when he continued seeing other women shortly thereafter. Since then, I'd cut his butt off completely. No sex, no cooking, no kids, and he was lucky to get any respect. I'd be a fool to bring any kids into a disastrous situation like ours because sooner or later, one of us was going to get tired.

Even though he hadn't admitted it, I knew he was getting tired of my late nights as well. At first, I started off by playing his own game with him. I wanted him to feel the pain I felt, so I stayed out late nights with my girlfriend,

Lea, and pretended that another man was occupying my time. Sometimes, I even splashed on men's cologne to make him think I was with another man, but it seemed not to bother Isaac at all. He never questioned me, but he'd always make remarks about me being with someone else. To me, his thoughts of me being with another man encouraged him to see more women. And according to Miguel, that's exactly what had been going down.

After playing my pretend game for so long, I finally started seeing Miguel. Sex between us only occurred three times, and when I realized he was just as bad as Isaac, and that using him for revenge was getting old, I'd been kind of keeping my distance. Miguel thought that his little hints about Isaac encouraged me to want to see him more, but there was nothing that anyone could tell me about my husband that I didn't already know.

A while back, I saw Isaac at McDonald's with Laquinta and their so-called child. I followed them back to her place, and to this day, he has no clue how I knew what I did. And if he really believed that little girl was his, then I was gonna let him keep on thinking it. She looked nothing at all like him, and Laquinta was playing him for the fool that he was. I hadn't said one word to him about my thoughts, but sooner or later, being with a low-class trick of her caliber would cost him dearly.

I sat in my office and stared out the window. It was rather late, but I didn't want to go home and stare at the walls on my anniversary. It was obvious from my conversation with Isaac earlier that he most likely made plans with someone else. I thought about calling Miguel or another friend of mine, Persey, who I'd been conversing with from time to time, but tonight, I simply didn't want to be bothered. I removed the clip from my hair and let my hair fall, then walked over to my desk, pulled out a bottle of Martel from the drawer and dimmed the lights.

I turned on some soft music and went over to the small sofa in the far corner of the room. After taking a seat, I removed my peach linen stilettos and propped my feet up on the coffee table in front of me. I unbuttoned my white silk blouse and leaned back. Thinking deeply about what Isaac was up to, I put the bottle up to my lips and tilted it. I gulped down a few sips of Martel and put the bottle on the table in front of me. I then reached for my cell phone clipped to my skirt and dialed his number. Surprisingly, he answered.

"What are you up to?" I asked.

"Trying to make my way home," he said, taking a few deep breaths.

"It's almost eleven o'clock. I'm surprised you're not home by now."

"I . . . I had a few stops to make. I should be there shortly, though."

"Why does it sound like you're having a difficult time breathing? Did I catch you at a bad time or something?"

"No, Cyd. I'm wiping my truck down. I got a spot on it and I can't get it out. Where are you?"

"I'm still at the office. I should be home within the next hour or so."

"Well, I'll see you whenever you get there. Until then, look in the bottom drawer of your desk. There's something in there for you."

I looked over at my desk. "Something like what?" I said, standing up.

"You'll see. Bye."

Isaac hung up and I went over to my desk to see what it was. When I opened the bottom drawer, there was a card with a single red rose taped to it. I removed the rose, sniffed it and opened the card. It wished me a happy anniversary and was signed by, "the man who still loves you, Isaac."

Hurt because things hadn't worked out as we had planned for them to, I stood dazed for a moment and thought deeply about him. Almost five minutes later, my concentration was broken by a slight knock on my door.

"Come in," I said.

When the door came open, it was Isaac. He walked in and turned up the lights.

"I see you got your card," he said. "You gripe about your secretary all the time, but she came through for me. I asked her to take care of that for me today, and I'm sorry I forgot about our anniversary."

I folded my arms in front of me. "Well, I'll be sure to thank my secretary, Isaac. But I . . . I thought you were somewhere wiping down your car."

"I was in the parking garage. My shortness of breath was from jogging up the steps to get to your office."

I smiled and took a seat in my chair. As I leaned back, Isaac came around next to me and leaned against the edge of my desk. Instantly, my whole attitude had changed. He'd stolen my moment of joy. Not only was smeared make-up on his shirt, but his pants were wrinkled and I could smell cheap perfume. To make matters worse, a used condom was dangling from his pocket.

"So, did you like your card?" he asked.

"Yes, I liked *her* card, but I feel so bad that I didn't get you one," I said. I turned to the small printer beside me and pulled out a piece of paper. I folded it in half and reached for a black marker on my desk. I wrote "Happy Anniversary" on the front, and on the inside, I wrote, "the woman who still loves you too, your wife." I handed it to him and smiled. "I hope that'll make you feel better."

He read the inside and laid the paper next to him. "Can we go home? Just for tonight, I'd like to go home together and hold you in my arms."

I stood up and leaned into his ear. I whispered, "Just

for tonight, huh? I was wishing . . . hoping for a lifetime of you holding me in your arms, but you ruined it for me. Just like you ruined our anniversary today by sticking your dick inside of another woman. How could you be so fucking selfish and conniving, Isaac? And then have the nerve to show up here like you're doing me a favor."

He moved his head back and looked at me. "I haven't been with another woman today, Cydney. How or why would you think that I'd spend our anniversary with someone else?"

"Because you are dirty like that and you know it. Besides, what makes today so darn special? You might have been with a woman the day before, but surely not today, right?"

He stood up. "Listen, I haven't been with another woman in quite some time. Yes, I flirt a lot, but that's as far as it goes. Lately, you're the one who's being doing all the cheating in this marriage."

I had to laugh because my husband seriously thought I was a fool. "Is there a possibility that the words 'quite some time ago' mean only a few hours ago? Isaac, before you answer, there is make-up on your shirt, and perfume all over your clothes."

He looked down at his shirt. "Maybe your make-up. And if I smell like perfume, it's probably yours too."

I reached for the dangling condom and smashed it in his face. "Well, I assure you that this doesn't belong to me. Now get the hell out of my office and take this useless card and rose with you."

Isaac wiped the condom from his face and held it in his hand. He looked at it as if he couldn't figure out where it came from. Of course, those were his exact words.

"I'm serious, baby. I have no idea—"

I took a deep breath, went over to the door and held it open. "Look, it's no surprise what I'm dealing with, Isaac.

You don't have to lie to me about your extramarital affairs because I already know they exist. There's no need to make my blood pressure rise or yours, so let's just call it a day and chalk up yet another anniversary as a loss."

Of course, he couldn't say much else. Didn't even have the guts to look at me as he left. All I could do was slam the door behind him.

I wound up spending the night at my office. Just so no one would know that I did, I rushed out about 5:30 in the morning. When I arrived home, Isaac was in bed, sound asleep. I thought about setting fire to his butt, but for me, those days were over. When he first started cheating, I'd gotten my clown on so many times and was starting to make a fool of myself. My clowning didn't change nothing about him, and neither did my tears. Once I decided to deal with his mess, I promised never to let him see me cry, sweat or act a fool again. Yes, it was hard to contain myself, but I had to do it. After seeing the condom in his pocket, I wanted to break his neck! But what good would it have done me? Isaac was going to continue being Isaac, and there was simply nothing I could do or say to make him the man I once truly loved.

Attempting not to wake him, I eased into the walk-in closet and search for a new outfit to put on. I reached for my silver blouse and gray pinstriped pants and headed to the bathroom to change. As soon as I got ready to close the door, Isaac called my name.

"Are you just now getting in here?" he griped.

"I've been here. You were just sleeping and didn't hear me come in."

He yanked the covers back, walked up to me and yawned.

"Listen, I'm sorry about the mix-up with the condom, but it seriously wasn't mine. Miguel was playing a joke on me and placed it in my pocket. Either way, our rule is to never, ever stay out all night. Every night, I come home to you and you come home to me, no matter what. Don't start changing the rules around here, Cyd, all right?"

In total disbelief, all I could do was stare up at him. I wanted to smack the shit out of him for constantly lying, so I did. He held his cheek and I spoke sarcastically, "You need to tell Miguel to stop playing games with you like that, especially on your anniversary. Didn't he know how I'd react to something like that?"

Isaac continued with his lie and rubbed his cheek. He got a kick out of my reaction, and the grin on his face showed it. "I guess you don't believe me, but I'll be sure to let Miguel know what his joke cost me. In the meantime, are we still going to this scholarship ceremony tonight? The folks at your job always trying to give out money to somebody, but as late as you work, they should be giving you a raise. Besides, I'm not sure if I have to work late or not, but if you still want me to go, I'll make some arrangements."

After all that had been going on, I totally forgot about the scholarship ceremony given by the executives at my job. Each year, they gave away $3000 to ten students who possessed the best athletic or artistic talent. Surely, I didn't want to go alone. I had to—no, *we* had to put on a front for everybody, but if Isaac wasn't going to come, I could easily say that he made an arrest and had to work overtime.

"If you could put your bitches—I mean your obligations off for a few hours tonight, I'd certainly appreciate it."

"I guess I'll have to." He smirked, and then stepped away from me to use the toilet. I quickly got undressed and hopped in the shower. As Isaac washed his hands, his eyes were all over me. I knew he wanted me bad, but at the rate he was going, he'd never have me again. My rushed shower lasted no more than five minutes, and I hurried to get dressed so I could head back to work.

I left the house without even saying goodbye. When I got to work, my boss, Darrell, was waiting in my office to greet me. He was a younger white man, was filthy rich, and held his position because his father was one of the stockholders. His girlfriend looked like Barbie, and his boyfriend could have easily been Ken. He and I got along extremely well, and he trusted me with the secret of his "on the down low" lifestyle. Not only that, but he considered me to be a true asset to the company.

"Good morning," he said, sitting on my sofa with his legs crossed. I laid my purse on the table and sat next to him.

"I don't know about it being a good morning, but I'm here and ready to go."

He patted my leg. "Cydney, it's always a good morning, my dear. Are you ready for the wonderful evening we have planned?"

"As ready as I'm going to get. Are you bringing your girlfriend or your boyfriend with you tonight?"

"Of course, my girlfriend. Not too many people know of my boyfriend, so don't say that too loudly. Besides, my girl's been kind of bitchy lately, but we'll see. What about you? Will Isaac be joining you?"

"Of course. He said that he wouldn't miss it for the world."

"I'll bet. You and he have such a wonderful relationship, and I hope that I find happiness someday like you have."

I stood up and could have choked for lying to Darrell. He was nice enough to share all of his business with me, and there I was lying as if I had the perfect marriage. Bottom line, I didn't want anyone to know what was really going on between us, and as much as I liked Darrell, I didn't trust him with my secrets. He was known for gossiping, and I couldn't take a chance at my business being spread throughout the office. Both Isaac's and my parents thought things were going well, and for the time being, neither Isaac nor I wanted them to know the truth.

"Well, sweetness," Darrell said. "Our meeting starts in about an hour. It's an all-day thing, so make sure you have breakfast and lunch all at once. Dinner will be served tonight, but I assure you that it'll be late."

"Thanks for the warning," I said. "I'll see you in a bit."

Darrell stood up and casually strutted out of my office. If he'd never told me he was gay, I wouldn't have known. He carried himself with the utmost class, had a body like Brad Pitt, and resembled him in many ways. I felt sorry for his girlfriend because she had no idea what was really going on behind closed doors. He said that he loved her, but there was nothing that he could do about his desire for men. I didn't quite understand it, but I had my own problems to deal with. At this time, all I could do was lend him my ear.

Darrell surely didn't exaggerate. The meeting lasted all morning and into the late afternoon. I didn't know what I was going to wear that night and thought I'd have time to stop by the mall and pick up something. When I rushed into my office, I looked at the clock and it was almost four. I had plenty of phone calls to return, but before I did, I called Isaac to make sure he was coming.

"Officer Conley speaking," he said.

"It's me. Are you going to be able to make it or not?"

"I . . . I'll try." He hesitated. "It's been a kind of wild today, but I'll put forth every effort to be there."

"Try hard. I don't want to—"

"Where's it at again?"

"At the Adam's Mark. As soon as you walk into the

lobby, you'll see us. I need you there by seven, no later than eight. Please."

"Like I said, I'll do my best."

"Lately, your best hasn't been good enough. I hope you'll do better."

He didn't respond, and because I had to return other phone calls, I hung up.

By the time I finished my calls, it was after five o'clock. I hurried to the Galleria and tried to find something to wear. Being a size fourteen didn't help much. Mostly all of the sexy and classy black dresses were for women whose dress sizes were in the single digits. I must have tried on twenty dresses before I came across a black one that was made strictly for me. It stretched around the curves in my hips, had a deep dip in the back, but met up with my neckline in the front. The trimming was black satin and matched a pair of black stilettos lined with tiny diamonds. Having little time to work with, I left the dress on and went to the make-up counter so the cosmetologist could work me up. She made my dark brown skin look flawless and arched my eyebrows to perfection. My lips were glossed, and my light gold eye shadow and liner gave my dark brown eyes a glamorous but seductive look. As for my hair, I left a part down the middle and let it fall on the sides of my face to my shoulders. My hair had a shine that wouldn't quit, and compliments came from everywhere. As I walked out, every woman that passed by me had something nice to say, and the men couldn't keep their eyes off me. One man nearly broke his neck as he tripped while trying to hold the door for me.

"You are stunning," he said. "Are you married?"

I smiled and twirled my fingers in the air. "Unfortunately, but thanks for holding the door for me." I kept on walking, and he continued to stand and look with the door pulled open.

By the time I reached the Adam's Mark, it was almost 7:45. I'd rushed to get there, but traffic was such a mess. Construction on the highway was down to one lane, so I knew Isaac was going to be a no-show, or use the traffic as an excuse not to come. However, when I walked inside, I saw him sitting at the bar. He sat next to one of my co-workers, and I watched him from a distance. The look of him sent chills throughout my entire body. He wore a black suit with a black silk shirt underneath it, and a few buttons were undone so you could see his chest. His wavy, coal black hair had been lined, and so was his thinly shaven beard. The tinted brown glasses he wore put him in a category all by himself . . . simply fabulous. It was so, so sad that a man so handsome on the outside had to be so ugly on the inside. I reminded myself of all the hurtful things he'd done to me over the years and quickly got back to reality.

Before making my way over to Isaac, I saw Darrell and his date sitting at a table. I stopped to chat and he couldn't stop talking. When he did, he stood up and asked me to dance. He gave me a disturbing look, as if something was wrong, so I couldn't decline.

We went to the dance floor, and Darrell quickly wrapped his arms around me.

"Cydney, on the way over here tonight, Jessica told me she was pregnant. Wha . . . what should I do? Please tell me, what do you think I should do?"

I was relieved. I thought Darrell was going to tell me he saw Isaac flirting with someone. Of course, I would have been embarrassed. "Darrell, I'm not sure what you should do. Maybe you should start with being honest with her. Honesty never hurt anybody, you know?"

"I can't tell her the truth, especially with her being pregnant. She's going to want to get married, and I am so, so screwed." Darrell twirled me around and pulled me closer to him. "By the way, did I tell you how gorgeous you look tonight? You look awesome."

"Thank you. And you don't look too bad yourself. The nervousness is causing you to sweat, though. Never let a woman see you sweat."

Darrell put on a wide smile and twirled me around again. As people watched us, we both laughed and agreed to have lunch tomorrow so we could talk. When the song was over, Darrell held my waist and escorted me off the floor. Immediately, Isaac walked up and pulled me by my hand.

"Isaac, you remember Darrell, don't you?" I said.

"Hi, Mr. Conley," Darrell said. "Good to see you again. Cydney is quite a dancer, isn't she?"

Isaac didn't say anything to Darrell. He looked at me and squeezed my hand tighter.

"Can I talk to you for a minute?" he said.

"Sure," I said, excusing myself from Darrell. We went outside and stood next to a lighted waterfall in front of the Adam's Mark.

"All I want to know is, are you sleeping with your boss?"

"Who, Darrell?" I said in disbelief.

"Yes, Darrell. By the way he was all over you, I can tell something is up with the two of you. And a white man, Cyd? Then, you've been here for almost thirty damn minutes and haven't even acknowledged me. If you wasn't going to say anything to me, then why did you ask me to come?"

"First of all, Darrell and I are friends. Secondly, I was on my way over to you, but he needed to speak with me about something important. Lastly, if you'd like to leave, feel free. Don't try to start an argument with me so that you can get out of here, Isaac. Please spare me the embarrassment, okay?"

I turned and Isaac grabbed my hand. Catching me off guard, he swung me around and sucked my lips into his. As I tried to pull away from his kiss, he held my head tightly and forced his tongue deeply into my mouth. I pushed him back and he backed away. I wiped my lips and stared at him.

"I'm here to pretend, so let's go inside and continue this charade," he said. "You look extremely beautiful tonight, and if you want another kiss like that one, you'd better be on good behavior."

"Trust me, I don't want another kiss like that tonight. And as long as you're placing your lips on other women's pussies, please don't put them on mine."

"It's too late to take it back," he said, opening the door for me. I rolled my eyes, stepped back inside, and the fakeness continued. You would have thought that Isaac and I had the perfect marriage. He stayed close by me, held my hand, talked to my co-workers like he had some sense and paid me many, many compliments in front of them. Basically, he bragged about what a wonderful wife he had and told them how lucky they were to have me. When he tried to sneak in another kiss, I walked his butt to the bathroom and checked him again. It wasn't that my husband wasn't a great kisser, but who in the hell wanted to kiss a man whose lips were all over St. Louis? I surely didn't, and until he was willing to make some changes, he didn't have nothing coming from me.

ISAAC

Cydney played me, and she played me good. After we left the Adam's Mark, we met up at home and stayed up talking most of the night. Our conversation flowed, and it appeared that she was ready to give in to me. Maybe the alcohol had her adrenaline going, but when it came down to it, she climbed in bed and went to sleep. Before going to sleep, I literally begged her to make love to me, but she refused. Hurt by her rejection, I left.

On my drive to Laquinta's place, I couldn't stop thinking about Cyd. Damn, she looked beautiful tonight! I hadn't seen her look that good in quite some time, and the dress she wore, it did justice for the curves in her body, and had me hard as a mountain's rock. By the way she looked at me, I was so sure that we'd make love tonight. I'd visualized removing her dress and tearing into it as I'd done so many times in the past. There was no doubt that making love to her was the best, and I was really starting to miss the relationship we once had. For now, though, Laquinta and the other on and off women in my life were there to fill the void.

The moment I arrived at Laquinta's place, I knew the attitude would be on. A couple of days ago, I'd promised her a visit and money, but was a no-show. Had Avena not wasted my time on my anniversary, I would've been able to make it to Laquinta that night. Since Miguel didn't show up for work yesterday, I couldn't wait to see him so I could tell him about my awful evening with Avena.

Laquinta quickly pulled the door open and searched me from head to toe. As handsome as I looked, I knew there was no denying me.

"You must have been out with the wife tonight, huh?" she said, turning away from the door. I barely discussed Cyd with Laquinta, so I didn't tell her if I was or if I wasn't. All I did was close the door and walk over to the couch. I removed my suit jacket and laid it next to me on the couch. After I sat back, I smiled at a woman with serious attitude standing in front of me. I slowly undid the buttons on my silk shirt and gave her *the look*.

"Come sit right here," I said, patting my lap.

Laquinta folded her arms and swung her micro-braids away from her face. She wore a red half T-shirt and hip-hugging blue jean shorts that showed her belly ring and a tattoo of cherries that pointed to down below. As she stepped my way, her Hershey's dark chocolate skin had a shiny glow about it that always turned me on.

When she reached me, she straddled my lap on her knees and dropped her red flip-flops to the floor. She placed her arms on my shoulders and stared me down.

"Do you have any idea how lonely I've been without you? I told you that your daughter was away with her grandmother, and that means I wanted some time alone with you. Then you never brought me the hundred bucks, so I haven't had anything to eat. I assume that you're going to take me to dinner tomorrow to make it up to me, right?"

I reached for my jacket and pulled out my wallet. I handed Laquinta two hundred-dollar bills.

"Please forgive me for my stupidity," I said, knowing that the extra hundred would keep her quiet. "Now, if you don't mind, I get enough gripe at home from my wife. I don't need to hear it from you too, and I apologize for not showing up when I told you I would."

Laquinta tossed the money on the floor and leaned in to my ear. She licked around it and stuck her pierced tongue deep inside. My head squirmed around, and I closed my eyes and dropped my head back. After her tongue left my ear, she massaged my chest and manipulated my nipples with the tips of her long fingernails. I wanted to taste her sweet lips, so I grabbed her face and brought it to mine. Momentarily, we smacked lips, and they were slippery wet.

When I reached for her shorts to take them off, she backed away. She walked around the coffee table and stood before me. I damn near melted in my seat as she pulled her top over her head and dropped her shorts to the floor. Her body was perfectly shaped, and there wasn't an ounce of fat on it. Teasing me, she rubbed her breasts together and turned around so I could get a view of her healthy, naked chocolate ass. When she reached back with her hands and pulled it apart, I jumped up from my seat.

I quickly stepped over the table and shoved her into the wall in front of her. Facing it, she turned her head to the side to kiss me as I pressed my body against hers. Always, the kiss was sweet, but not as sweet as her pussy was. I knew how rough she liked it, so I reached in my pocket for my handcuffs. I pulled her arms tightly behind her and placed the cuffs around her wrist. More than excited, I dropped my pants to the floor and pressed my dick against her butt. I moved her braids away from her neck and softly bit it.

"Spread your legs," I ordered. She obeyed my command as I reached around to her front and roughly massaged her breasts together. "You have the right to remain silent. Anything you say can and will be used against you in the bedroom. You have the right to see any man that you wish to, but no man can fuck you like the one you've appointed to do it for you today."

"I know how good you are to me, Isaac," she moaned. "Fuck me good, though, baby. Do it good."

With her legs still apart, I rubbed one hand on the side of her hip and swayed it across her ass. My fingers entered her from the back, and I worked her until she was moist. Actually, she was more than moist, as the juices from her insides made a loud, gushy sound. I removed my fingers, squatted down low behind her, and separated her cheeks. Diving right into it, I licked her insides from front to back. She was on fire and could barely keep still. Her legs trembled, and she bent over further so I could go in deeper with my tongue.

"Damn, Isaac," she cried out. "Why do you do this to me? I . . . I'll never be able to give this up . . . never."

After finishing my business, I stood up and licked my lips. "And I'll never ask you to give this up either. That would be depriving me too, and we gon' do this every hour," I said, placing my dick inside of her to relieve us. "Every minute." I gave her several good, hard and lengthy strokes. "Annnd . . ." I strained to keep myself from exploding. "And every second that we can."

Laquinta nodded in agreement, and as I continued to sex her from the back, she worked me like a pro. During sex, I loved the way she made me feel. It was the after effects that always bothered me.

* * *

I hadn't gotten a lick of sleep, and I had a hard time getting out of Laquinta's bed. For now, the rule about going home every night had gone down the drain. If Cydney felt as if she didn't have to come home, neither did I. I was sad that things had turned out so badly for us, and as my guilt started to kick in, all I could think about was being with my wife. Cydney knew how to please me better than anybody, but at this point, pleasing me was the last thing on her mind.

Once I changed into my uniform in the locker room, I sat on the bench, dropped my head into my hands and closed my eyes. When I felt myself nodding off, my thoughts switched to my amazing night with Laquinta. I didn't mind dropping money by her bedside because the sex was surely worth it. And even though she had her ghettofied ways, she was still a sweet person who knew how to please her man. According to my friends who'd met her, they said I'd stooped to an all-time low, comparing her to Cydney. But just because she was on welfare and living in a low income apartment, that didn't classify her as stupid. She had brains, she kept herself and her apartment clean, and she took care of our daughter. I was on cloud nine thinking about the head job she'd given me, and my thoughts prompted me to pick up the phone and call her. After our eventful night together, of course, she was asleep.

"I knew you were probably sleeping, but before I got busy today, I wanted to thank you for alleviating some of the pressure I've been under."

"No need to thank me, Isaac. I just wish I didn't have to sit around and wait for you to come by and see me on your time. You know I want us to be together, but I'm willing to wait and see what happens. Besides, every time you get upset with your wife, that's a bonus for me. Your sex be off the chain, and you certainly know how to put something on a sistah's mind. You've been doing a lot of that lately, so I suspect that things aren't going too well at home. Whenever you're ready to call it quits with her, just let me know."

"As much as I feel for you, Laquinta, I don't want to make you any promises. Cyd . . . my wife and I have been together for a long time, and our marriage isn't going to end overnight."

"Well, we've been at this for over two years now. I'll remain patient because I love you like that. As long as you continue to take care of me and your daughter, I'm cool."

"I know, and I appreciate your patience. Now, take your sweet self back to sleep and I'll most likely see you later."

"Later, as in sex later or take me out on the town later? You looked so nice earlier, and it kind of frustrated me knowing that you'd been out with her."

"As much as I would like to, you know I can't be flaunting you around like that. I wish I could, but there's too much at stake. My wife knows a lot of people, and if possible, I'd like to spare her any embarrassment."

"Now, that hurt. You putting her feelings before mines is quite painful. Don't tell me no, but just think about it. I'd like to go anywhere . . . somewhere other than being cooped up in here all day."

"No offense, baby, but why don't you go look for a job or something? Work might keep you busy, but, uh, it's just a suggestion."

"Isaac, it's not that I don't want to work, but daycare costs a fortune. If I can live here nearly rent-free, take care of our daughter, and live a stress-free life because all of my bills are paid, then I'm cool. Stressing myself with work doesn't sound tempting to me right now."

"Then what about school? An education never hurt anybody."

"I'm twenty-eight years old and going back to school is not on my agenda. Hell, I barely made it out of high school, and you think I'm interested in going to college? Please."

Her pussy had been so good to me that at times, I forgot what I was dealing with. "Baby, I gotta go. Keep my spot warm for me until I can get there to see you."

"Always," she said, and then hung up.

I held my cell phone in my hand and took a deep breath. When I heard a whistle, I turned and saw Miguel walking through the door.

"You're late," I said. "And what was the purpose for your absenteeism yesterday?"

"Since when did you become the boss?" he joked while opening up his locker. "If you must know, I'm late because I caught a flat on my way to work, and I didn't come in yesterday because I had to fix my sister's car."

"Well, hurry up and change. Sergeant Armstrong wants to see you."

"Yeah, I know. On my way to the locker room, he told me to stop by his office."

"I wonder what's that all about," I said, looking at him suspiciously.

Miguel shrugged his shoulders and hurried to change.

When Miguel and I stopped at Armstrong's office, he was on the phone and asked us to wait outside in the hall. With his door closed, we waited for him to end his call.

"That fat white motherfucker makes me sick," Miguel said. "I can't wait to kiss this damn job goodbye."

"I thought you liked your job. You just said the other day that this was the best job ever."

"Fool, you know why I like my job. And it's the same

reason why you like yours. The part I hate is being told what to do and how to do it. Armstrong be talking down on the brothas around here, and frankly, I don't like it."

"I know what you mean, but most of our time is spent on the streets. Realistically, Armstrong shouldn't be a problem for either one of us."

"I guess," he said, looking through the dusty blinds to see if Armstrong had ended his call. He had, and immediately pulled the door open.

"Officer Conley, what are you doing in here? I didn't ask to speak with you. I asked for Officer Spencer to come see me."

"But we partners, though, Sarg. You don't mind if I stay to see what's up, do you?"

He sat in his squeaky, busted-up leather chair and pointed his finger at Miguel. "Again, I've been getting some complaints about you. One about you, Conley, but—"

Miguel quickly spoke up. "Complaints about what? I'd like to know."

Armstrong picked up a small stack of papers. "On last Friday, you handcuffed a guy on Sarah Avenue, and busted his nose." He thumbed through to the next page. "On last Tuesday, you tossed a guy through a windshield, and witnesses said that he was very cooperative with you. During our last conversation, and still being investigated, a lady claimed that you patted her down and touched between her legs. And a drug dealer said that both of you guys stole some money from him. These actions might require me to put the both of you on suspension. If any of this is proven to be true, I assure both of you that you're out of here."

"Like I told you the last time we spoke, all that was justified, Sarg," Miguel responded. "With the exception of patting down a woman and stealing money from a drug dealer. You know that's against the rules, and whoever filed those complaints lied."

Armstrong looked at me. "What's going on, Conley?"

"Haters. That's what's going on. Miguel and me aren't well liked on the streets because we handle our business and handle it well. You can tell by how many criminals we've placed behind bars, and even you can agree that the streets of St. Louis are a lot safer because of us. Miguel busted that brotha's nose because he'd punched him in the face. The other guy went through the windshield because he tried to run from us by jumping over his own car. The witnesses were there after the fact and didn't see everything that happened. As for the drug dealer, please. All the money that we found, we turned in every last dime. I don't know anything about a woman being searched down, but it was probably a complaint from a woman whose feelings were hurt because her sexual advances were turned down."

Armstrong appeared to be very attentive to what I was saying. He respected me more than he did Miguel, and I knew he'd appreciate my "honesty."

"Both of you, get to work. If I get any more complaints, we're all gonna have a talk, and it won't be a pleasant one. I hope Internal Affairs doesn't get involved, and any officer who gives this precinct a bad name is going to have his head on the table. Got it?"

We both nodded and turned to leave. I straightened the cap on my head and Miguel slid his silver-framed glasses over his eyes. After that, we smiled at each other and jetted.

We were no more than two blocks away from the station, and there was trouble. A man and woman were outside of a parked car, going at it. He grabbed her by the arm and she swung her purse on the side of his head to hit him. It looked like a robbery attempt to me, but Miguel insisted that it was a disputing couple.

"Man, leave them alone," he said. "We got bigger fish to fry."

I placed a piece of Juicy Fruit gum in my mouth and slowly drove up next to the parked car and flashed my lights. Both of them turned their heads and looked in our direction.

"Is there a problem?" I asked while looking at the lady. She snatched her arm away from the man and rolled her eyes.

"No, nothing I can't handle."

"Are you sure?" I said. "I can always get out of the car and handle your business for you."

The man spoke up. "She cool. We just had a li'l disagreement, that's all."

"Well, cool out and get in your car and go home. That kind of stuff don't look good out here on the streets."

Both of them nodded, and the woman walked over to the passenger's side of the car to get in. I drove off, and Miguel looked at his watch.

"There goes five minutes of wasted time down the drain. They gon' go home, fight some more, and be fucking by the time the sun goes down. I get so tired of wasting my time on these domestic violence calls, but some of these women know what they be dealing with."

"I agree, but that's what we get paid for. You just never know when you might be saving somebody's life the moment you step up to them." Miguel looked out of the window and I slammed on the brakes. We both went forward.

He quickly turned his head. "Man, what the fuck—"

"I forgot to tell you about Avena."

"Who? Who the hell is Avena?"

"You know, that dark-skinned honey who lives in North County," I said, driving off.

"You mean the non-fucking ho who I still have night-mares about?"

"Yes, yes, that's the one. Man, you should have seen how fast I gathered my shit and left! The foreplay started off cool, but when we got to her bedroom, I put my dick inside of her and she went wild. I pumped three to four times and she had an orgasm. When I tried to get my shit off, she barely let me finish. I asked for some head, and she damn near chewed my dick up. That was the first time I ever had to pull out of a woman's mouth."

We cracked the hell up.

"I told you, didn't I?" he yelled. "What planet did she come from?"

"I don't know, but what a waste. I damn near broke my neck running to the door. I was so out of it that I tripped and left the condom in my pocket. Cydney saw it, and I got busted like a motherfucker."

"I know. She told me," he said laughing.

"When?" I said, stopping at a red light. "When did you talk to Cydney and what did she say?"

"Man, it was . . . yesterday. I called to tell you that I wasn't coming in, and she asked me about the condom. She said you told her I was playing a joke on you, and I agreed that I'd done it."

"Thanks for having my back. I was meaning to call and let you know what was up, but I forgot."

"Well, I took care of it for you. Like I always do."

Later that day, we were scoping the streets in down-town St. Louis and got a call about a shooting on Cass Avenue. When we got to the crime scene, a seventeen-year-old was lying on the ground with a bullet in his shoulder. He was squirming around in pain, and after I rushed the dispatcher for an ambulance, I kneeled down next to him to find out what had happened. Miguel was talking to several people standing around, but as usual, nobody saw anything.

My attention remained focused on the teenager. "Listen, man, tell me what happened. You're losing a lot of blood, and I got an ambulance on the way to help you."

He painfully held his shoulder and squeezed his eyes together. "Ced and one of his boys shot me. I got jacked for some of his money, and he was upset."

"Where does Ced live?"

The teenager told me, and as soon as the ambulance came, Miguel and I made our way through the apartment complex to look for Ced.

I knocked on the door, and Miguel and I held our hands close to the gun holsters on our sides. The door came open, and as always, it was a female who opened the door with a baby on her side.

"Is Ced here?" I asked.

She moved aside and we walked in. The apartment was a mess. Filthy walls, busted-up furniture, and it reeked of piss. When this big black dude with nappy dreads came out, I assumed he was Ced.

I pulled my gun and aimed it at him. "Come sit down on the couch and tell me what just happened."

"I'on know what you talkin' 'bout," he said, continuing to stand up.

I got louder. "I said come sit down on the couch and tell me what just happened!"

He gritted his teeth that showed his gold grill. "And I said—"

Miguel fired right into the wall next to him, and Ced

ducked out of the way. The woman started screaming, and the baby cried. "Get down on the motherfucking ground," Miguel yelled. "Both of you!" He quickly grabbed the baby and put her in a playpen. I covered him. "Isaac, you be too damn nice to these fools. Now, my partner asked you what the hell just happened! We need some answers, now!"

"One of my other boys shot that punk for smokin' up all of his money. He gone and said he wat'en comin' back. Can't tell you where he is 'cause I don't know."

Miguel handcuffed Ced, and I cuffed the woman. As they lay on the floor, we stepped over them and slowly made our way through the apartment. The rest of the place was empty, but when I noticed a stack of money on the dresser, I made a motion for Miguel to check it out. He went over to it and picked up the stack. He flipped through it and nodded.

"About two, maybe three," he whispered.

Our rule was to only tamper if it was more than five G's, so I moved my head from side to side.

"Just a couple of hundred, okay?" he whispered again.

I nodded, and Miguel counted out several hundred dollars and stuck it inside his pants. We hurried back into the tiny living room and pulled both Ced and the woman from the floor.

"What's up with all this money, cuz?" I asked. "With money like this, I know there's a stash of dope somewhere."

"That's my girl's money. She do hair, and we've been saving for a new place."

"Is that right?" I said, looking around. "Yeah, you could surely use a new place. But too bad it won't be a place of your choice."

I shoved Ced to the door, and Miguel waited around so

the chick could call a neighbor to come get her baby. Shortly after, a friend came for the child. In the meantime, Ced and his lady were hauled off to jail until we got to the bottom of where the money came from, and who was responsible for shooting the teenager. I was certain that once a search warrant had been issued, the two of them would go to jail for a long, long time.

CYDNEY

I could feel that things were starting to change even more between Isaac and me. I hadn't seen or talked to him for two days, and normally, he'd always make his way home or at least call. His days away prompted me to give myself to Miguel once again. I felt horrible on the inside, but having sex with him wasn't bad at all. During sex, everything was fine. It was afterwards that ate at my insides. Miguel always wanted to cuddle and talk, but I was always anxious to get the hell out of there. He insisted that he understood my pain, but nobody did. So for now, I was dealing with it the best way I knew how.

Early Saturday morning, I rolled over in bed, and Isaac wasn't there. I didn't expect for him to be, but I surely thought I'd hear from him by now. According to Miguel, Isaac was still alive, so I wasn't worried about him being in any major trouble. Having a busy day scheduled, I put on my gray sweat pants and an old family reunion T-shirt. I left my hair in rollers, but covered my head with a white scarf. After I tied it, I went into the kitchen, poured some orange juice and grabbed my clippers to do some work in my garden. As I passed by the stairs to the atrium, I heard loud snores. I slowly crept down the stairs and saw Isaac lying on our contemporary lime green sofa, sound asleep. Hell, I didn't even know he was home. I guess he'd gotten tired of sleeping in bed with me, and that was fine by me. I headed back upstairs and made my way outside to the garden.

After spending nearly two hours clipping, cutting, trimming and planting, I was exhausted. Sweat rolled down my back, and the sun baked me with every minute that passed by. When I heard Isaac's old race car start up, I looked by the garage, and he was backing it into the driveway. He was shirtless, and had on a pair of khaki shorts that fell a little below his knees. The shorts revealed his muscular and thick, sweaty calves. He looked at me, and without saying one word, he turned his head. I got back to work on my garden, and he started to work on his car.

Another hour had gone by, and we remained silent. I was in dire need of some cold water, so I dropped my tools and headed inside to get some. Before going inside, I stopped to ask Isaac if he wanted some too. He lifted his head from underneath the hood of his car.

"Yes, thank you," he said, wiping his sweaty forehead. My eyes searched his dirty and sweaty body, and I had to admit, it looked tremendously good. Too bad I was upset with him for staying away from home, and even though I said I was going to let him know how I felt about it, I'd changed my mind. The less hurt he knew I was, the better.

Instead of water, I made both of us a tall glass of cold cherry Kool-Aid. And after popping a few grapes into my mouth, I picked up the glasses to take them outside. Just as I did, the phone rang. I looked at the caller ID, and it was my mother-in-law, Loretta. I knew she was calling to see if we were planning to attend the surprise birthday party for Isaac's dad, so I answered.

"Yes, Mother, we're still coming," I said.

"Hello, dear. I was just calling to make sure. It's still early, but I'm putting together some last minute preparations."

"Is there anything I can help you with? If so, please let me know."

"On your way, just stop by the grocery store and pick up an extra bucket of vanilla ice cream. We never seem to have enough ice cream. Oh, and don't forget the candles. I always forget the candles."

"I won't forget. If there's anything else you can think of, let me know."

"Thanks, Cydney. You're such a wonderful daughter-in-law. I'm blessed and I know it."

Her words brought tears to my eyes. "Mom, I'll see you later, okay?"

"Where's that son of mine? Let me speak to him."

"He's outside working on that raggedy race car of his."

She laughed. "He's been working on that car since he was sixteen years old. Don't bother him. I'll just see him when he gets here."

"Okay, but I'll be sure to tell him that you called."

Loretta and I ended our call, and I headed back outside to give Isaac his glass of Kool-Aid. When I got there, I was surprised to see Miguel next to his car, talking to him. It made me nervous, but I maintained my composure.

"Hi, Miguel," I said, handing the glass of Kool-Aid to Isaac. He thanked me, and Miguel couldn't pass up an opportunity to wrap his arms around me.

"What's up, Cydney?" he said. He squeezed me tight and kissed my cheek. I spoke back and quickly backed away.

"Loretta called and wanted to make sure we're coming to your father's surprise party. She wants us to bring ice cream and candles."

Isaac nodded and squinted his eyes from the bright sun shining in his face. His hands were covered with greasy motor oil, and he reached them out at me.

"Come here," he said, playfully trying to grab me. I backed away and laughed.

"You'd better go wash your hands if you want to touch me," I said.

"I am. 'Cause I for surely ain't getting nowhere with this damn car."

Just a little playfulness between my husband and me made Miguel uncomfortable. I smiled at him, and he gave me a fake smile back. Afterwards, I walked away and continued working in my garden.

I was just about ready to wrap things up when a thick thorn stuck me in my index finger. I yelled out loudly and looked at the blood as it dripped down my finger.

Isaac had given up on his car, but he and Miguel were still outside talking. I headed inside the house, squeezing my finger to stop the bleeding.

"Let me see it," Isaac said. I stuck my finger out to him, and he wiped it with a nearby paper towel. He attempted to remove the thorn, but I pulled away.

"Ouch, that hurts," I said.

"Then be still."

He continued to doctor me up, and once he removed the thorn, he wiped my finger with another paper towel and then placed the tip of my finger in his mouth. He sucked it and teased it with his lips. I slowly pulled my finger away.

"Thank you," I said.

"It feels a whole lot better now, doesn't it?"

"Yes. But a Band-Aid can take care of the rest."

I walked inside and went to the master bathroom to get a Band-Aid for my finger. I opened the closet, placed the

Band-Aid on my finger and then closed it. Once I did, I saw Miguel standing right by the door.

"You know my feelings are hurt, don't you?" he said.

"Well, I'm not trying to hurt your feelings, Miguel. Sorry if I did." My eyes searched behind him for Isaac. "Would you mind going back outside? I don't want—"

"I told Isaac I had to use the bathroom. He knows I might be a minute, but I thought I could come in here and sneak a little kiss." He leaned in, but I pushed him back.

"Not in my house, Miguel. I don't play games like that."

"Game? This ain't no game, baby. When you need me, I'm always there for you, so you've got to be there for me."

He leaned in again, and just to get him off my back, I gave him a tiny peck on the lips.

"Aw, you can do better than that, Cydney. Give me one of those kisses you gave me the other night. Now, that was something to remember."

I was getting nervous. "Miguel, I can't. Later, all right?"

He ignored me and forced another kiss on me. Since I didn't stop him, he got a bit more aggressive and started rubbing his hands all over my ass. When his hands went up my shirt and touched my breasts, I begged him to stop.

"Please, Miguel. Not like this . . . not in my home. I'll call you later. I promise."

Miguel ignored my demands. He backed me up to the wall and raised my T-shirt over my head. I couldn't scream because any noise from me would alarm Isaac. Miguel knew that as well, and kept on with his persistence. He sucked my breasts, and once he had those wet with his saliva, he slightly backed up and snatched my sweatpants down to my knees. Deviously, he unbuckled his pants and unzipped them. I pleaded with him again.

"Miguel, we can't do this. Isaac has plenty of guns around here, and he wouldn't think twice about using one if he walked in on this."

"You ain't ever been worried about Isaac using his gun, Cydney. Now, step out of your pants so we can get this over with. The more time you waste, the riskier this gon' get. I promise to make it quick."

At this point, all I could do was give Miguel what he wanted. I stepped out of my pants, and after he put on a condom, he stepped up to me. He lifted me against the wall, inserted himself and pumped away. I straddled him, in disbelief that this was happening.

"Come on, baby, and work with me. You worked good for me the other night, and I need for this pussy to make me come. You want me to come, don't you?" I slowly nodded. "Good. And I want you to come too."

I put forth a little more effort to make Miguel come, but I also knew he wanted me to talk dirty to him. He loved dirty talk, and required it every time we got together.

"Yeah, baby," he said, stroking me. "Give me some more of this good pussy. I want you to wet my magic stick. I want you to come."

"I'm coming," I said, faking it. "Your magic stick about to get slippery wet, baby. Just keep fucking me. Please don't stop fucking me." I'd gotten rather loud, and Miguel sped up the pace. He closed his eyes and sucked in his bottom lip. As my back slammed hard against the wall, I took a hard swallow. I regretted ever giving myself to him. This had to be one of the biggest mistakes of my life. Once he came, he took a deep breath and lowered my legs to the floor. I quickly stepped away from him and eased up my pants. I stood in front of the mirror and placed the palm of my hands on the sink. While zipping his pants, he came over to me and whispered in my ear.

"That was good. I wish Isaac would have come in on us, and you should have too. After all he's done to you, I don't know why you want to spare his feelings. If and when you need me again, you always know where to find me." He smacked my ass and kissed my cheek. After he flushed the used condom down the toilet, he walked out.

Still, I was in disbelief. I didn't ever think Miguel would pull a stunt like that. I was so wrong about him, and from that moment on, he would never be able to touch me again.

Feeling grimy, I took a shower and changed into the clothes I intended to wear to my in-laws' house. I put on a pair of khaki shorts with a cuff at the bottom, and a sleeveless, ruffled white button-down shirt. I pulled my hair over to rest on my left shoulder and slipped into my open-toed flat brown sandals.

I was hoping and praying that Miguel had left, but when I got outside, he was leaning against Isaac's car while talking to him. I put the long strap to my purse on my shoulder and stepped up to Isaac.

"I'm going to the store to get some items your mother asked me to get. Do you think you can be ready by the time I make it back?"

"How long will it take you? Why don't you just wait on me so we can go together?"

Honestly, I wanted to get the hell out of there and away from Miguel. But Isaac insisted that I wait for him.

"Give me a few minutes to shower and change and I'll be ready. It doesn't make sense for you to go all the way to the store, and then come back and get me."

I agreed to wait, and Isaac told Miguel he'd see him that night. Miguel slammed his fist against Isaac's and gave me a wink before walking to his car. I turned my head, relieved when I saw him drive away.

Isaac was ready to go in no time. He wore his dark

blue, well-pressed polo shorts and a sky blue T-shirt neatly tucked inside of his belted shorts. His phone was clipped to his shorts, and I knew his gun was tucked somewhere as well. He never left home without it, and I always felt safe when we were together.

Since he decided to drive his white truck, I hopped inside as he held the door open for me. He closed it and got in on the driver's side.

"So, what store do we need to go to?" he asked while backing out of the driveway.

"You can go to Schnucks, if you'd like. All she asked me to bring is some ice cream and candles."

Isaac nodded and drove to Schnucks, which was at least two miles from where we lived. When we got there, he told me that he'd go inside to get the items, and I opted to stay in the car. I asked to use his phone, just so I could call Loretta and see if she needed anything else. When I called her, she told me to bring several bags of ice. I knew she'd add to the list, so I told her I'd get it, and ended the call. As soon as I opened the door to get out, Isaac's phone vibrated. I thought it was Loretta calling me back, but when I answered, it was a chick asking to speak with Isaac.

"Who is this?" I asked.

"Who is this?" she snapped.

"This is his wife."

"And this is his lover."

"Well, nice to hear your voice, lover. He's busy right now. I'll be sure to tell him you called."

I hung up, angry that another woman would have the nerve to ask for my husband when I answered his phone. The boldness and lack of concern was unbelievable! More than anything, my frustrations lay with Isaac because he had no business giving out his phone number to begin with. Since she called herself his lover, I assumed it had to be Laquinta. Besides, I knew her voice from speaking with her in the past, and I was positive that it was her. I made my way inside the store to find Isaac and to pick up a few bags of ice. As soon as I put the ice into a cart, his phone vibrated again. It was a different number, so I picked up. It was another woman asking to speak with him.

"May I ask who's calling?" I responded.

"Avena," she said properly.

"Avena, when Isaac gave you his number to call him, did he tell you he was married?" She didn't say a word. "Hello?" I said.

"May I speak to Isaac, please?"

"Hold on a minute," I said, pushing my cart up to where he stood in line. I placed the phone on his ear and picked up a magazine. I pretended to be occupied.

"Hello," he said. After hearing her voice, he looked at me. "Let me hit you back later." He paused. "I don't know, but I can't talk right now." For a few more seconds, he held the phone to his ear and then hung up. He looked at me as I continued to page through the magazine.

"I take it that my mother wanted some ice," he said, looking into my cart.

"Uh-huh," I replied, not looking up. "She wanted some ice, and your lover wants you to call her back too."

"My lover? Who's my—"

"I don't know. When I asked, that's what she told me her name was. You might want to check your caller ID."

He searched the numbers, and after seeing who it was, he clipped his phone back to his shorts. I kept my mouth shut, especially because of what had just happened between Miguel and me.

As usual, we had a blast at my in-laws' house. Isaac's two brothers and their wives were there, and his sister and her fiancé were there too. One of his brothers had two kids, and the other had three. Along with my father-in-law, Jake, his friends and other family members, the backyard was pretty packed. Isaac and his brother, Carl, did most of the barbecuing, and all of the ladies stayed in the kitchen, whipping up desserts and making side dishes. The huge birthday cake for Jake was enough, but Loretta always went out of her way whenever she planned a party.

From working in the garden all morning, I was exhausted, and removed the apron from around my waist. I poured a glass of lemon iced tea and headed to the backyard with Carl's wife, Peggy. She was a white woman, but her race didn't matter to anyone in the family, except for Isaac. He had a thing for women with a dark complexion, and a white woman or light-skinned black woman didn't stand a chance. All we cared was that she loved Carl, and everyone else in the family very well knew she did.

I watched Isaac and his brothers having a good time as they laughed and cooked the meat. A huge part of me felt as if this was where I belonged, but I knew that at the rate our marriage was going, all of this would someday come to an end. We could only put up a front for so long, and while we were in the kitchen talking earlier, Isaac's mom noticed something about me. She said that she'd talk to me later, and I hoped that she couldn't see through the bullshit act that Isaac and I had put on for everybody.

Peggy sipped from her glass of tea and put it down on the table. After she dabbed her son's mouth with a napkin, I asked if I could hold him.

"He is so cute," I said, reaching for him. "How old is he again?"

"He just turned seven months. I can't wait until he at least starts walking."

"Oh, I'm sure. He's big to be seven months, and so, so cute," I said, rubbing his nose with mine.

"Cydney, when are you and Isaac going to start a family? You guys have been together a long time, and I'm surprised that you don't have any kids yet."

I looked over at Isaac, who was still laughing and joking around with his brothers. Yes, I wanted children, but not like this. Every time we came around his family, I envied each and every one of their relationships. "We're still holding out, Peggy. I've been trying, but it just hasn't happened yet."

"Well, don't give up. And any time you need a little practice, you can always borrow mines."

I smiled, and Loretta yelled for everyone to come inside so we could sing "Happy Birthday" to Jake. I gave the baby back to Peggy, and Isaac came over and whispered in my ear.

"Don't go getting any ideas," he said playfully.

"Shut up talking to me," I whispered as we held hands and went inside. Isaac stood behind me and wrapped his arms around my waist. A part of me felt so uncomfortable, but then again, his arms felt nice. We all sang "Happy Birthday" to Jake, and once we were finished, he had to make a speech, like always.

"Thank you, thank you, and thank you again," he said. "I thank y'all for remembering this old man, and Loretta and I are so blessed to have a family as close and loving as all of you. To see my sons laughing and playing like they did when they were kids, and my daughter who's soon to be taken away from me by another man, all I can say is I'm grateful." Everybody laughed. "Anyhow, I hope that God blesses me with many more years of being with everyone, and many more grandbabies too." He looked at me and Isaac, and all I could do was smile. "Sons, keep on making me proud. I know that the good women that you've chosen to be by your sides are the reason that all of you have been successful in your careers and in your everyday lives. If it wasn't for Loretta, only Lord knows where I'd be." He teared up, and she squeezed his hand. "Anyhow, keep on loving each other, and let's pray for many more close and loving generations to come."

We all bowed our heads to pray, and as Jake kept on with his touching words, my eyes started to fill with tears. I blinked to clear them, but I couldn't stop several tears that had rolled down my cheeks. When Isaac felt a tear drop on his arm, he leaned to the side and looked at me. I closed my eyes, and once Jake was finished, I quickly stepped away. I went into the bathroom and closed the door. Hurt and pain was everywhere inside of me, and I didn't know how to stop it. There was a knock on the door, and I knew it was Isaac.

"Cydney," he said. "Open the door."

I hurried to wipe my face and cracked the door. "What?" I said.

"Are you okay?" he asked.

"I'm fine. I just need to use the bathroom, that's all."

"Are you ready to go?"

"Yes, please, I'm sorry. After your father cuts the cake, I'd like to go home, if you don't mind."

He stepped away from the door and I closed it. Before leaving the bathroom, I gathered myself and took a deep breath. I walked out as if nothing had bothered me.

Once the cake was cut, I told Loretta I had the cramps real bad and needed to go home and lie down. She told me to call her so we could talk, and after we said goodbye to everyone, we left.

The ride home was by no means quiet. Isaac's phone rang so much that he was forced to turn it off. I kept my cool by looking out the window until we made it home.

As soon as Isaac pulled in the driveway, I got out of the car. I rushed inside and went into our bedroom to get ready for bed. Surely, Isaac noticed my mood. He climbed in bed behind me and attempted to comfort me, but I pulled the covers over me.

"I know that being at my parents' house was difficult for you, Cydney, and I appreciate you going there with me."

"What are we going to do about this marriage, Isaac? All of this lying and pretending is driving me crazy."

"Do you want a divorce? I'm telling you right now, for the record, it's not what I want."

I lay on my back and looked at him. "Then why do you continue to do the things that you do? You act as if you don't care, and—"

To quiet me, he leaned down and kissed me. For the first time in many, many months, I kissed him back. Hatred for what he'd done to me roamed in my head, and after moments of kissing, I broke our embrace.

"Let me make love to you," he said, already touching my breasts. "I've missed touching your body and loving your insides, Cyd. Just let me make things right between us."

He kissed me again, and as things got heated, he removed my nightgown. Maybe it was time for us to give our marriage another try. The visit to his parents' house gave me hope that things could be the same for us as they were for his parents and siblings. A part of me knew Isaac wanted the same thing too, but I wasn't sure how all the hurt we'd caused each other could be forgotten.

Either way, I made my way on top of him, and he touched all over my naked body, particularly my ass and hips. He closed his eyes and massaged me with his hands.

"I love you . . . I miss this feeling," he moaned. "You will not regret—"

I lowered myself to kiss him because I knew Isaac's words were a lie. I knew I'd regret giving myself to him.

We'd been there and done this before. In knowing so, I got my head on straight and got off his hardness. I lay on my back, and he moved between my legs.

"What's wrong?" he asked.

"Isaac, as much as I want to, I can't do this with you."

"What do you mean, you can't do this?" He got angry. "Do you feel how hard I am? Don't you know how bad I want you? You're my wife, Cyd, and I shouldn't have to beg you like this. Every time we get close to making love, I have to beg you to continue."

I couldn't say one word. I just stared at him. He lowered himself and brushed his lips against my inner thighs. I knew he wanted to love my insides, and as I started to think about how well he could perform, I also thought about Miguel being inside of me earlier. I scooted back and pressed my tightened knees close to my chest.

"I'm sorry, baby. I will not give myself to you under these conditions."

He quickly stood up. "Fuck it then, Cydney. You playing this 'turn me off then turn me on' game, and I don't have time for the bullshit. When I leave you for someone else, please don't be mad at me."

"How could I be mad, Isaac? Realistically, you've already left me for someone else, haven't you?"

He walked out, and moments later, the front door slammed.

ISAAC

My blood was boiling, and I was furious! To hell with Cydney and her games. I saw how hurt she was at my parents' house, and I felt inspired and encouraged by my dad's words. He had a lot of faith in me . . . in us, and I felt as if my being able to make love to my wife would be a turning point for me. The whole time I was at my parents' house, I kept thinking, *To hell with Laquinta.* I was going to try hard at removing myself from that relationship, and work on not pursuing other women, but so much for that thought! How could I give up my other fulfilling relationships if Cydney would never give me a chance to make things right? Didn't she know that I had needs too? I guess not, so fuck it. Until she was willing to make some changes, I'd keep on doing what I did best.

I told Miguel that I'd help him out at the club that night, working security. However, Cydney had me so angry that I didn't feel like working at all. I still had on the casual attire I'd worn to my parents' house, so I made my way over to the club just to see what was going down.

When I got there, it was crammed inside. I saw Miguel

sitting on a stool with his uniform on. He was talking to several females who were all over him. As I stepped up to him, he excused himself from the ladies.

"Where are you going, Terrence?" one of the ladies asked, referring to Terrence Howard. He hated to be called Terrence, so he corrected her. "It's not Terrence, baby. It's Miguel." He turned to me. "What took you so long, and why aren't you in uniform?"

" 'Cause me and Cydney got into it. I don't feel like working, and I stopped in to give you the word."

"Is everything cool? I mean you ain't have to bust her up, did you?"

"Naw, nothing like that. I just get tired of begging for sex from my own damn wife, that's all."

"Shit, I would too, but, uh, come here. You've got to see this," he said, walking me through the crowd.

Smiles, "hellos," and flirting eyes were all over the place. Cydney didn't know what the hell she was missing out on.

Miguel stopped in front of the bar and told me to look over his shoulder. I checked the dance floor and saw nothing that caught my eye. He told me to look harder, and that's when I saw Laquinta. She wore a thigh-high, body-hugging, black jean dress with silver buttons down the front. The top buttons were undone, and a healthy part of her cleavage showed. Her braids were neatly pulled back, and showed her pretty chocolate face. When she saw me, she left her dance partner and strutted her way to me. I gazed at her oiled, slim legs and at the wooden high-heeled shoes that gave her much height. Before she reached me, she was stopped twice. She ignored the brothas and made her way to me.

"You know what I'm about to ask you, don't you?" she said.

In deep thought, I placed my hand on my chin. "Why am I here, and why haven't I returned any of your calls?"

She used her small purse and hit me in my arm. "You got it. So, why haven't you called me? And I didn't think you liked coming to nightclubs."

Miguel interrupted. "I asked him to come help me out tonight, but since he won't be helping me, I'm gone leave y'all at peace." He stepped away, and I looked Laquinta up and down.

"You know you got it going on, don't you?" I said. "Turn around."

"I'd like to think I got it going on," she said, turning around. "But maybe not as much as I think, since you won't return my phone calls."

I didn't really hear what she said, as I was too busy thinking about what she had on underneath. "You don't have on any underclothes, do you?" I asked.

"Why don't you reach underneath my dress and see?"

I moved her as close to the bar as I could and reached underneath her dress. All I felt was a bare, soft ass.

I gave her a serious look and whispered. "Baby, you don't know what you do to me, do you?"

Laquinta laughed and held my hand on her ass. She pulled my hand up to her hip.

"I have a thong on, Isaac. If you would have searched beyond my butt cheeks, you would have felt it."

"Hey, that's even better. What color is it? And please don't tell me red."

"Okay, then I won't tell you," she said, removing my hand. "But I'll give you a hint."

"What's that?" I smiled.

"You gave them to me on Valentine's Day."

"Then they're red. I gave you some red ones on Valentine's Day."

"Lucky guess," she said, getting ready to walk away. I lightly pulled her arm.

"Do you want something to drink?"

She nodded and I gave her a hundred-dollar bill. I asked her to get me a Corona, and she stood by the bar to get our drinks.

I'd seen Miguel getting into it with some fellas at the door, so I stepped up to where he was. When I asked if everything was cool, he assured me that it was.

"Yeah, I got everything under control. I told these punks they can't come in here with no damn tennis shoes on."

One of the brothas quickly spoke up. "And all I'm saying is we've been in here with tennis shoes on before. What's the big damn deal?"

"The big damn deal," I said, "is you too close to my partner's face and you disrespecting him. He don't like to be disrespected, do you, Miguel?"

"Hell, naw. It pisses me the fuck off. Sometimes, I get all crazy and shit and start beating niggas asses for no reason."

"Now, y'all don't want that to happen, do you?" I said, moving them back towards the entrance. "Just go get your Stacy Adams on and we won't have no problem letting you in."

The three youngsters talked all kinds of shit before leaving. I stepped back over by Miguel and took a seat on a stool.

"Guess who had the nerve to call me today?" I said.

"Who?" he asked.

"Avena. Cyd answered my cell phone and it was her."

"What did she want?"

"I don't know and I don't care. I haven't called her back, nor do I intend to."

"She gon' keep bugging your ass, trust me. After a while, she'll give up."

We laughed, and when two light-skinned chicks entered the club, Miguel nudged me.

"Now, I know you don't like 'em like that, but you've got to appreciate women who put that much time and effort into looking good."

I had to admit, the ladies' beauty and figures did cause me to take a double look, especially the one who had on a pair of white pants that revealed a tattoo on her lower back. Her fishnet white top only covered her breasts and left her midriff and back bare. As soon as they walked towards us, I asked for their IDs. Miguel reached for one, and I reached for the one that seemed to catch my eye.

I worked the Juicy Fruit gum and looked at the young woman's name on her ID. "Sidney, huh?" I smiled.

She reached for her ID. "I thought you were supposed to be checking my age, not my name. But now that you know it, do you mind sharing yours?"

"Isaac. And don't hurt nobody up in here tonight, Sidney. As fine as you are, I know that might be impossible."

She smiled and looked back at her friend, who was conversing with Miguel.

"I'm going to the restroom. Meet me there," she said.

Her friend nodded, and before walking away, she gave me one hell of a look. I watched her ass. All these panty-less women were driving me crazy. As my eyes followed her to the restroom, Laquinta came up and turned my head.

"Your drink," she said, handing it to me. "I know damn well you ain't up in here flirting with anybody."

"Hell, naw, baby. I know her from scoping the streets. She's one of my connections."

Damn near choking on my lie, I took a sip from my

Corona and set it on the table next to me. Laquinta stood close by me and sipped on her drink. Once Miguel got up to see about something, she took a seat on his stool. All kinds of females that I knew from working the streets came in, and every time one of them would hug me or get close to me, Laquinta got bent out of shape. After a while, I asked her to move away from me.

"Oh, you would like that, wouldn't you?" she griped.

"Look, I don't need you sweating me, baby. Go and have yourself some fun. You claim you don't get out that often, so go dance and enjoy yourself."

Pissed, she rolled her eyes and stepped away from me. I expected her to try to make me jealous, and that's exactly what she did. She stepped to every brotha that looked her way. She flirted and gave her phone number to many. Hell no, I wasn't jealous. I knew I could have her pussy any day, any time, and any moment that I wanted it. That's why I was working on something else for the night. It was either Sidney, or this other chick I'd seen while driving the streets with Miguel. I didn't know her name, but she kept her eyes on me, and I couldn't stop looking her way either.

As my eyes searched the crowded club, Sidney came up to me and leaned on my shoulder.

"Do you work here often?" she asked.

"No, I don't work here at all. My partner in crime does, and he asked me to come help him out tonight."

"Oh. So, you both are police officers, huh?"

I nodded and could see Laquinta watching me from a distance.

"Well, this is my first time here. It's okay, I guess. My girlfriend comes here often, and since I'm from L.A., you know our clubs be popping way more than this."

"I bet they do," I said, sitting up straight so she could

move her arm from my shoulder. She did, and seconds later, Laquinta walked up to us.

"Isaac, baby, what time are you leaving? I'll be ready to go soon, and I wondered if you'd take me home."

Now, she knew better than to front on me like that. I looked at her and stared. "How did you get here? However you got here is the same way you're going to get home. I'm not leaving yet."

"Well, I'm ready to go," she snapped. "Since you call yourself my man, I'm asking you to take me home now!"

I was already going to make Laquinta pay for calling my phone and telling Cydney she was my lover, but even more so now that she kept frontin' on me. Yes, Cydney had confronted me about Laquinta before, but I never admitted to having an ongoing relationship with her. Cydney was always left to assume, but Laquinta's phone call kind of validated things for Cydney. No doubt, I was pissed.

"Laquinta, I'm not your man. As a matter of fact, I'm a married man. Don't be coming up to me with this attitude like I owe you something. I don't owe you a damn thing, and a ride home tonight will not come from me."

Her feisty ass had the nerve to smack me, and hard too. It was loud and turned many heads in the club. I jumped up from my stool and snatched her collar. I pulled it, and we made our way outside. I shoved her against the brick wall and placed my hand above her head.

"What in the fuck is wrong with you?" I said. "You don't put your got-damn hands on me like that, woman!"

She pouted and shot daggers at me with her eyes. "You shouldn't be up in there flirting with no bitches right in front of my face. I don't give a shit what you do when I'm not around, but don't be disrespecting me like that."

"If you want respect, Laquinta, you've got to give it.

Don't you ever, ever put your hands on me again! Now, I'm going back inside. As for you, you're going home. Get in your car and go home because I'm not letting you back in this club tonight."

"You don't have no control over where I go," she said, walking away to go back inside.

I pulled the back of her collar. "Don't make me hurt you, all right? I said go home and I'll be there in about an hour. We can finish this conversation up then!"

She snatched away from me and tried desperately to go back inside. I was getting furious with her, and gave her a hard shove backwards. "Please save yourself the embarrassment. I don't want to hurt you out here, baby, but you're leaving me no choice. Go home, and I swear to you that I'll be there in an hour, okay?" I spoke calmly.

No doubt, she was pissed, but by the look in my eyes, she wasn't about to challenge me. The last time she did, she paid dearly for it, and I wound up apologizing for many, many days. As she seemed to calm down, I escorted her to her car, and not saying one word to me, she left.

When I got back inside, Miguel was waiting by the door, cracking up. I already knew what it was about, and all I could do was shake my head.

"You heard it, didn't you?" I asked.

"Man, that smack was so loud, I heard it over the music. I looked up and thought I was gon' have to come peel her ass up off the floor. You should have fucked her up for that one. She was way, way out of line. I don't recall you ever saying Cydney went out like that, and she's your wife."

"I know," I said. "Laquinta will pay for it later, though. I bet she'll never try that shit again."

As Miguel and I continued to talk, Sidney and her friend came over by us. She had a set of keys in her hands, and it appeared that they were getting ready to leave.

"Leaving so soon?" I asked.

"I am," she said. "My friend isn't. She's staying, and I'm using her car to go back to the hotel."

I picked up her hand and removed the keys. "It's dangerous for a woman to be by herself at night. I'll take you back to the hotel. You'll be safe with me."

"Not after watching your girlfriend smack you the way she did. If she sees us leave together, she might knock me upside my head or something."

I laughed and handed the keys over to her friend. "I'll take Sidney back to the hotel. She's in good hands, and whenever you get there, she'll be there waiting for you."

"Is that cool?" her friend asked. "Miguel said that once the club closes, he'd follow me to the hotel, so I'll meet you there."

"That's cool." Sidney said, and I followed behind her as she left.

By 4:30 in the morning, I had already taken Sidney to the hotel, fucked her, and was on my way to Laquinta's house. Sidney was too damn easy, and the moment we stepped into the hotel room, her clothes were off. I'd been teasing her in the car, and her insides were on fire for me. The only problem was, she came too quickly. After that, she really wasn't much good. She got tired, and I had to do all of the work. I didn't mind because some of my frustrations were taken out on her. The rest, I saved for Laquinta.

I knocked on Laquinta's door at about 4:45 in the morning. She opened it, still in the dress she'd worn at the club. Saying nothing to me, she walked over to the couch, sat yoga style, and placed a pillow in her lap. Since she was partially in the dark, I turned on the lights so I could see her. No doubt, she was upset.

"If you gon' sit there and pout, I can just leave."

She folded her arms. "Where have you been, Isaac?

You told me you'd be here in about an hour. It's damn near five o'clock in the morning!"

"I don't need to be reminded of the time, and I don't answer to nobody but my wife. Hell, I barely answer to her, so you know damn well that you ain't got nothing coming."

She got up, stomped to the door and opened it. "Fuck you and your wife, Isaac! You don't ever have to answer to me, and both of you can go to hell!"

I pointed my finger at her and slammed the door. "Leave my wife out of your mouth, all right? As a matter of fact, if you ever call my phone and she answers, hang the motherfucker up! You know the rules, Laquinta, and how in the hell are you going to try and keep tabs on a married man? It can't be done, sweetheart, and you're making a fool out of yourself trying to keep me in line."

"What did I ever do to you but love you? I've put up with your mess, and I've allowed you to walk all over me. Not once—"

"Not once did I ask you to do shit for me, Laquinta! I didn't ask you to love me. You did that on your own. Hell, I didn't even ask for a child, but you lied to me about being on the pill and gave me one anyway. You knew I was married, and when I gave you money for an abortion, you used it for something else." Angry, I knocked over her floor lamp and it smashed to the floor. The light went out, and Laquinta came back over to the couch. She plopped down, furious with me.

"So, now you're making me pay for it, Isaac? Is that what you're doing? Putting all the blame on me? Well, I'm not the one to blame. You need to take a look at your own self," she griped then covered her face.

"I do take responsibility for what I've done. Truthfully, I'm the one who's a fool for taking care of a baby that might not be mine." I stepped up to her and removed her hands from her face. "She ain't mine, is she, Laquinta? Erica looks nothing like me."

"You're just afraid to face the facts. You're hoping that she's not yours so you can have an excuse to end this with me and work things out with your wife."

"I don't keep coming here because of Erica, Laquinta. And whenever I have a blood test done, you'd better hope and pray like hell that she's mine. Up until recently, I haven't asked you for a blood test because I trusted that you wouldn't lie to me. But the more and more I look at Erica, I have doubts. If she's not mine, some serious shit gon' go down between you and me, you understand?" I said, grabbing her face.

She snatched her face away from me. "I said she's yours, and if she's not the reason you keep taking care of me, then why do you do it?"

I pulled Laquinta up from the couch and unbuttoned her dress. Once I pulled it off, she stood before me in her thong. I pulled it apart in the back until it tore. It fell to the floor, and I grabbed her pussy and squeezed it in my hand.

"This is what's causing me to do the crazy-ass things I do. You know I'm hooked, but you've got to stop causing me so much grief, especially since I get enough of that at home. If not, I swear I won't have no problem letting you go. Just . . . just stop tripping with me, baby, and I promise you that everything will be all right."

I stuck my fingers inside of Laquinta and she hiked up on the tips of her toes. Unable to handle my touch, she sat back on the couch and opened her legs. I got on my knees and placed her opened legs on my shoulders. I pecked her thighs, and before loving the inside of her slit, I looked up at her.

"I'm sorry for some of the hurtful things I said to you. At times, I get carried away and I later regret some things I say and do."

"Me too," she said, lowering my head down to her good stuff. I pushed her widened legs close to her chest and went to work. "I . . . I'm sorry for putting my hands on you, and it will never," she took several deep breaths, "never, ever happen again."

I stopped for a moment, just to confirm my words. "You'd better make sure it never happens again, and I mean it."

Anxious for her, I resumed my business.

CYDNEY

One thing I knew about Isaac, when mad or not, he meant every word he said. His last words to me were, if I didn't get my shit together, he'd leave me for someone else. I wasn't too worried about it, but there was no way I'd let him have the final say-so in this marriage. While he was away the night before, I thought hard about where our marriage was headed. The only answer I could come up with was nowhere. Isaac wasn't willing to make any changes, and at this point, neither was I. Finally, reality had set in, and if I ever intended to be happy again, I had to be honest with myself and with Isaac about how miserable my life was. I was tired of pretending, and keeping up this charade in front of our families was getting ridiculous. It was only a matter of time before the truth would come to light. I could tell that Isaac's mom and mine could see right through us. I knew they'd be hurt by my decision to end our marriage, but Isaac left me no other choice. Certainly, my happiness was more important than anyone else's.

Sunday was supposed to be a day of rest, but not in my household. Around one o'clock in the afternoon, Isaac strolled in looking and smelling as if he'd been soaking in sex. He walked right past me and headed for the shower. As he stood and let the hot and steamy water pour on him, I stood in the doorway.

"Wash all of her residue off you, please. And once you're done rinsing, make sure you wash yourself again."

"Cydney, I'm tired. I'm not up to arguing with you today."

"I'm not going to argue with you, Isaac, but it's time that either you or I left. Which one of us is going to be the brave one? That's the question."

"Well, I'm not going anywhere," he said. "This is my house, and I'm staying right here."

"Fine," I said, walking away and into my closet. "And make sure you can pay the bills in *your* house too."

I pulled out my suitcase and laid it on the bed. Isaac turned off the water, grabbed a towel and wrapped it around him. He looked at me as I entered the closet and pulled out some clothes. Saying nothing, he dried off his body, moved my suitcase aside and got in bed. He turned his back to me and pulled the sheets over his head. I continued packing up more necessities, and since I had so much stuff, I knew I'd have to come back for many of my belongings later. Either way, the suitcase was filled to capacity, and I pulled it off the bed so I could go.

As soon as I made it to the entryway of our bedroom, Isaac yanked the sheets off his head and yelled my name.

"What?" I yelled back and turned.

"Why are you being so silly? This—"

"Silly? Do you think this is a game or something, Isaac? You're the one who's silly for treating this marriage as you have, and you'll be hearing from my attorney soon."

"Whatever," he said, pulling the sheets over his head again.

I cut my eyes at him and continued out the door.

The moment I left, I knew my whole life was about to change. The first thing I did was check into a hotel for the night, thinking about how to move forward. Monday, I'd go into work and ask Darrell for some time off. I was sure he'd give it to me, but maybe it was time for me to be honest with him about my situation. I wasn't happy about sharing the truth, but I didn't feel good about constantly lying to my boss, who had been nothing but honest and upfront with me.

As I sat at the hotel, looking through some travel brochures, I tried to decide where I could go for the next week or two. I'd had the brochures sent to me a year ago, as I'd thought about trying to patch up things between Isaac and me. That never happened, and what a waste of time it would have been. Either way, I wanted to go somewhere nice, quiet and relaxing. The kind of place I was thinking of would surely cost me a fortune, but a vacation for me was long overdue. When I came across a brochure from the Four Seasons Resort in Maui, it instantly caught my eye. After I got on my laptop and researched the packages, I was sold. Fifteen thousand dollars was a lot for a vacation, but no one deserved it more than me.

Surprisingly, I slept like a baby that night. My head was clear and my mind was focused. Yes, I'd thought about my failed marriage to Isaac, and the thoughts of it hurt deeply inside. However, I couldn't allow it to consume me, and I was more than anxious to take my trip.

When I got to my office, I buzzed Darrell and told him that we needed to talk. He came right in and closed the door behind him.

"You sounded anxious, Cydney. I . . . I hope you're not leaving the company—are you?"

"No, nothing like that, Darrell. I'm happy with my job. But sadly, it's my marriage that's in question."

"What?" he yelled, taking a seat on my sofa.

I stood up, folded my arms and gazed out of the window. It hurt me like hell to even think about discussing my issues, but at the same time, it felt good to get things off my chest. "Yes, Darrell. I think it's time for me to throw in the towel. Isaac and I have had problems for many years, and I haven't been happy for quite some time."

"Cydney, noooo. Every time I see the two of you—"

"It's been an act, Darrell. He doesn't love me anymore, and I've fallen out of love with him. I didn't call you in here to discuss my marriage, but I wanted to know if I could have some time off. I need to clear—"

"Sure, sure," he said hurriedly. "Take as much time as you need. I'm sorry about this, and I certainly had no idea."

I walked over and held my arms out for a hug. Darrell stood up and embraced me. "Darrell, please don't tell anyone about this. I'd like to keep everything under wraps until I decide what to do."

"I wouldn't tell a soul."

Darrell walked away to pour us some coffee, and after he handed the cup to me, we both took a seat.

"So," I said, "how are things going with you and your girlfriend?"

"It's a disaster. I've asked her to marry me, but I'm still seeing someone else. She's so darn emotional, and the thought of hurting her is killing me inside."

"Darrell, you've got to be honest with her about your feelings. Marrying her is not the answer, trust me. Right about now, I'm not one to give advice, but you'll be so much happier in the long run if you start by being honest. It's better to hurt her now than hurt her later."

Darrell agreed, and we stayed in my office most of the morning discussing his situation and mine. To my surprise, I felt comfortable speaking with Darrell. He said that Isaac was a fool, and was taken aback when I told him I'd been sleeping with someone as well. He was in total disbelief, but even though he was, he wished that Isaac and I somehow could work out our issues.

The prime oceanview suite at the Four Seasons Resort in Maui was the best. As soon as I got there, I pulled off my white straw hat, sat on the soft, queen-sized bed, and fell backwards. I looked up at the ceiling fan and wanted to scream for not doing this sooner. The room was to die for. It was furnished with bright, tropical colors and had an view of the white sandy beaches. White French doors separated the bedroom from the living room and adjacent dining room. Nearby was a built-in bar for my drinking pleasure, and I surely intended to make use of it. The bathroom was made of marble, and the entire room had to be at least three thousand square feet. No doubt, I was in heaven.

I stepped outside on the balcony and checked out the amazing scenery. What a beautiful sight it was, as the blue waters and flowered gardens brought tears to my eyes. This was a moment for Isaac and me to enjoy together, but so much for that. I'd planned to make the best of my vacation, and I hurried to unpack so I could change into my swimming gear.

It didn't take long for me to change into my peach-and-white one-piece swimming suit and sheer wrap that tied around my waist. I'd thought about wearing my white straw hat, but instead, I brushed my long hair over to the side and let it rest on my right shoulder. As I stood looking at myself in the oval-shaped glass mirror, there was a knock on the door, and my cell phone rang at the same time. I'd forgotten to turn off my cell phone, but I rushed to see who it was. I'd told Darrell to only call me if there was an emergency, but when I looked at the caller ID, the caller was anonymous. I answered the phone as I opened the door. I heard Miguel call my name as my personal server came into my room with fresh flowers.

"Hold on," I said to Miguel and lowered the phone to my side. I looked at the server. "Thank you. The flowers are beautiful."

He walked them over to a crystal floor vase by the balcony and put them inside.

"We do this for all of our guests," he said while arranging the long-stem flowers. "And if you need anything else, please let me know. My name is Mylee."

I walked up to him. "And my name is Cydney. I won't be needing anything else right now, but if I do, I'll be sure to call."

The Asian man smiled, nodded and made his way to the door.

"Call the front desk, Cydney. They will page me if you need anything."

I nodded, and once he closed the door, I put the phone back on my ear.

"What is it?" I said.

"Damn, baby. Your tone would imply that you're mad at me about something. You not returning my phone calls would mean the same, and I hate to be ignored."

"Miguel, your game is over. Just in case Isaac hasn't already told you, we're getting a divorce. Now, like I told you the other day when I did return your phone call, I'm taking a vacation to Maui. I need some time alone, and what we had . . . we have no more. You're gonna have to find another one of Isaac's women to toy with because this one here is out of the picture." Not wanting Miguel or anyone else to ruin my vacation, I disconnected him. Before I turned off my phone, I at least called my mother to let her know my whereabouts.

"Maui," she yelled.

"Mom, I promise I'll be back in a week, or maybe two."

"Okay, but you should have told me this before. You know how I feel about you riding on those planes. Anything could have happened to you."

"Sorry, but my boss was in a rush," I lied. "We almost missed our plane, and as soon as we got here, I had to attend a conference. I'm on my way to another one now, so I have to go, okay?"

"Where's Isaac?"

"Uh, he . . . he's on his way here. He got caught up at the station and had to take a separate flight. I'm expecting him soon. Normally, he doesn't attend my business trips with me, but we needed some quality time together too."

"Well, that's good. At least he'll be there with you. Be careful and call me as soon as you get back to St. Louis."

"I will, Mom. Love you."

"I love you too," she said, and then hung up. Feeling awful about lying to my mother, I wiped a few tears that had fallen then turned off my phone. I tossed it on the bed and left the room so I could enjoy the rest of the day.

No doubt, by the end of the day, I knew why this island was considered paradise. I'd done everything from snorkeling to horseback riding. After taking a helicopter ride and going on a scenic waterfall hike, I was exhausted. While on the helicopter, I met a black lady named Dez, who was taking a vacation as well. She and I met up for drinks, chat and dinner on the beach.

"My Charles has only been gone for three months, and my life hasn't been the same without him. I needed this vacation badly," Dez said while sipping her wine.

"I'm sorry for your loss. From what you said earlier, Charles sounded like a wonderful husband."

"He was. I couldn't ask for more."

I wanted to change the subject because this was a time for us to enjoy ourselves and not think about the hurtful things in our lives. Dez's husband had prostate cancer, and her deep thoughts of him caused me to think of Isaac.

For a while, we sat quietly. That was until the waiter came over and placed lobster tails in front of us.

"Now, that should get us in the mood," Dez said, looking at the lobster. She was a beautiful woman who put me in the mindset of Patti Labelle. Richy-rich was written all over her, but no matter how hard she tried, a bit of sadness still covered her face. I could tell she was much older than I was, but the way we clicked, it didn't even matter.

Dez fell back in her chair while chewing her food. She placed her hand on her chest. "Girl, this is delicious, isn't it?"

The taste of the lobster made my mouth water for more. "It's more than delicious. I just hope there's plenty more wherever this came from."

We laughed and continued on with our dinner and chatting.

Not intending to, I sat at the table and spilled the beans about Isaac's and my relationship to a complete stranger. When I told Dez about some things that had transpired between Isaac and me, she appeared to be in disbelief. Several times, her mouth hung open, and she kept moving her head from side to side.

"Umph, umph, umph," was all she could say, and after hearing myself tell it all, that's all I could say too.

"How does a marriage get that bad?" she asked. "There is no way in hell I would have put up with that mess. Your husband is out of line, and you haven't been no saint either. Two wrongs don't make a right, Cydney."

"I know it doesn't, but being with someone else, at times, made me feel a lot better."

"Only for the moment, I'm sure it did. But you've got to be better than he is. So many people think that revenge is the answer, but by taking that route, all you're doing is hurting yourself. Being married for thirty-one years, Charles and I had bumps too. Early on in our marriage, he cheated on me one time. I did the three p's and prayed for him, packed my bags, and pitched him. I left and told him that when he worked out his *issues*, I'd be waiting for him. Honey, that man missed those meals, he missed having his clothes washed and laid out for him, and let's not go there with the sex." She laughed. "But when he figured out that no woman would love him like I did, he got his mess together. We went to counseling, and after that, everything was fine. It took time for us to heal, and if he ever stepped out on our marriage again, I knew nothing of it. Any man who is capable of keeping their mess outside of the home is all right with me."

"Well, you wouldn't like Isaac at all. His mess is all over the place. He doesn't care what I know about his infidelities, and I can't understand how or why I haven't divorced his butt yet."

As open as I was with Dez about my marriage, I hadn't told her that I'd already left Isaac and wanted a divorce. Instead, I wanted to hear her thoughts.

"Timing, Cydney. When the time comes for you to let go, then you will. Then again, that time might not ever come. You can't base that decision on what I say, or what others say, but you have to do what feels right for you."

"I agree," I said as we held our glasses up and clinked them together.

Dez and I hung out until dawn. The beach was still crowded with partygoers and couples who were there on their honeymoon. The sky was too beautiful, and to go inside would have been a sin. Basically, I had no choice because if I yawned one more time, I was bound to fall asleep in the white wicker chair. Dez gave her good-byes and said she'd see me in the morning. We agreed to meet up early for breakfast and take a boat ride in the Pacific Ocean.

After drinking a bit much, I was a slight bit tipsy as I made my way back to my room. I squeezed my tired eyes together, and when I opened them, I squinted at a tall, muscular white man, dressed in a pure white uniform. He removed his hat and placed it underneath his arm.

"Are you all right?" he asked, walking up to me as I stumbled down the hallway.

"Yes, I'm fine," I said, staring into his olive green eyes. Simply put, he was gorgeous. His tan glowed, and his dark brown wavy hair gave me good chills. He put my arm inside of his and escorted me.

"Where's your room?" he asked.

I pointed down the hall, and he helped me to it. After I slid my card inside the door, it popped open.

"Thank you, but I'll be okay," I said. "I just had a little too much to drink. It's nothing a little sleep can't cure."

He smiled at me with his pearly whites and waited until I went inside. Not even getting his name, I closed the door and stepped away from it. Surely, I waited for a knock, but I could hear him walk away.

Once I got settled in for the night, something inside of me felt funny. In deep thought for a moment about the

"Superman" I'd just seen, I stood on the balcony and gazed at a dark but beautiful sky. The soothing breeze made my pink silk nightgown cling to me, and caused my long hair to blow all over my head. A moment later, I stepped inside and closed the doors to the balcony. Tired, I went into the bedroom and sat on the edge of the bed. I wondered what Isaac was up to, and assuming that he was with one of his lovers, I tightly closed my eyes.

ISAAC

I was lonely as hell, and couldn't believe Cydney had finally walked out on me. Reality had set in, and it was time for me to put up or shut up. I had to make some changes, and my first effort started with avoiding Laquinta's calls. I had no desire to be with her, and Cydney's whereabouts had my mind consumed.

As for Cydney, I didn't know where in the hell she'd gone. It was as if she'd fallen off the earth or something. Worried, I called her mother, Gloria—that's when she told me Cydney was on vacation. She asked why I wasn't with her, and why I didn't know where she was.

"Gloria, I didn't know she had left because we've been having some issues in our marriage. It's nothing we can't work out, though."

"I hope so, Isaac. Cydney told me she was on a business trip with her boss. She also said that you'd be joining her, so I'm really surprised by your phone call. Are you sure—"

"Look, Mom, please don't stress yourself out about this. I'm sure that Cydney didn't tell you the truth because she didn't want to worry you. Lately, we've been having some differences, but again, it's nothing that we can't work out."

Gloria let out a deep sigh. "Isaac, take care of my girl, okay? A mother knows her child, and during our conversation, I could sense that something wasn't right. Lately, Cydney's been so short with me, and I don't like the idea of her lying to me. I want you to know that her dad and I are there for you all, if you need us."

"Thank you. And if we need you, we'll let you know."

Gloria hung up, and I held the phone in my hand. My conversation with Gloria made me crazy. If Cydney was with her boss, I wasn't sure what the hell was going on. Cydney had been gone for almost a week, and she'd never been away from me for so long. For business purposes, maybe a day or two, but this was ridiculous. We were still considered husband and wife, and for her to be away for so long, I knew another man had to be occupying her time. More than anything, I knew that coochie was hot! I hadn't dipped into it for quite some time, and I knew her insides were burning. I tried not to let my hurt show, but as I sat at my desk doing nothing, Miguel interrupted my thoughts.

"Are you ready to go?" he asked.

"Go where?" I asked.

"Fool, it's time to hit the streets. Since your mind is twisted, how about you let me drive today?"

"Sounds like a plan to me," I said, standing up. I put on my hat, and Miguel handed me a piece of Juicy Fruit gum. I thanked him.

"What's been on your mind?" Miguel inquired as we got in the car.

"Cydney," I said, closing the door behind me. "Several days ago, she left, and I haven't heard from her."

"Well, call her. I'm sure she has a cell phone, doesn't she?"

"I've called her several times, but she won't answer her phone. After three days of calling, I gave up."

Miguel put on his seatbelt and started the car. "Well, you just might have to find a replacement for her soon."

I looked straight ahead in deep thought. "And you might be right. Besides, fuck her. She ain't satisfied my manly needs in a very long time, and I should've kicked her to the curb a long time ago."

"Right . . . right, especially if she's been satisfying another motherfucker too. Do you think she's giving it up to someone else?"

"I have my suspicions, but then again, Cydney's so . . . she's so . . . so innocent and self-righteous and . . . "

"And sneaky, sexy, secretive and seductive. I'm telling you that trusting a woman of her caliber will get you in a lot of trouble."

"I agree, but why do you think you know so much about my wife? Now, she's all of the above, but how would you know?"

" 'Cause I see it in her eyes, playa. Every time I see her, her eyes tell me that she's got just as many skeletons in her closet as you have."

I sat quietly and thought about what Miguel had said. Maybe I did give her too much credit, but even though I figured she'd stepped out on me a few times, no other man could ever replace me. Miguel was just speculating and looking at our situation from the outside. Of course he'd view things the way he did.

It was less than one hour after we left the police station when we found ourselves chasing after a youngster who had been selling crack. I ran as fast as I could down the alley to catch him, but the motherfucker had to be a track star. He was gone in the wind, and Miguel had run off in a different direction to catch him. Moments later, it all came to an end when a German Shepherd rushed out of his dog house and bit at the youngster's leg as he attempted to climb over a fence. I hurried and grabbed the dog by his collar. When Miguel ran up, he quickly dropped the youngster to the ground and kneeled deeply into his back.

"I can't brea-breathe," the youngster gasped.

Miguel slammed his fist into his face. "Shut the fuck up! You don't need to breathe."

The owner of the dog rushed out, and I handed him over to her. He continued to bark and growl at us.

"Would you mind taking the dog into the house?" I asked.

"Not until the officer over there calms down," she said. "I saw him sucker punch that boy in the mouth."

Miguel turned to the side and looked at her. "Good. And you gon' see me punch him again," he said, slamming his fist into the youngster's face again. He looked damn near unconscious, and I walked over and slightly pushed Miguel back.

"Get off him," I said. "Let him get up so he can breathe."

Miguel hesitated, but then scooted back and stood up.

"Ol' punk-ass nigga," Miguel said. "You can run, but you for damn sure can't hide."

The youngster staggered off the ground, blood drizzling from his mouth. I knew Miguel was anxious to get at him, so I hurried and placed the cuffs on him. As I shoved him to the alley, he looked angrily at Miguel.

"I'm gon' get that ass, nigga. You betta watch yo' back 'cause I'm gon' knock that ass," the youngster said.

Miguel hated to be challenged by brothas on the street, and he rushed up to us. He snatched the youngster away from my grip and tripped him to the ground. He used him as a punching bag, and pushed me back when I tried to intervene.

"Move back, Isaac," he said while stomping. "I—could—have—had—a—heart—attack, chasing after this fool."

"I'm calling the newsroom," the woman yelled. "This is ridiculous!"

Miguel stopped. "Take your ass back inside and mind your own damn business! This motherfucker is a criminal, slangin' drugs in your neighborhood, and you out here trying to protect him! One more word from you and I'm going to arrest you for interfering with a police matter. Now, the choice is yours." He spoke sternly.

I looked at the woman, who was so ready to open her mouth. "Just go inside, please. We'll wrap this up and be out of here in a few minutes." Knowing that we didn't need any more reports made to the sergeant, I gave Miguel a frustrated look. "Go get the car, all right?"

Before leaving to get the car, he gave the youngster one last kick in the stomach. The youngster rolled over on his back and continued to mouth tough words. I couldn't quite understand it, because to me, now was the time to shut the fuck up.

Miguel came back with the car, and after searching the youngster from head to toe, I put him in the back seat of the car. He had a plastic bag full of rocks in one pocket, and rolled up money in the other. I tossed both items to Miguel, and he held them in his hands. When we got in the car, he sat for a moment and counted the money.

"One hundred, two hundred, three hundred . . . thirty-seven hundred dollars." He looked at me, and then turned to face the youngster in the back seat. "Man, what you doing with twelve hundred dollars on you, huh?"

"Kiss my ass," he said. "You can take all my shit. I'on give a fuck. There's mo' where that come from, partna."

"Aww, so you snitching now, right?"

"I ain't doing or saying nothing. A rookie-ass cop like you can't break me down, nigga. You living in my world, my day, and on my time."

Miguel looked at me and laughed. All I could do was shake my head at how amazingly stupid some of our young people had gotten. I turned to the youngster and made myself clear. "You damn right we can't break you. We can't stop none of you motherfuckers out here from doing what you doing. But when your ass go to prison over this petty shit, we gon' see who gon' break down. It for damn sure won't be me or Miguel."

"Fuck you, man, and no thanks for the shitty advice. If anything, I'll see both of you crooked fools there with me too. Word on the street . . . it's going down. Both of you suckers going down."

"Well, thank you for the heads up," I said. "But for the time being, the only person who'll be getting fucked, and not in a good way, is you."

Miguel and I headed back to the station to book the youngster. His comment in regards to Miguel and me going down kind of bothered me. It wasn't the first time that I'd heard those words, and as Miguel seemed to be getting more aggressive, I knew I'd better watch my back.

Once the youngster was settled into his new home, we left, made a couple more arrests and gave out several tickets. There were always good things about my job, as we saved the day when we found a lost dog for a little girl who'd had him for years.

The work day was nearly over, and since I couldn't stand to be alone anymore, I made arrangements to pay Laquinta a visit. Before Miguel dropped me off at her place, he stopped by his loft to get some clothes to take to the cleaners. I hadn't been inside his loft since he'd got it, but it was obvious that a police officer's salary alone couldn't buy the expensive furnishings he had. He'd gone overboard with the money we'd been taking from time to time, and definitely had no shame flaunting.

"This is off the hook," I said, looking around at the contemporary style loft. The color scheme for the living room was gray, burgundy and white, and stainless steel dressed up the open kitchen. His bedroom was in the far corner, but was sectioned off by room dividers. I sat at the kitchen's island and waited for Miguel to gather his things.

"Why don't you get something to drink, Isaac? I got some Coronas in the fridge."

Rather thirsty, I got up and went to the fridge. I reached for a Corona and removed the cap then looked around for the trash can. When I found it, I dropped the cap inside. Immediately, I couldn't help but notice a piece of paper with Cydney's name written on it. Underneath her name was the address to her office. I held the piece of paper in my hand and wondered why Miguel needed my wife's work address. As I stood there thinking about it, he came into the kitchen and startled me.

"What's that?" he said, walking up to me. He took the paper and held it in his hand. "Aw, that," he said, throwing it back in the trash.

"Why do you have Cyd's work address written down?" I asked abruptly.

"I . . . I was looking for you and I wrote down her work address so I could call information and get the number."

"Normally, information will give you a phone number as long as you know the name of the place. The exact address really isn't needed."

He got defensive. "Shit, man, what's the big damn deal? That day I took off work, I couldn't reach you, so I called her. I . . . I really can't remember why I wrote down the address."

I sipped from the Corona bottle and listened to Miguel stumble over his words. His reaction didn't really sit right with me, but since I knew that Cydney would never, ever be involved with a man like Miguel, I wasn't worried.

"Are you ready to go?" he asked.

"As soon as I finish this," I said, guzzling down the rest of the Corona. Afterwards, I dropped the bottle in the trash and felt uneasy as it fell on top of the piece of paper.

After Miguel dropped off his clothes at the cleaners, he got a call from one of his lady friends and rushed me over to Laquinta's. My truck was still at the police station, so I asked him to pick me up in the morning, and he agreed to it.

With Cydney heavy on my mind, I knocked on Laquinta's door. When she opened it, Erica was on her hip, and she quickly passed her over to me.

"Here," she said. "I smell my cake burning." She rushed off to the kitchen, and I followed behind her with Erica on my side. She was a beautiful little girl with chocolate skin, big dark brown eyes and a melting smile. Unfortunately, I didn't see one ounce of my features on her. But I was the only daddy she knew, and until I decided to dig further for the truth, things had to stay the way they were.

I kissed Erica on her cheek and gave her the strawberry Blow Pop I'd gotten at the corner store earlier. She never said much, but I could tell by her smile that she was happy to see me.

"Would you like for me to remove the wrapper?" I asked.

She nodded, and I put her on the floor to remove it. Laquinta pulled the burnt cake from the oven and tossed it on the stove.

"Damn," she said. "I knew I shouldn't have been running my mouth on the phone that long. I told Dee I had something to do!"

"Well, I always told you that mouth of yours was gon' cause you some trouble." I gave the Blow Pop to Erica and picked her back up.

"I know you ain't complaining about my mouth, are you? It works wonders for you, so you'd better watch what you say."

I snickered and turned to go into the living room. "Handle your business, baby. Burnt food or not, I'm eating, because I'm hungry."

Laquinta laughed, and after removing my shirt and holster, I sat on the floor and stacked blocks with Erica. When Laquinta yelled that dinner was ready, I picked up Erica and we went back into the kitchen. I placed Erica in her high chair and took a seat at the table. With the exception of the cake, the mac and cheese, baked chicken, green beans and dinner rolls looked delicious. Laquinta knew how to throw down in the kitchen, and she knew that the way to my heart was through my stomach.

"So, how was work?" she asked while feeding Erica some green beans.

"Work is always work. And how was your . . . day?"

"It was cool. I missed my baby, and I'm glad she's back now. I'm even more excited that her daddy's here now. I hadn't heard from you, and I thought you'd forgotten about us."

I kept my head down and continued chowing down on my food. Once my plate was cleared, Laquinta took it and put some more chicken and green beans on it.

"That's enough," I said as she piled the green beans high.

"Are you sure? You went through that first plate too fast for me."

"I'm positive. I'm already overdoing it, but I haven't eaten all day."

Laquinta smiled and brought the plate to me. After she

put it in front of me, I reached my hand around her waist and put her on my lap. I kissed her cheek and squeezed the side of her thigh.

"You'd better stop being so good to me. You know I'm bound to take advantage of you, don't you?"

"Sounds exciting to me. I love it when you take advantage of me, and you do it all so very well."

We kissed, and afterwards, she wiped her fingers around my lips.

"I'm pleased that you're enjoying my food, Isaac. I bet your wife doesn't cook as good as I do for you."

I stared at Laquinta. "How many times must I tell you to leave my wife out of your mouth? Lately, every time we get together you start running your mouth, and it really irritates the fuck out of me. Get off my lap."

"All I said—"

"Get off my lap!"

"No problem," she said, getting up. She went to the other side of the table and took a seat. I got back to eating my dinner, and she continued to feed herself and Erica.

We sat in silence, and once I finished, I got up and put my plate in the sink.

"Since you cooked, I'll clean up, all right?" I said.

"No, thank you," she said with attitude. "I can handle cleaning up, just like I handle everything else."

"And what's that supposed to mean?"

"It means I've been handling my business and your business too. Erica can't survive off two or three hundred dollars a month, and if or when I decide to go back to school, daycare is going to cost a fortune. Food alone—"

As Laquinta continued to rant, I reached in my back pocket and pulled out my wallet. I counted out one hundred and fifty dollars and laid it on the table.

"This is all I can do right now. In the meantime, stop griping and get a job," I said, and then removed Erica from her high chair. I left the kitchen and went back into the living room to play with her.

I could hear Laquinta cleaning up in the kitchen. I played with Erica for an hour or so, and once she got sleepy, I scooted back on the couch and laid her on my chest. Within minutes, she was knocked out, and soon after, I feel asleep too. With Cydney being on my mind, I dreamed about her being with another man. I saw him making love to her, and when he turned his head, I'll be damned if it wasn't Miguel. I quickly opened my eyes and saw a blurred vision of Laquinta standing in front of me. She wore a sheer black short negligee trimmed with hot pink fuzz. The negligee did nothing for me, and neither did the hot pink panties underneath, or the high-heeled shoes with pink fuzz balls on top. Ignoring the fact that Erica was still lying on my chest, Laquinta started to remove her panties.

I quickly sat up. "We are not about to get down with Erica in the same room as us."

"I agree," Laquinta said, reaching for her. "That's why she has a bedroom."

Laquinta picked up Erica and carried her off to her bedroom. Moments later, she came back. Simply not in the mood, I lay back on the couch, placed my arm on top of my forehead, and closed my eyes. When she stepped up to me, she pulled my arm, and I dropped it to my side.

"What?" I said.

Of course, since I wasn't up for fucking, she got mad. "What is up with you, Isaac? Your attitude is horrible."

"Not as horrible as that . . . that whatever the hell it is that you have on. That's what's horrible."

"You son of a bitch! You need to get your butt off my couch and out of my apartment. Come back when you're in a better mood, all right?"

"You mean come back when I want to fuck you, right? Damn, baby, I just don't feel like it tonight. We don't have to fuck every time I come over here, do we?"

"Since when? That's why you come over here, ain't it? Now all of a sudden your wife must be dishing it out and you don't have time for me. I'm getting sick of this shit, and you'd better get your act together real soon or else I'm outtie."

Laquinta went into her bedroom and slammed the door. I could tell she was getting tired of me, and frankly, I was getting tired of her. More than anything, I was fed up with my thoughts of Cydney. Her being away was causing me much headache, and I couldn't help but take my frustrations out on those around me. Unfortunately, Laquinta just happened to be the closet person to me, and after I tossed and turned on the couch, I got up to go apologize. Admitting that I was wrong always made her feel better, and she'd become such a forgiving woman. She played the tough-cookie role quite often, but her cookie always managed to soften from my words.

"I'm sorry for disrespecting you," I whispered while walking into her dark room. She didn't say a word. "Quintaaa," I teased. "Baby, did you hear me?"

"Don't Quintaaa me," she griped. "I knew your happy-go-lucky ass would come in here apologizing."

I eased in bed behind her. My right hand touched her naked body, and I inhaled her strawberry fragrance. "I might not have liked your negligee, but your body smells awfully good," I whispered.

She lay on her back and looked up at me. "What was so wrong with my negligee? I know you didn't hate it that much, Isaac."

"Red is your color, not pink," I said. I made my way on

top of her. "Next time you want to excite me, wear red, okay?"

She reached down to unbuckle my pants and opened her legs. "How about next time, I wear nothing at all?"

"That'll work too."

I placed my lips on Laquinta's, and the night was long, hot and filled with energy. Sex between us was so energetic that I was too tired to get up for work. When Miguel called and said he was on his way, I had to drag myself out of bed and into the shower. Even after a shower, I still wasn't feeling up to going to work. I sat on the edge of Laquinta's bed and slowly got dressed. Since she was in the kitchen feeding Erica, I reached for my cell phone and dialed Cydney's number. After one ring, her voicemail came on, so I knew her phone was off. I spoke sternly.

"You need to call me back. I don't know where the hell you're at, but a phone call to let me know you're okay won't hurt either. Call me!"

I closed my phone and looked up at Laquinta standing in the doorway.

"I'm almost afraid to ask who you're begging to call you back. You kinda sound like me when I be calling you, but—"

I stood up and stepped into my pants. "Let it go, Laquinta. We had a wonderful time last night and this morning, so don't go ruining the moment."

She folded her arms. "Miguel's outside. He blew the horn twice, but I guess you didn't hear him."

Rushing, I grabbed my shirt and kissed Laquinta on the cheek as I passed by her. I hurried into the kitchen, gave Erica a kiss and opened the fridge.

"An apple a day might keep your bitches away," Laquinta said.

"Naw, we don't want to do that," I said, reaching for the apple. "But I'll take one anyway."

I put the apple in my mouth, bit into it, and winked at Laquinta on my way out.

Miguel was blowing the hell out of the horn. When he saw me rushing to the car, he stopped. I got in the car, dressed in my white T-shirt, and my blue pants were un-buttoned.

"I can tell you had a long, long morning. Sleep was not on your agenda last night, was it?" He laughed.

"Messing around with Laquinta, it never is. I just can't believe your ass is on time. I for surely thought you'd be late."

"Not since Sarg has been on my ass. You can be late, but not me. He's looking for any reason to fire me."

"You think?"

"Oh, I know. I can tell when a motherfucker don't like me, Isaac. I get all kinds of vibes and shit."

I nodded and agreed.

"So, you seem to be in a better mood today," he said. "Ol' girl must have laid it down good for you."

"Like I said, she always do, but I still have to listen to her gripes about Cydney. Man, I get so tired of hearing that shit."

"It comes with the territory, Isaac. The other woman will always use your wife as ammunition against you. By the way, where is Cydney? I know you said she stepped, but you still ain't heard from her?"

"Not one word. I'm so mad at her ass that I don't know what to do. Being away this long is out of character for her. She's got to be seeing—"

"Man, she probably ain't seeing nobody. You know how bitches be playing them games all the time."

Stunned by Miguel's choice of words, I turned to him.

"Bitch? Hey, look, don't disrespect my wife by referring to her as a bitch. She's far from being a bitch, and if she is one, then I'm the only one who can call her that. You straight up out of line, and you don't even know her like that."

"Excuse the hell out of me. You know how I get sometimes, man, but no offense to you or your wife."

"Like hell, nigga! That was very offensive to me. We might have our problems, but she still my motherfucking heart!"

"For a man who I just picked up from fucking his other woman all damn night long, I don't know what kind of heartfelt love you got for Cydney. Whatever it is, it sho' looks fucked up to me."

"That's because you don't understand what my heart needs versus what my dick wants. Personally, I don't give a shit what anybody thinks, but I know Cydney better be making her way back home soon. If not, I'm gon' send a search party out to get her, and once she's found, it ain't gon' be pretty."

Miguel laughed, and so did I. He apologized for calling her a bitch, but said at times that's how he referred to women. Deep down, his apology was not accepted, but for the time being, it just had to do.

CYDNEY

Shame, shame on me for being so indulged with my new companion. Captain Raymond Lee Burg was his name, and since that night we bumped into each other, he'd been occupying my time. I knew there was something special about him, and the next morning, a card and flowers were placed outside of my door. The card asked me to meet him for breakfast, and after I told Dez I'd catch up with her later, I ate breakfast with Raymond and spent the entire day with him. The only time I'd been alone was when I went back to my room for bed. He wasn't trying to take me to bed, and I wasn't trying to give it up to him either.

During our first conversation at breakfast, I asked him not to inquire about my reason for being in Maui, and even though he wanted to know, he avoided any and all questions about my personal life. To be fair, I didn't want to know if he was married, but by our second day together, he told me he wasn't. All I knew was that he was the captain of a yacht that transferred visitors from one island to another. Other than that, all we knew was each other's names, that our skin color was different, and that we were having one hell of a good time together.

It was late, and I stood on the top deck of a yacht named Majestic while looking at the dark sky and many miles of ocean water. My vacation would end in two days, and I dreaded going back to the life I had before I came. I'd received many calls from Isaac, and without listening to any of his messages, I deleted them. Miguel had the nerve to call as well, and his messages were deleted too. For now, what was in the past would stay in the past. I felt like a new woman who needed a new beginning.

Being with Raymond helped me forget about my many troubles, but more than that, just getting away from the headaches gave me time to think about what I really wanted. Basically, I'd been a fool. I should have ended it with Isaac the second time he cheated on me. The first time was forgivable, but after I forgave him, he took my kindness for weakness and used it to his advantage. His doing me wrong caused me to jump out of character and do him wrong. Two wrongs never made it right, but I wound up causing more hurt and damage to myself by being with Miguel. Maybe even spending this time with Raymond was a big mistake, but for now, it felt good, and I was happier than I'd been in a long, long time.

As I stood in deep thought, peering over the rail, I felt his arms slowly ease around my waist. His chin dropped to my shoulder, and he whispered close to my ear.

"What thoughts could make your eyes water, but not allow the tears to fall? I've been watching you for nearly ten minutes and I could see—"

Not wanting to discuss my issues, I turned to Raymond and placed my finger on his lips. "Are you finished for the night?" I asked.

"Yes. It's late, and you'll have to stay the night with me in the stateroom. You don't mind, do you?"

"Of course not," I said.

Raymond kissed the back of my hand, and we went to the lower deck of the Majestic. Earlier, I'd been in the pilot's house and office with him. We'd had dinner in the dining room and had a few drinks in the lounge. The Majestic was made in Italy, and was dressed in cherry oak glossy wood. It was unlike anything I'd ever seen before, and nothing prepared me for the master stateroom. I was stunned by its beauty, and stood with my mouth nearly wide open.

"This . . . this is awesome," I said, gazing at the glass mirrors, the cream satin bedding ensemble that dressed the king bed, the Jacuzzi in the corner of the room, and the humongous flat screen television built into the cherry oak wall. It was obvious that he had some serious money.

Raymond loosened his hand from mine and removed his hat. He laid it on the bed and rubbed his hands together.

"Feel free to look around, and if you see anything you'd like to take home with you, let me know. I'm going to take a shower and I'll be right back, okay?"

I nodded and continued to search the room. He didn't really mean for me to take home anything I wanted, did he? I felt like a kid in a candy store, as many of the pictures on the walls, the furniture and gold accessories had to be priceless.

Raymond removed his shirt and walked over to a closet. He slid the glass door over and pulled out two white cotton robes. As he made his way over to me, I couldn't help but admire his tanned, thick body that showed one hell of a six pack. The top button to his white pants was unbuttoned, and the smooth look of his skin was eye-catching. He reached out and handed the robe to me.

"I don't have anything else for you to change into, but if you wish to relieve yourself of your swimming suit, you can wear this."

By the looks of him, I wanted to wear nothing, but for now, the robe was appropriate.

"Thank you," I said, looking into his seductive eyes. He smiled and headed for the bathroom, leaving the door open. I watched as he stripped naked and stepped into the shower. He had a nice and tight, nail-gripping ass, and before he turned around to his front side, I stepped over to the bed and took a seat. The satin comforter felt like cotton rubbing against my skin, and so did the robe as I removed my swimming attire and put it on. I cuddled myself in the robe and stood up to tour the remainder of the suite. There was a picture of the Majestic framed in gold. I wanted it for memories, but I was sure that the picture was close to Raymond's heart. Another drawing of the Majestic was on the other side of the room, and when I looked down on a desk underneath it, I saw a picture book. I opened the book and there were pictures of the Majestic being made. There was an older man who looked just like Raymond in the picture, along with two other men who could have been his siblings. As I turned the page, I saw pictures of people who appeared to be visitors on the Majestic, but I also noticed a lot of pictures of one woman in particular. She'd been in several pictures with Raymond, and surprisingly, she was a black woman. Not quite as dark as me, but her skin was a caramel brown. Her model-shaped legs and body made me think of Tyra Banks, and when I saw her kissing Raymond in one of the pictures, that's when I closed the book. I looked around some more, and when the lights dimmed, I saw Raymond standing in the bathroom's doorway with his robe on. To set the mood even more, he went over to the entertainment center and turned on some music. It was the soothing voice of Luther Vandross, and I couldn't help but laugh.

"Now, you know that if I wasn't here, you'd be listening to some classical music or something."

"Are you kidding me?" He smiled. "I love Luther Vandross' music. I was devastated when he passed away, but his music lives on in my heart."

"Mine too," I said.

Raymond came up to me and held out his hands. "Let's dance. I'm not that good, but anybody can slow dance, right?"

"I guess . . ."

He reached for my waist and clinched one of his hands together with mine. I placed my hand on his shoulder, and we slowly moved from side to side. There was silence for a long while, and Raymond stopped to look in my eyes.

"Why are you so tense and uptight? Are you frightened by what might happen?"

"No, I'm not. It's just that I wasn't expecting to come here and experience all of this. I don't know what's going to happen, and frankly, I don't care. But I'm grateful for the good time you've shown me."

"Same here," he said, starting to move again. We continued on in silence until the song was over.

Raymond loosened his embrace and walked away to turn off the music. He then stepped over by the bed and removed his robe. Wearing only his black Calvin Klein boxer shorts, he sat on the bed and leaned his back against the glass mirrors behind him. After combing his fingers through the sides of his curly hair, he looked up at me. He patted the spot next to him and smiled.

"I promise you that I won't bite. We will do nothing that you don't wish to do."

I reached for the hair clip in my pocket and pulled my long hair together. Once I clipped it, I made my way onto the bed and up to Raymond. He opened his arms, and I laid my head on his chest.

"Now, that wasn't so bad, was it?" he said.

"Not at all. Don't take this personal, but I've never been this close to a white man before. I work with several awesome white men, but I've never been in bed with one before."

"Does the color of my skin really matter? Maybe it does to some people, but to me, it's never made the difference."

"So, you've dated a black woman before?"

"Several. It's my preference, and I find black women very attractive. My relationships have been difficult because you all are so worried about what others might think. Am I wrong or right?"

"You might be on to something." I laughed.

"Oh, I'm very much indeed on to something. Even you have to admit that a black man has no problem stepping outside of his race, but a black woman is skeptical."

"Maybe. But it's an individual choice. You can't put all black men and women into one classification. For me, the color of someone's skin doesn't matter either. I haven't thought much about dating anybody because I've been with the same person for a very long time. Besides, I never really noticed white men paying attention to me anyway."

"Trust me, as beautiful as you are, they've paid attention to you. Maybe you didn't want to notice, but I'm sure you can tell me the last time a black man showed interest. All I'm saying is there are always options. Don't limit yourself to only one option when there are plenty of options you can have."

"If I did limit myself, I wouldn't be here with you, would I?"

"You're here with me because I took the initiative. I'm pleased that you accepted my offer, but realistically, so many of you don't. Maybe after this experience, things will change."

I sat quietly and took in what Raymond had said. At least we both agreed that skin color wasn't a factor. I was enjoying every moment with him, and that's all that mattered.

"So, did you find anything you'd like to take back with you as a souvenir?" he asked.

I rubbed my hand across his six pack and looked down at his goods. "I would like to take the picture of the Majestic home with me." I pointed to it.

Raymond sat up and pointed to the picture as well.

"That picture?"

"Yes, that one."

He stood up and walked over by it. "This one?"

"I don't see any other picture over there. You said feel free to take anything."

"But not this one. This is my . . . my everything," he said, gazing at the picture. He stood for a few minutes, and then went to the other side of the room. He picked up the picture book and sat up in bed next to me. He opened to the first page and smiled.

"You can have one of these pictures of the Majestic. How 'bout that?"

I pretended as if I hadn't seen the pictures, and looked down at them. "Are those pictures of the Majestic being made?"

"Yes," he said, flipping the pages. He pointed out his father and two brothers. Another white woman in the picture was his sister, and when he looked at the picture of him and the black woman, he hesitated, but then he told me her name was Sheila. I couldn't help but ask who she was.

"She . . . she was my wife. We're divorced, and we've both moved on."

"You don't have to go any further, Raymond. Days ago, we agreed not to share our personal lives, and I don't wish to do it now."

Raymond closed the book and placed it on the floor. Once we got back into a comfortable position, I laid my head on his chest again and he rubbed my hair back.

"I'm glad I met you, Cydney."

"Same here, Raymond."

For a long while there was silence, and once I closed my eyes, his fingers combing through my hair stopped. I looked up, and Raymond had fallen asleep.

It was my last night in Maui. I hated to leave, and Raymond hadn't said much about it. As usual, we spent the entire day together, bike riding, scuba diving and lying on the beach. I looked around for Dez, but I didn't see her. When I went to her room earlier, it appeared that she'd already checked out. I wanted to say goodbye to her, but I guess Raymond had occupied much of my time. Just as I stepped away from her door, Dez's room server came up to me.

"Cydney Conley?" he asked.

"Yes."

"Mrs. Dez wanted me to give this to you." He handed me a card with a pink rose attached to the top.

"Thank you," I said and opened the card.

It was an encouragement card that advised me that when times got rough to search deep within myself and look to the Man above. She signed her name, and wrote several words inside.

I see that your new man is keeping you busy. Have a wonderful time, and pay attention to your surroundings.

Sometimes, some things may be too good to be true. Don't get lost in a fairytale, and I wish you all the best. It was a pleasure getting to know you.

Dez.

I closed the card and smiled. I knew Dez could see how vulnerable I was, and frankly, so could Raymond. Either way, all I intended to do was enjoy myself that day, for whatever the future held, I had no clue.

Later that day, after a quick dinner, Raymond and I decided to work it off by playing tennis. I went back to my room and changed into a pair of white cuffed short shorts and a white half shirt that showed my midriff. My waistline wasn't as fit as some of the women on the beach, but it was still a shapely waistline. I put my hair into a ponytail and placed a white sweatband around my head.

As soon as I left my room, I saw Raymond waiting at the end of the hall for me. He was engrossed in a conversation with a woman who seemed to make him uncomfortable. She had a drink in her hand, was dressed in a thong bikini, and was all over him. I slowly made my way up to them, and he stepped back to introduce me.

"Sherri, this is Cydney. Are you ready?" he asked me.

"As long as you have the rackets." I smiled.

The white woman looked at me in disbelief. Her eyes searched me up and down. She cut her eyes and touched Raymond's arm.

"Is this why you haven't called me?" she asked.

"Sherri, I haven't called because I'm not interested. I will take you and your friends back to the island tonight. Right now, if you'd excuse me, I have plans."

She stepped back, and Raymond and I walked away. Hell yes, I was on cloud nine. Raymond was one fine man, and the women on the island couldn't help but stare. I guess it was something he was used to because he didn't seem to give the stares much attention.

When we got to the tennis courts, Raymond reached for two rackets and removed his shirt. He handed one of the rackets over to me, and reached into the pocket of his white shorts. Pulling out a black sweatband, he wrapped it around his head.

"You're not going to be mad at me for beating you, are you?" he asked.

"Listen, I may not be Serena Williams, but I know how to play tennis. Don't you get mad at me for beating you."

He laughed, and we both made our way to the middle of the court to play. I served first, and Raymond came back with a hard ball that stayed in bounds. I didn't have time to rush over to it, and we both laughed.

"Okay, since I can't stop admiring you, I'm having a difficult time looking for the ball. Maybe you need to put your shirt back on," I said, making excuses.

He bent over and got ready for me to serve again. "If I can ignore the black thong you have on underneath your shorts, then you can deal with my bare chest."

"And how do you know what color my thong is?"

He stood up and placed the racket underneath his arm. "Because I looked. You don't mind if I look, do you?"

"Then look at this," I said, hitting the ball over the net. It caught him off guard, and he missed it.

"Okay, so now you want to cheat, huh?"

"I have a feeling that it's the only way I'll win."

We laughed and got down to business. It was obvious I was no match for Raymond. He was playing like Andre Agassi, and I was no competition for him. I tried hard, and once I twisted my ankle, I had to call it quits. I sat on the ground and rubbed my ankle.

"Are you okay?" Raymond said, rushing up to me.

"I'm fine. I know you want to laugh, so go ahead and do it."

Instead, we both smiled, and he told me to wrap my arms around his neck.

"You are not about to pick me up. If you help me off the ground, I promise you I can walk."

Raymond helped me off the ground and held my waist. He put my arm on his shoulders and helped me back to my room.

"I'll call a doctor to come and look at it," he said.

"Trust me," I said, limping. "It's not that serious. All I need is some ice and to elevate my foot for a while."

When we made it back to my room, Raymond opened the door and we went inside. He helped me to the bedroom, and I sat on the bed. He went over to the bar and placed some ice on a towel. After he wet it, he came over and kneeled down in front of me. He removed my tennis shoe and then my ankle socks. After holding my foot in his hand, he placed the cold iced towel against my swollen ankle.

"You might need a doctor to take a look at this, Cydney."

"I said no. The ice is fine."

Raymond continued to hold the ice against my ankle, and he reached for my other tennis shoe to remove it. I felt so cared for, and looked down at him proudly taking care of me. Knowing that our minimal time together was running out, I reached out to touch his wavy hair. It started to curl, and as he continued to hold his head down, I knew he felt my advances.

"What are you doing Cydney?" he asked while moving his head away from my touch. He looked seductively at me with those panty-dropping green eyes.

"I . . . I, before I go, I want to satisfy your needs and mine."

Raymond looked back down at my ankle and held it in his hand. He laid the towel on the floor and opened it. He then reached for a piece of ice and held it in his hand.

"Are you positive that this is something you want to do?" he asked. "You're not obligated to do anything, and just being with you these few days have truly been more than I could ever ask for."

"I'm more than sure about this, Raymond. If I had any doubts, I wouldn't do it."

I pulled my shirt over my head, and Raymond looked at my perky, thick breasts filling a Victoria's Secret black lace bra. My nipples were erect, and once I unsnapped the bra in the front, my breasts were clearly in his view.

He leaned forward to kiss me, and I'll be damned if it wasn't one hell of a kiss. His lips were soft, and his tongue was light as it turned inside of my mouth. As we kissed, his hands went up and cupped my breasts. He removed my bra, pressed my breasts together, and wet my nipples with the ice.

Getting more anxious for him, I reached down to the zipper on his shorts and unzipped them. He broke our kiss, removed his hands from my body and leaned back. He took another gazing look at my breasts and placed some more ice cubes in his mouth. He leaned in again, and I scooted back on the bed. He lay over me and looked down at me. I smiled and watched him lower his mouth to my breasts. The ice cubes, along with the coolness from his mouth, caused me to tremble. He sucked them so good, and licked the melting water as it rolled down my sides. When the water rolled towards my belly button, his tongue followed the water and he took lengthy sips.

Already, this man was making love to me. His touch was gentle, and I hadn't felt this way since Isaac and I stopped making love. I closed my eyes from the feeling, and felt Raymond easing down my shorts. I lifted myself to make it easier, and when my shorts came off, I lay there in my thong. He winked at me and stood up to remove his shorts. He wasn't no Isaac, but whoever said white men couldn't hold a candle to any black man was a lie! Raymond certainly could, and he reached for more ice and crawled between my legs.

"If this gets too cold, let me know," he said.

He put the ice cubes in his mouth and lowered his head. My thong remained on, but he teased me with them on. I could feel his tongue and the cold ice pressing against my inner walls, but since I wanted to feel more, I reached for the string on my thong and pulled on it. Raymond assisted me and pulled them down. He dove right back into me, from my front side to turning me over on my back side. The electrifying feeling made me crazy. I rolled on my back and started heavily breathing in and out. The heavier I breathed, Raymond's licks, slurps and sips got more intense. And just when I was on the verge of coming, Raymond stopped. He wrapped my legs around his waist and went inside of me. Seconds later, I came, and after changing positions, I came again. Giving him much pleasure, I gave him a lengthy ride. Since his dick was so far up inside of me, it was a damn good ride at that. The lovemaking was unbelievable, and never in my wildest dreams did I expect to experience something so intriguing with a white man.

Nearly an hour later, Raymond and I were drenched in our own sweat. The room was hot, but filled with steam. He was back on top, and my legs were wrapped tightly around his waist. He looked down at me and kissed the tip of my nose.

"Don't go," he said, taking deep breaths. "You can't just walk out of my life like this. I have to know . . . are you married? Are you a happily married woman?"

"I . . . I'm married, but not happily married. I came here to get away from my husband. Please don't make me talk about him right now, though. We can talk about him later, okay?"

Raymond got on his knees and remained between my legs. He separated them with his hands and held them far apart. As I watched his insertions inside of me, he moved his head from side to side and closed his eyes.

"Ohhh, Cydney," he moaned. "You have no idea how your insides feel."

I was tense, and my pussy was sensitive to his strokes. "No . . . no, I don't, but I know how good your dick feels inside of me. I've got to come, Raymond. We've got to come . . . come again."

Raymond dropped my legs, scooted in closer and worked my pussy and my breasts. Within a few minutes, I let loose, and his body jerked while on top of mine.

He sighed and rolled on his back. He put me on top of him and held my waist.

"I'm serious, Cydney. Why don't you stay for a few more days? You can't leave after sharing what we just did."

"Raymond, I wish I could stay. I have a job to get back to, and my family is probably worried sick about me. I haven't spoken to anyone since the day I got here."

"Then call them. Tell them you'll be back soon. Just not now. At least give me a few more days with you."

I laid my head on Raymond's chest and thought about it. Yes, I wanted to stay, but I knew it was in my best interests to get back and put closure to my marriage. I told Raymond just that, and after continuously giving me reasons to stay, he finally said he understood and left well enough alone.

The sunlight coming through the room made me aware that it was time for me to go. Raymond was still asleep. I eased out of bed to take a shower and soak my sore ankle. Before I did, I stood at the end of the bed and looked at his lower body covered in white sheets. What a man, I thought. Why couldn't I take him back to St. Louis and be done with it? Or why couldn't I just stay here forever and never ever go back to the bullshit at home? Saddened by my departure, I walked, limping slightly, into the bathroom and ran some water to soak my ankle. After thirty minutes, the soothing water eased my pain, so I headed for the shower.

For whatever reason, when I got into the shower, I felt like crying, so I did. I knew going back home would mean arguing with Isaac and facing the fact that our marriage had failed. I knew I'd have to explain to our parents that things just didn't work out for us, and the thought of it tore at me.

Ready to get it over with, I hurried to gather myself and dolled up my face with a touch of make-up. When I made my way back into the bedroom area, I saw that Raymond had left. I thought he'd gone into one of the other rooms, but when I checked those, there was no sight of him. Wondering where he'd gone, I went to the door and opened it. On the ground were some flowers and a card identical to the ones he'd given me several days ago. I picked up the cards and flowers, and when I opened the card, it read:

I'm not good with goodbyes. Have a safe trip back home. Our time together was precious.

Love, Raymond.

I'd hoped to personally say goodbye to him, but I guess this was his way of not dealing with our departure. Maybe it was best this way, and after realizing that it was, I gathered my things and got dressed to go.

* * *

As soon as the plane touched down in the Lou, I began to dread getting off. Since I'd been gone, I'd deleted fifty-four messages from Isaac and twelve from Miguel. My mother had called three times, and my mother-in-law called once. I figured Isaac had probably told them something, so before speaking to them, I wanted to see him first. No sooner than getting in my car at the airport and driving downtown to catch him at the station, I spotted his truck at a BP gas station. I pulled my BMW next to it, and when I looked inside, the truck was empty, but a car seat was in the back.

I parked by a nearby pump, and as soon as I opened the door to go inside, Laquinta came out with her daughter resting on her hip. Laquinta had on a short and skimpy blue jean skirt and a jacket to match. Her weave was parted down the middle and draped down the sides of her face, onto her shoulders. I'd often worn my natural hair the same way. Ghetto fabulous and all, no doubt, she was headed for Isaac's truck. She put her daughter in the car seat and appeared to struggle with it. Wanting to get a closer look at her daughter, I stepped over to her and offered my help.

She turned. "It's okay. I got it," she said.

"Girl, trust me. It's no problem. My baby's car seat is so difficult, and besides, you have her facing the wrong way. The police will pull you over and ticket you for improperly seating your child."

She chuckled and allowed me to help. "And to think, my husband is a police officer and he hasn't said one word to me about her car seat," she said.

I wanted to choke on my spit, but instead, I turned the car seat around and the little girl faced the seat. I buckled her in and got a good look at her. I couldn't tell if she was Isaac's child or not, but she really didn't look like him. I didn't know if it was me not wanting her to, or realizing that she didn't have any of his features.

"There you go," I said, smiling at the child. I looked at Laquinta. "You need to tell your husband that he should be ashamed of himself for not showing you this before. And by the way, what did you say your name was?"

"Oh, I'm sorry. My name is Laquinta, and my daughter's name is Erica."

"Nice to meet you, Laquinta. My husband is a police officer too. What's your husband's name? Maybe my husband knows him."

She hesitated. "Isaac Conley."

My forehead wrinkled and I squinted. "Are you sure? I thought Isaac Conley was married to someone else. I met his wife before. Did . . . did they recently get divorced or something?"

Laquinta seemed panicked, and reached for the gas pump to pump her gas. "I don't know nothing about that, but thanks for your help," she said.

For the hell of it, I stepped up to her. "It's a small world, isn't it, Laquinta? I'm Isaac's wife, Cydney Conley, and the last time I checked, we were still married. If it wasn't for *your* child in the back seat, I'd take this truck and ram it up his ass for allowing you to drive it. However, I'm being awfully nice today, so when you see him, be sure to tell him that I'm back in town, and how nice it was to finally meet you."

She put her hand up in my face. "Whatever, lady. You need to take your issues up with your husband and not with me. He's the one sniffing after my behind, so your gripes are falling on deaf ears."

"Oh, you heard me loud and clear, especially when I tell you that child is not his. It's been a pleasure seeing what kind of trash my husband has stooped to, and for the record, you need to put that little girl off on somebody else. Have a splendid day, Laquinta, and don't forget to tell *your* . . . my husband I said hello."

She put up her middle finger and tooted her lips. She watched as I got in my car and drove off the parking lot. Since chatting with her, I'd changed my mind about going to see Isaac. Instead, I drove to my office to see how much work I had to look forward to.

ISAAC

I was waiting for Laquinta to pick me up from the police station, but she was late. It wasn't often that I let her use my truck, but since she had to take Erica to the doctor, I let her use it. That was more than three hours ago, and she still hadn't shown up. I was tired and ready to go home, and if she didn't show up soon, I was going to let out my frustrations.

As soon as I decided to take my police car home, she pulled up in front of the station. She smiled at me as I yanked on the door and pulled it open.

"Don't ever ask to use my truck again," I said. "Move over. I'm driving."

She moved over and sat on the passenger's side. I got in and drove off. "I was late because I took Erica to see her grandmother. My mother asked me to take her to the store, and I couldn't tell her no."

"But you can leave my ass standing out here waiting for you, right? Like I said, don't ask me again. I'm tired. I had a long, rough day at work, and I'm ready to go home."

"I'm sorry, boo," she said, rubbing the side of my face. "You know I can always make it up to you later."

"No thanks," I said. "I'm not in the mood."

"So, are you dropping us off or are you staying with us?"

"I'm going home tonight. I need some rest. Besides, my dick hurt from fucking you so much."

She laughed. "Naw, your dick hurt from making love to me and fucking all these other hoes in St. Louis. You might need to go get checked, if you know what I mean."

"Woman, I will mess you up if you ever give me something. That wasn't just a hint from you, was it?"

"Baby, I'm good. All good. Ain't nobody tapping into this but Officer Isaac Conley. Besides, a woman doesn't need nothing else as long as she got you, right?"

I smiled. "Why you over there trying to stroke my ego? We still ain't fucking tonight, but tomorrow night you'd better be dressed in red."

She laughed, and so did I. When I yawned, I looked in my rearview mirror and noticed a car full of thugs behind me. I stopped at the red light and they pulled up beside me. The driver lowered the window and yelled Laquinta's name. She lowered the window.

"What's up, boo? Where you niggas headed?" she yelled.

"To go shoot some hoops." He leaned forward and looked over at me. "Is that yo' man?"

"Something like that," she said. "Tell Jo-Jo to holla at me, and don't y'all hurt nobody, all right?"

Before he could respond, when the light turned green, I drove off. The car sped up and paced beside me.

"Raise my window," I said.

Laquinta hesitated, but she did it anyway. The brotha driving the car kept yelling her name, and when he swerved over close to me, I put my foot on the brake. He stopped too, and quickly reacting, I pulled my truck over in front of him and got out. I'd previously changed my police shirt, but still had on my pants and holster around my waist. As I approached the car, the driver looked shocked. I leaned down and looked inside the car.

"Is there a motherfucking problem here?" I asked, showing them my badge.

"Naw, I was just trying to holla at ol' girl."

"Well, it looked to me like you were trying to mess up my truck. Why don't all of you step out of the vehicle?"

As soon as I said that, frustration showed on their faces. The driver got out first, and when the other brotha got out on the passenger's side, the one in the back got out and broke out running. I aimed my gun at the other three and dared them to run.

"I promise you that if either of you run, I have no problem shooting first and taking names later! Now, get down on the ground!"

It was just my luck that another police car was driving by. He turned around, and when I told him I needed back-up, he called for it. I hated for a motherfucker to run, and I wanted so badly to go after the fool who'd taken off. He was long gone, and there was nothing I could do. After the three fools were patted down and searched, we saw that one had a bag of marijuana in his pocket, another had some crack, and a gun was found underneath the driver's seat.

Laquinta had gotten out of the truck to see what was going on, and I yelled and told her to get back inside. If her ghettofied, stupid ass had not lowered my window, none of this would have happened. I was damn mad, especially since my work day was already over. By the time we wrapped things up, it was almost an hour and a half later. Once the tow truck came for the car, I got in my truck and slammed the door.

"I often wonder why I even fuck with you. How stupid

can you be, lowering my window, yelling out of it like some damn fool while riding with a police officer? You knew damn well that those fools were going to clown!"

"I didn't know nothing, and you'd better stop yelling at me like you my damn daddy. Just take me the fuck home, Isaac."

"You damn right I will. And maybe you do need a fucking daddy in your life or something. Maybe your daddy should have been around to kick your ass for being so stupid. "

She slapped me hard on my face. "My Daddy has nothing—"

I reached over and tightly grabbed her neck. "Do you remember what happened the last time you hit me?"

She couldn't say a word. All she did was scratch my hand and try to pull it away from her throat. I jerked her head back and let loose.

"I'm through fucking with you, Laquinta." I said, driving off. "This shit just ain't working out for me, and if Erica wasn't in the back seat of this car, I would fuck you up."

She coughed and held her throat. "Good," she said. "You don't even have to take me home. You can let me and my baby out right here, Isaac."

I looked at her with disgust. "If I was just a brotha on a date with his woman, I could've gotten killed back there. Your so-called friends were strapped, and could've driven me off the road. With or without Erica in the back, they didn't care. In the meantime, you need to check your damn self and get it together. Don't fucking call me until you do."

When I stopped at the red light, Laquinta opened the door and got out. She slammed it and started walking down the street. When the light changed, I pulled over and drove closely to the curb.

"Would you quit tripping and get in the car? You look like a hooker trying to get picked up." She ignored me and kept on walking. "Quintaaa," I joked. "Erica is starting to cry for you."

She kept on walking, so I parked the car and ran up to her. I put handcuffs on her and escorted her back to the truck.

"Take these cuffs off me, Isaac. I'm in no mood to be playing around with you."

I put her inside the truck and got back in on the driver's side. "When I drop you off at home, I'll take them off."

"Then hurry it up," she said angrily.

"I will, but why you still mad at me? I told you I ain't fucking with you no more, didn't I?"

"Trust me, I ain't gon' cry, and I for damn sure ain't gon' lose no sleep."

"And neither will I."

I drove Laquinta home, and as soon as I removed the cuffs, she got out of the car. She walked around to the driver's side to get Erica, and I stood close to her as she opened the back door.

"What do you want from me?" I asked. "I've been trying to figure it out for a long, long time."

She turned to face me. "I don't want anything from you, Isaac. Nothing right now, but I would like to slap that smirk off your face since you think this shit is so funny."

"So, you want to smack me again, is that it?"

"Yes, hard, very hard for being a motherfucking jerk."

"Then do it. If it makes you feel better, then smack me."

With no hesitation on her part, she smacked my left cheek hard. It stung a bit, but I held my stare.

"Hit me again."

She smacked me on the left cheek and came up with her other hand to smack me on the right. My face burned, but I continued to hold my stare.

"Do you feel better yet?" I asked.

"Much better," she said.

"Good," I said, pulling her hair back. I squeezed it tightly and gave her a long, hard, wet kiss. She shoved me back and wiped her lips.

"If I forgive you for the abuse and for almost getting me killed today, maybe I'll see you tomorrow. If not, then I might need some time to heal," I said.

"Take all the time you need, Isaac," she said, removing Erica from her car seat. "Your mind needs all the rest it can get. Besides, I'm sure that since the sheriff is back in town, you'll be missing in action anyway."

"Sheriff? What Sheriff?"

"Your precious little wife. Today, I saw her at the gas station and she introduced herself to me."

I was stunned. "And you're just now telling me? Where . . . what did she say?"

"She went off on me. What did you expect her to say?"

"What the fuck does 'went off on you' mean? Were you driving—"

"Yes, Isaac. I was in your truck and she got her feelings hurt. She wasn't too thrilled to see Erica. "

"I can't believe you didn't tell me," I said, hurrying into my truck. I knew that listening to more of what Laquinta had to say would piss me off. Instead of feuding with her again, I jetted. I called Cydney's cell phone, and finally, she answered.

"Where in the hell have you been?" I yelled.

"Isaac, I'm busy right now. I'll call you later."

"Busy! What the fuck—"

She hung up on me, and I called her right back. This

time, her voicemail came on, so I knew she'd turned off her phone.

First, I drove to our house. I didn't expect her car to be there, and it wasn't, so I drove to her office. Her car was parked in the parking garage, along with a few other cars. It was late, but I didn't care. Problems in our marriage or not, Cydney had some explaining to do. No matter what, I would've never, ever left her for ten whole days without calling.

By the time I made it to her office, from a distance, I could see Darrell sitting on the couch while looking in the direction of her desk. I walked fast and stepped inside the doorway.

"Do you mind if I talk to my wife alone?" I asked. Darrell looked at Cydney for approval. "What in the hell are you looking at her for? I asked you to leave."

"In case you forgot, Isaac, this is his place of business. You need to calm down, and please don't come in here demanding anything from either of us."

"Cydney, it's okay. Just close the door so that no one will hear you. Mostly everyone is gone, with the exception of the cleaning crew. If you need me, I'll be in my office."

Darrell walked past me, and since I didn't move aside, he brushed up against me. After he left, I slammed the door.

"How dare you bring your lousy butt up in here treating my boss like dirt?"

"Fuck your boss, Cydney! Is that the motherfucker you went on vacation with? Your mother told me you'd taken a vacation, and I know damn well you didn't go alone!"

She folded her arms. "What's it to you, Isaac? Before I left, we separated. Now, I've had time to think about things, and this marriage is over. I want a divorce. We need to get this unsalvageable marriage over with as soon as we can."

"All of a sudden, it's like that, huh? You sitting over there glowing and shit. Motherfucker probably fucked your brains out every single day you were away, and now, you want a divorce? It ain't going down like that, baby. I've put too much into this marriage, and I'm damn well gon' get something out of it!"

She laughed. "What a joke, Isaac. Tell me, what is it that you've put into this marriage but a bunch of nonsense and hurt? I can't believe those words even fell out of your mouth, after I saw your new wife and daughter at the gas station today. Didn't she tell you?"

"I let a friend of mine use my truck to take her daughter to the doctor. Now what? You're making something out of nothing to justify your own deceiving."

"Well, Laquinta must be one hell of a good friend. When you first got that truck, you wouldn't even let me drive it. As a matter of fact, I've never driven it. But I guess after being with you for so long, she can pretty much get anything that she wants from you. And her precious child . . . she's quite gorgeous. She looks nothing like you, but I guess the pussy is so powerful that it's not only cost you your marriage, but it also has you taking care of a child that isn't really yours."

"I know she's not mine, and I'm not taking care of nobody. I had sex with Laquinta a few times, and that's because your ass was tripping. Don't blame me because you wasn't being the wife you should've been. I had needs, Cyd, and you was never there for me."

"Boo-hoo-hoo, Isaac. I'm done disputing this issue with you, and let's just get this over with so we both can move on."

I was somewhat hurt by her coldness, but more than

anything, I could tell she'd been with someone else. I went over to her desk, turned her chair to me, and straddled it with my arms.

"Who is he, Cydney? I want to meet the motherfucker who's got you speaking a different language. He's got to be a bad-ass brotha to take what's mine, and I swear to God that when I see him, I'm gon' break his neck for interfering where he don't belong."

"Back away from me, Isaac. You have no right—"

I shook Cydney's chair. "Who is he?" I yelled. "Whoever he is, you will not have one damn day of peace with him! I'll make sure of that. And if a divorce is what you want, then you'll get it! It's still not going to stop me from kicking his ass each and every time I see the two of you together."

"You've lost your mind, and I'm not going to stand for that kind of tone or your threats. Leave, Isaac, or I'll have you arrested."

"Do what you feel is necessary, Cydney. You sitting here all proud and shit, glowing, and pussy probably ain't even dry yet from giving this nigga my loving. I can't believe you'd put somebody before me, and whether I saw other women or not, I never put any of them before you. Never!"

"That makes me feel so special, Isaac, but I beg to differ. The day you decided to sleep with them, you put them before me. Now," she said, backing me up so she could stand, "would you please leave so I can get some work done?"

I stood next to her. "Are you coming home?"

"That's your house, not mine. Remember, I don't live there anymore."

"It's our house, but if either of us decide to leave, it'll be me. There's no need for you to be sleeping at your other man's house when you have one to go to."

"I agree. So, when you have all of your things packed, call me so I can come home."

"I'm on my way there to pack them now. Are you coming?"

"I said call me when you're on your way out."

"In about two hours, I'll be packed and gone. I hope you haven't forgotten your own address."

Cydney turned her head, and I left her office. Little did she know, I wasn't going no damn where. Starting tonight, we were going to work this shit out and somehow save our marriage.

CYDNEY

Now, what kind of fool did Isaac take me for? I knew that when I got home, none of his things would be packed. What I didn't know is that he'd whipped up a little dinner for us, served out some wine, lit some candles and thought his actions could win me over. I told him to shove dinner where the sun didn't shine then went downstairs to get some sleep.

I was exhausted from my trip, and I couldn't stop thinking about Raymond. My mind was consumed with the thoughts of him, and as much as I tried to forget about what we shared, I couldn't. I didn't have a phone number to call him, nor did I have an address to write him a letter. I felt the need to hear his voice, and for him to hold me in his arms one last time. Before I'd left Maui, I'd planned on making love to him, but that was cut short by his abrupt departure. Maybe I was reading too much into this and he left because he'd gotten what he wanted. I couldn't have had that much of an impact on him, and the more I thought about it, the more I began to believe that maybe I was fooling myself.

As for Isaac, I was starting to pity him. After seeing again how trashy and low class Laquinta was, I lost respect for him. I never, ever understood why, when a man cheated, he had to find the worst kind of woman to cheat with. That's what hurt the most, and for a woman like that to have my husband in her possession for so long, that was a no-no. As far as I was concerned, she could have him. He was getting out of control, and I was sure that she was getting the backlash of his frustrations. Hell, the other woman always does. It might not be that day, or the next, but she'd soon regret that he ever came into her life.

I'd been home from my trip for almost two weeks. Isaac was attempting to play the "reformed" husband's role and had been coming home straight from work. When I mentioned him moving out, he claimed he'd been looking for a place to stay. He even removed a few pieces of clothing from our closet, but when I saw the clothes in the back seat of his truck, I knew he was full of it.

Since he thought I was joking around with him, I stayed late nights at the office so I didn't have to see him. He continuously called to see when I was coming home, but more than anything, he was trying to make sure I wasn't out anywhere messing around.

On Friday, it was getting late, and I was more than tired. Due to my taking such a long trip, my work was backed up. No matter how late I stayed, I still couldn't get caught up. My administrative assistant, Carol, had been working overtime to help. She was an elderly white woman who came highly recommended by Darrell. I knew he was doing a friend a favor, but she wasn't much help to me at all. Around seven o'clock, I told her she could go home.

Before she left, she brought my mail to me and laid it on my desk.

"Since you were in a meeting, I forgot to give the mail to you. I already looked through it, but it wasn't anything too important. There was a package delivered for you, but it's too heavy for me to lift."

I thumbed through the mail, and it was the same ol', same ol'. I followed Carol out of my office and went to get the package she mentioned. She put her purse on her shoulder and pointed to the wrapped item. I looked at it curiously, and when I moved it forward, I tore off a piece of the paper. Immediately, I noticed that the frame looked familiar, and I tore off more paper. It was the picture of the Majestic.

My heart raced. "What time was this delivered?"

"About two . . . maybe three hours ago."

"Who delivered it?"

"A guy from UPS."

"Are you sure?"

"Positive."

"How did he look?"

"He was a black, tall guy with—"

"Are you sure?"

"Yes, Cydney, I'm positive."

I looked at the picture again and could only smile. As I tore off more paper and looked down, I saw a tiny folded piece of paper taped to it. I reached for the paper and read it.

Meet me for dinner tonight. I'll be at Cardwell's in Clayton at 8:00. I'm anxious to see you, so don't be late.

I looked at my watch, and it was already 7:30. I rushed into my office and grabbed my purse. Carol waited for me, and we walked to the elevator.

"That was an awfully pretty picture, Cydney. Who sent it to you?"

Carol was always being nosy, so I lied. "My father-in-law sent it to me. He knows how much I love yachts."

As soon as the elevator opened, I stepped on it. But when it opened in the lobby, Isaac stood waiting for me to get off.

"I was on my way up to keep you company. Now that you're leaving, you don't mind if I take you to dinner and a movie tonight, do you?"

"Isaac, I really don't have time. I have to meet a client for a late dinner, and after that, I'll be home. It shouldn't take long at all because I'm tired and anxious to wrap up this meeting."

Isaac walked me to my car and promised me that upon my arrival, a bubble bath would await me.

"Thanks," I said and quickly shut my door. I drove off and looked at him in my rearview mirror. How or why did I feel so guilty? After all the things he'd done to me, I had the nerve to feel sorry for him.

By the time I made it to Cardwell's, it was already 8:20 P.M. The valet parked my car and I went inside. I expected Raymond to be waiting at the door, but he wasn't. And when I looked around the dining room, I didn't see him. Maybe I was too late. I went back over by the door and looked outside. Still, there was no sign of him. Giving it one last shot, I asked the maitre d' if reservations were made for Raymond Burg. He said yes and directed me to where Raymond was. I followed and the maitre d' opened the door to a private dining room. It was small, and there were only two other couples dining in the area. The maitre d' pulled back the chair for me and told me Raymond would be joining me shortly.

I took a seat, and soon, my heart melted. He came into the room awesomely dressed in a black tailored suit and white crisp shirt underneath. No tie was needed, and the suit fit every bit of his muscular frame. His hair was neatly lined, and everyone in the room could smell the money on him. I couldn't even get out of my seat to stand, so he stood up next to me and fumbled with the silverware.

"If my asking you to come here makes you uncomfortable, I'm sorry. I had to see you again, Cydney, and I didn't mean to intrude in your life."

Intrude, I thought. Hell, he'd just saved the day and didn't even know it. "I . . . it wasn't a problem, Raymond. I'm glad you came."

"Did you get the picture?"

"Yes. And thank you," I said, finally standing up. I pulled my beige pin-stripped suit jacket together and reached out for a hug. Raymond wrapped one arm around me and whispered in my ear. "Can I make love to you tonight?"

I backed away. "We . . . we'll see," I said, playing hard to get. The answer was really yes, got damn-it, yes! But I didn't want to appear desperate. More than anything, I couldn't let him know that the thoughts of him had been occupying my mind twenty-four seven.

I sat back in my chair, and Raymond walked around the table to take a seat. With his fingers, he combed the sides of his curly hair back and picked up the menu. After looking at it for a few minutes, he lowered it and looked at me. I pretended to be occupied with my menu.

"You are so, so beautiful," he said. "Why couldn't I stop thinking of you after you left?"

"I don't know. Maybe because you left the room before saying goodbye to me?"

"I hope you aren't upset about that. I was being selfish and I wanted you to stay. After you left, I got your information from the front desk. I know it's confidential, but the Captain has access to many things on the island."

"Okay, Captain. What is it that you really do for a living?"

"Are you positive that you want to know? In Maui, our lives were supposed to be such a secret."

"Yes, I want to know. I'd like to know everything about you."

"Are you prepared to share everything about you?"

"Maybe."

"That's not fair, but I didn't expect for you to be. Anyhow, I'm in the family business of building luxury yachts. Since I love them so much, I often volunteer to navigate them from one island to another. I'm thirty-seven, and I have homes in California, New York and Washington. My family's beachfront properties are all over the world, but you'd be surprised that I have rental property right here in Lake St. Louis and on the south side." He placed his hands behind his head. "Other than that, I'm divorced. I have a son, and this suit I have on is so, so uncomfortable. I only wore it to impress you, and the only time I like to dress this way is when I wear my captain's uniform."

I smiled and shook my head. "You have such a great sense of humor. The suit looks really, really nice, but you didn't have to wear it to impress me. I'm already impressed, but I'm curious to know why your marriage didn't work out."

He leaned forward and placed his elbows on the table. He clinched his fingers together and stared at me from across the table. "I assume you want the truth, right?"

"It helps."

"I don't want you to look at me any differently, but my wife divorced me for having extramarital affairs. She has our son, and I have never forgiven myself for being such a jerk. I was young and stupid, Cydney, but now I know better. If I ever have the opportunity to find love again, I'll never repeat what I did in the past."

Of course, Raymond's news didn't sit right with me, and I did not want to deal with a man who had cheated on his wife. Once a cheater always a cheater, I thought. As I sat quietly, the waiter was right on time when he came over and took our orders. I ordered prime rib, and so did Raymond.

"Cydney," Raymond said, "you're too quiet. Now that I've shared some things with you, you have to share some things with me."

"There's really not much to share," I said hesitantly. "I . . . I don't—"

Just then, a voice interrupted. "Hey, baby," Isaac said, leaning down to kiss my cheek. He looked over at Raymond and held out his hand. "I'm Cydney's husband, Isaac. And you are?"

Raymond didn't say a word.

"Raymond Burg," I said, shocked. "Raymond, this is my husband, Isaac. I mentioned my dinner plans with a client tonight, and Isaac said he might join us."

Raymond slowly reached his hand out and shook Isaac's. "Nice to meet you," Raymond said.

"Really?" Isaac said, taking a seat. "It's cool to meet you too, Raymond, and I'm elated about finally meeting the man who's been occupying my wife's time. Shocked, more like it."

Raymond remained cool, calm and collected, but I knew Isaac was fishing. "Well, business is business, Isaac. I've been thinking about investing in the company your wife works for, and her boss told me to speak with her about it."

"Now, why would he do that?" Isaac asked.

"Because I've been there for quite some time, and other than Darrell, nobody knows the business better than I do."

"Bullshit, Cydney. From a distance, I've been watching the two of you, and your body language said business wasn't being discussed." Isaac sat back in his chair and looked down at his gun holster. He then looked up at me. "Tonight, you and Raymond got a choice. Either he leaves, or else I'm gon' get up and put my foot in his ass or yours. At least I'm giving everybody here some options."

I knew that Isaac was about to trip, and I didn't want Raymond involved in our mess. I looked across the table at him as he sat sternly. He wasn't about to move.

"I am starving," Raymond said. "I can't wait until the food gets here. How about you, Cydney?"

"Raymond, I'll have to take a rain check. If you wouldn't mind leaving Isaac and me alone, I'd more than appreciate it."

Raymond stared at me, and I could see the fire in his green eyes. He dropped the napkin on the table and stood up. He came over to my side of the table, placed one hand on the back of my chair, and the other on the table. He then leaned down in front of me.

"If you put your lips on my wife, your ass will hit the floor. I dare you," Isaac said furiously.

Raymond's eyes shifted up to Isaac, and then turned to me. Isaac's words didn't scare him at all. "You deserve better. I'll call you tomorrow, okay?"

I nodded, and Raymond looked deep into my eyes. His eyes dropped to my lips, and as I could feel him wanting to lean in, I slowly moved my head from side to side.

Isaac stood up, and Raymond backed away from my face. Before leaving, he gave me one last look and was gone.

Isaac sat down in the chair and gazed at me. "A white motherfucker, Cydney? You went behind my back and slept with a white man?"

"Must we sit in this restaurant and put all of our busi-

ness out there? If you have something to say to me, you
need to say it in the privacy of our own home."

"Oh, I got plenty to say. Now, let's get out of here so I
can go home and say it," he said.

Sparing us the embarrassment, we headed for the door.
The maitre d' said that Raymond had settled the bill, so I
thanked the maitre d' and apologized for the inconve-
nience. I waited for the valet to bring my car, and Isaac
walked to a nearby parking garage to get his. I'd thought
about avoiding Isaac and getting a room for the night,
but I felt a need to stand up to him. How dare he inter-
rupt my dinner engagement and make any demands of
me, especially after all he'd done to me? Thinking about
what had happened, I hurried home so we could talk.

As I made a left turn to get on the highway at Ladue
Road, a silver Jaguar cut me off. The driver told me to
pull over, and since I thought I'd bumped his car, I did.
When the back door opened, Raymond got out. He
opened the driver's side to my car and squatted down beside me.

"I'm sorry for what happened back there, but your
husband irritates the hell out of me. Will you . . . can you
follow me?"

"Now?"

"Yes, now."

"Raymond, I don't think that's a good idea. Isaac could
be somewhere watching me, and with me wanting a divorce, I'd hate for him to have any ammunition against
me. When are you leaving?"

"Tomorrow. I can always come back, but I was hoping
to see you while I was here."

"Then maybe tomorrow, okay? Tonight is not a good
time. I'll be paranoid all night long."

Raymond looked disappointed. He gave me the same

stare he'd given me at the restaurant. When his eyes
dropped to my lips, I moved forward to kiss him. As usual,
his kiss made me melt like butter. I wanted so badly to let
him make love to me, but the thoughts of my crazy-ass
husband wouldn't let me. I broke our intense kissing and
told Raymond I'd most likely see him tomorrow. He got
back into the Jag, and the driver pulled off. For a while, I
followed, and then merged onto Highway 70 to go home.

CYDNEY

Saturday or not, I got out of bed early and headed for work. Today would be a catch-up day for me, and since no one would be in the office, I could get plenty of work done. When I got home the night before, Isaac wasn't even there. I just knew he'd come in acting a fool, but he didn't. Him not being home gave me a little time to sleep, but the thoughts of Raymond weighed heavy on my mind. I wanted to see him today, but then again, I had to clear up this mess with Isaac and do it fast. He was getting out of control, and I knew that somebody was bound to get hurt. If Raymond allowed me just a few more months, I could very well be free to do whatever I desired to do.

On my way to the office, my cell phone rang. It was Miguel. Since I'd been home, he'd backed off. I guess he was in the mood to mess with me this morning. Trying to see what the enemy was up to, I answered.

"What?" I said sharply.

"Now, that ain't no way to talk to me after all I've done for you, is it?"

"Make it quick, Miguel. I'm busy."

"When am I going to see you?"

"Never. I told you that I'm not dealing with you any-more, Miguel, and the same goes for Isaac."

He laughed. "That's a lie and you know it. You'll never leave Isaac, Cydney. He's got you wrapped around his finger like the rest of his bitches. Don't think for one moment that I've forgotten about you because I haven't. I've just been busy working on a li'l something else. For now, you and Isaac are on the back burner. Trust me, I'll be in touch with you real, real soon."

He hung up, and I tossed my cell phone over to the passenger's seat. If I could ever take back my involvement with him, I surely would. All I could ask myself was, what in the hell was I thinking?

When I arrived at my office, the moment I walked in, I looked at the picture of the Majestic. I tore off the re-mainder of the paper and pushed the picture into my of-fice. I already had a place for it on my wall, but it was so heavy that I had to wait for someone in maintenance to hang it for me. For the time being, I placed it against the wall right in front of my desk.

For the next several hours, I got down to business. Next week was going to be a breeze for me, as I'd filed all of my papers, reorganized my desk, and reviewed all of the insurance claims that required upper management's attention. Bottom line, Carol wasn't worth a damn, and since I had to do her work too, her salary was a serious waste.

By the time I got finished reviewing one hundred and twenty claims, it was already getting late. I got up to pour another cup of coffee, and when I got back to my desk, I looked down at the picture. I'd been looking at it all day, and I figured by now that Raymond had already left.

As I was in deep thought, I heard laughter. When I

looked up, it was Darrell and his male companion. Darrell walked in, but his companion stayed by the doorway. By the looks of both of them, you'd never know their preferences.

"Cydney, I didn't know you were coming in," Darrell said.

"Yes, I wanted to get caught up on my work. You don't mind, do you?"

He looked at his watch. "Did you know that it's almost eight o'clock? How long have you been here?"

"Since eleven. I plan to wrap up a few more things, and then I'm leaving."

"No, you leave now. You can finish up on Monday. You look very tired, and you've got to get your beauty rest."

I was feeling awfully tired, so I stood up and reached for my purse on my desk. "Would you walk me to the elevator?" I asked.

"Sure," he said, excusing himself from his companion. He failed to introduce me, but I already knew what was up.

We walked to the elevator, and I couldn't help but pry. "So, is this thing between you and him official?"

"Yes, it is, Cydney. I took your advice and told my fiancée the truth. She was devastated, but I had to be honest with her."

"What about the baby?"

"There was no baby. She lied about being pregnant, only so I would marry her."

All I could do was shake my head. I told Darrell to have a good evening and I'd see him on Monday.

"You too, Cydney. And be careful driving. It's raining cats and dogs."

"I will."

From my office, I'd seen and heard the thunder, but I guess I hadn't paid much attention to the rain. The park-

ing garage saved me, but when I drove out of it, the rain
came pouring down. The streets were extremely slick,
and as soon as I got on Highway 40 to go home, the highway was at a standstill. There was an accident, and I
crawled my way through traffic. By the time I reached the
Forest Park exit, I was frustrated and got off. Going
through the park was like going in circles, but anything
beat staying stuck in traffic.

As soon as I merged off to go through the park, another car followed closely behind me. The streets were
dark, and all I could see were headlights. Trying not to
panic, I figured the driver must have had the same idea I
did. Soon after, my cell phone rang. I reached for it, and
when I looked at the caller ID, the caller was unknown.
Instead of letting it go to voicemail, I answered.

"Cydney?"

"Yes."

"Pull over."

I looked in my rearview mirror and recognized the
voice as Raymond's. Honestly, I didn't appreciate being
followed, but I pulled my car over to the curb. Having no
umbrella, and feeling uneasy about being on a dark
street, I stayed in the car for a moment. When I saw Raymond walking toward my car with a huge black umbrella,
that's when I got out. I walked to the back of my car, and
that fast, my wet hair was flat on my head. He walked up
and covered both of us with the umbrella. I pulled my
hair over to one side and blinked my wet eyelids.

"Raymond, I have to be honest. I don't like being followed like this."

"And I don't like to sneak around either, but I wanted
to see you before I left. Before I contacted you, I had to
be sure that Isaac wasn't anywhere around. As I said before, if I've made you uncomfortable in any way, I have
no problem allowing you your space. Just say so."

"It's not that, but all this sneaking around and popping up out of nowhere stuff is making me extremely paranoid. I need time, Raymond. Time to resolve my issues with Isaac. Just allow me some time, okay?"

"It's whatever you want, Cydney. But will you come back to my hotel with me tonight? Just for . . . only for a few hours."

Before I could answer, the thunder roared and the rain fell heavily. Even the wind kicked up and blew the umbrella up. Raymond tried to hold on to it, but after it wouldn't cooperate, he let it go. We got drenched, and Raymond squinted his eyes.

"Can we go now?" he asked. "There's no need—"

"I can't, Raymond. Not—"

He moved forward and kissed me. Wanting . . . needing his touch, I pulled on his wet hair and sucked his lips into mine. He backed me against the trunk of my car, and his hands started to wander. After he yanked at my red silk button-down blouse, the buttons popped off, and my blouse came apart. Raymond rushed to lower his head, and pulled my right breast from my bra. He massaged the left one, and placed his mouth on the other one. We both wanted each other so badly that the rain didn't seem to matter. As he sucked my breast, I leaned my head back and closed my eyes. The rain beat down on my face, and when Raymond reached for my skirt to pull it up, I stopped him.

"Let's . . . let's go to your room," I moaned.

"No," he said. "I'm enjoying you right here."

His hands went up my skirt, and he felt how wet my insides were. I was too thrilled to make him stop, but I suggested getting inside of the car. As we stepped to the other side of my car, Raymond opened the door. I scooted backwards on the back seat, and Raymond crawled inside. His white casual shirt was drenched and clung to his body. To feel him like I wanted to, I unbuttoned it, and he pulled it off. He was too tall to close the door, and when he lowered himself between my legs, the door being open gave him plenty of room. Hurrying, he pulled down my panties, and I kicked them off my feet. He tasted me first, and since the moment was so intense, it didn't take long for me to come. Afterwards, he moved up closer to me, and I spread my legs farther apart. He unzipped his pants, and I was relieved. My pussy was a slippery, wet mess. The look on Raymond's face showed pure satisfaction. He tightened his eyes, and never failed to entertain my breasts while he stroked me down below.

"Cydney, Cydney, Cydney," he moaned. "What are you doing to me?"

"The same thing you're doing to me," I whispered.

As he continued to wet my nipples, I lifted his face and brought it to mine. I sucked on his bottom lip and twirled my tongue around in his mouth. He accepted my taste, and I couldn't imagine myself being anywhere but right there with him.

"Raymond, what are we gonna do? Why do you have to live so far, far away? I need you . . . I need this."

"Me too," he said softly. His words caused me to work even harder, and within moments, his six pack was moving in and out, and his body jerked. He dropped his lips to my neck and kissed it.

"Wonderful. Just wonderful."

I smiled, and when we heard the sound of wet tires driving on the pavement and saw shining lights inside of the car, I panicked. Raymond looked up, and his eyes slowly followed the car as it passed by us.

"Who is it?" I whispered.

"I don't know. She's gone."

I let out a sigh of relief, and Raymond backed himself out of the car. I quickly sat up, and after he zipped his pants, he got back in and closed the door. He sat next to me and put his arm around my shoulders.

"Are you cold?" he asked.

"Freezing," I said, trying to button the few buttons on my blouse. "The rain has me extremely cold."

He sat shirtless and placed his hand on his lap.

"Come over here and straddle me," he said.

"Why? Haven't you already had enough?"

"I'll never get enough of you, Cydney, but I just want to hold you. I can't hold you from the side."

I straddled Raymond's lap, and my breasts were directly at his face. When I sat back on his lap, he smiled. He looked up at me with his seductive eyes.

"You have the juiciest and most succulent breasts I've ever seen." He held them in his hands. "Your nipples are . . . they're perfect."

"Oh, by how much and how well you suck them, I can tell how much you like them."

"I can't help it. I'm a breast man." He let go of my breasts and gripped my ass. "I'm an ass man too, but your breasts are irresistible."

When I heard another car coming, I slid off of Raymond's lap. The car slowly drove by us. It was another woman with her kids.

"We'd better get going," I said, touching Raymond's leg.

He lifted himself and pulled his wallet out of his pocket. He took out a card and handed it to me.

"Now you have no excuse not to call me. Whenever you're ready to see me again, I'll come back. I hope you'll work out your situation with Isaac real soon because I don't know if I'll be able to stay away for long."

"I'll do what I can. But more than anything, I'll be sure to keep in touch."

We both leaned in for a kiss, and it was an unforgettable one. Afterwards, we got out and walked around to the driver's side of my car. Raymond opened the door for me, and after I got in, he said goodbye. I watched him go back to his car and get inside. Once I drove off, he followed. At the end of the street, I made a left and he made a right.

MIGUEL

Just who in the hell did Cydney think she was, trying to drop me like a hot potato? If she was planning to leave Isaac, she would've done it a long, long time ago. Bottom line, she wasn't planning on doing shit but having her cake and eating it too. I hated a woman who was that damn devious, and if she thought I was going to sit back and be made a fool of, she was sadly mistaken.

See, when I partnered with Isaac almost a year ago, things were pretty cool. That was until I took him over to my family's house and he met my moms, along with my twenty-nine-year-old sister, Trinity. I immediately noticed their attraction for one another, but I made it clear to Isaac that she was hands off. I knew what kind of playa he was, and I didn't want her to get caught up like the other tricks in his life. But what does a playa normally do? He stepped to her anyway. Had sex with her several times behind my back, and when he got tired, he kicked her to the curb. She wound up getting her feelings hurt and got pregnant by him. He gave her money for an abortion, and then told her he wanted nothing else to do with her. From the get-go, I told her he wasn't no good. Since then, I wanted to hurt him for going against my wishes, but Trinity made me promise not to get involved. Isaac has no idea that Trinity gave me the down low about their relationship, and I was damn mad about it. I couldn't stay out of it, and the only way I could get back at Isaac was through my involvement with his wife. She was an easy target, and since I knew so much about his extramarital affairs, I knew her life was chaotic.

At first, Cydney welcomed me with open arms. Sex between us occurred a few times, but then she started feeling guilty. For what? That's what I wanted to know. How could she feel guilty when he was the one constantly fucking around? Either she was just plain old stupid, or deep down, Cydney loved Isaac more than she loved herself.

Either way, I'd had enough. She wasn't as receptive to my advances, so I had to back off. I didn't know if telling Isaac about being with his wife would cause as much damage as I intended, but I wanted to send him over the edge like I was when I found out about my sister. When he found Cydney's work address on that piece of paper, I was just about ready to spill the beans. I intended to give her address to my connection so he'd know where to find her. We came up with another plan, so I ditched the address, not knowing Isaac would see it.

After a long night at the club, I went to Denny's for an early breakfast. I sat impatiently waiting for my companion to come. The motherfucker had straight up been tripping lately, and if he didn't get his shit together soon, I was gon' put my foot in his ass.

Just as my food was placed on the table, he walked in. I removed my silver-framed glasses and placed them on the table.

"Well, it's about time," I said, looking up at him. "Why haven't you returned my phone calls?"

He slid into the booth and sat across from me. "Because I've been busy. I told you that I wanted out of this mess, so I wish you'd stop calling me."

"What's wrong? You done got pussy whipped? I should have known that Cydney was too much for you to handle. But you and I have a deal."

"Yeah, well, the deal was over when she left Maui. I'm on my time now, and it has nothing to do with you."

"So, you think you can play me like that? We had a deal, Raymond, and it ain't over until I say it's over. Now, I'm about to blow this thing wide open. I need you to help me follow the plan. Got it?"

Raymond laid a bag on the table and looked over at me. "There's your money back. I don't want it nor do I need it. Cydney's a very nice woman, and she's not going to divorce Isaac for me or for anyone. Besides, he's already found out about me, and he's working to save his marriage. I'll bet the money that's in your bag that he'll save their marriage, so that means your plan has failed. It's time to go back to the drawing board, but this time, don't include me."

"If you would've never come to St. Louis, he wouldn't have found out about you this soon. You fucked up my plan, and why, Raymond? Cause you had to come here and fuck her again, didn't you? Yesterday, you didn't return my phone call because you had sex with her again."

Raymond moved around in the booth and clinched his hands together on the table. He gave me a serious but stern look.

"Face it, Miguel, you chose the wrong man for the job. If I could, I would take Cydney from Isaac and make her mine. I could love her the way she deserves to be loved, and I regret like hell that you've involved me in something so conniving. Once I check on my family, I'm out of St. Louis for a while. I'm glad that I don't live here anymore, and seeing your face is starting to really irk me. When I get back to Florida, I'm sure you're dying to tell Cydney all about me. When you do, I hope you mention what a wonderful woman I think she is."

"You are a sorry excuse for a man. And you're right, once Cydney finds out that you spent time in jail for money laundering and drug trafficking, she's going to wash her hands and be done with you. Since then, your wealthy family disowned you, and I was the one who supported you the entire time you were in jail. We've been friends for too long, Raymond, and you owe me to see this thing through."

"You supported me because you knew I was innocent. My father and you were behind that bullshit, and I was the one who had to take the fall! You're still on his payroll, Miguel, and all I have to do is tell the police about your little pick-up tomorrow. You didn't think I knew about it. But if you have a problem excluding me from your little game with Cydney, everyone will know what kind of person you really are, so back off. Both you and my father can go to hell!"

Raymond eased out of the booth and gave me a devilish look. "And you have the nerve to wear that police uniform and call yourself a cop," he snickered. "What a fucking joke." He walked away.

"And a damn good cop at that," I yelled.

I chewed my eggs and realized that despite all of my efforts, I was back to square one.

ISAAC

I tried hard to put the thoughts of Cyd in the back of my mind, but her being with a white man was hard to swallow. The way she looked at him and he looked at her, that shit didn't sit right with me at all. Since then, I'd been just about watching her every move. Yesterday, she managed to slip out on me because I had to go check Laquinta for ringing my phone like she was crazy. I wound up spending the night on the couch, but the only reason I stayed was because Erica was sick. She had a cold, and since dick was the only thing on Laquinta's mind, I held Erica in my arms for the entire night. When I got home, Cyd was gone, and I'd been trying to catch up with her all day. I knew she wasn't at work on Saturday, so going to her office was out of the question. I waited and waited for her to come home, but up until two o'clock in the morning, she was a no show.

When I heard the front door close, I turned in bed and looked at the clock. It was 7:15 in the morning, and I yanked the covers back and got out of bed naked. I walked down the hallway and noticed the doors to the kitchen swinging. I saw Cydney leaning against the kitchen's counter, drinking a glass of water. Her hair was nappy and pulled back into a ponytail. Her clothes were wrinkled, and I could see her nipples poking through her ripped silk blouse that had only a few buttons connected. She looked my body up and down and placed the glass on the counter.

"What in the hell happened to you?" I asked.

"Nothing," she said, walking past me.

I grabbed her arm. "Nothing? You mean to tell me that you're going to walk in here looking like you've either been raped or fucked, and *nothing* is the best you can come up with?"

She snatched her arm away from me. "Nothing happened to me that I didn't want to happen to me. Now, back off, Isaac. I don't want to hear it this morning."

She walked away, and I followed her to our bedroom.

"Well, damn it, Cyd, you're going to hear it! This game you're playing needs to stop, right now! Why would you come in here like this? You know that you being with another man is killing me! Especially a white—"

"Well, you should've thought about that when you started having your rendezvous. I can't—"

Before she stepped into the bathroom, something clicked. I swung her around and tightly held her arms. "Did you have sex with him in the rain? Is that why your hair and clothes are like this?"

"Let go of me, Isaac," she yelled. "You're hurting my arms."

"Good," I said, reaching for her skirt. I pulled it up and saw she didn't have on any panties. When I ripped the rest of her blouse, her bra wasn't there. I was furious, and couldn't control myself.

"Get your ass in the shower," I yelled, while shoving

her over to it. "Wash all of this motherfucker's scent off you!"

She tussled with me and tried to push me away. When she bit my hand, I pushed her hard against the shower's wall. I walked off to our bedroom, grabbed my gun and came back. Livid, I aimed the gun at her.

"Take off your skirt and turn on the water!"

Tears started to fall from her eyes as she stared at me and slowly dropped her skirt. She reached for the faucet and turned on the water. With her back against the wall, I stepped inside of the shower, laid my gun on the shower's seat and picked up a towel. I lathered it with soap and started to wash her body.

"Here you won't even make love to me, but you gon' give your shit up to someone else? What sense does that make, and I'm your husband? Turn around," I yelled. Cydney slowly turned around, and I lathered up her backside. Her ass was like a melon, and I could tell she'd been losing weight. It was for him, of course, and that made me even angrier. I dropped the soapy towel and pressed my body against hers. I kissed the side of her neck and touched all over her body. She closed her eyes and trembled.

"Isaac, please don't," she said.

"Please don't what? Are you saying that I can't make love to you?"

"No, you can't. I don't want this anymore," she said. "I . . . I don't want to make love to you anymore."

"Does my touching you hurt you that much? Does it cause you to tremble the way you are? I can't believe that you don't have no desire to make love to me anymore. Do you at least still love me?"

Having my attention, she turned around to face me. "I will always love you, Isaac, but my heart is moving in another direction. Your touching me hurts me deeply. My body yearns to have the husband I had years ago, but not the one who stands before me today. I'm sorry, but I just can't give myself to you under these conditions. You've hurt me so much that I have nothing left."

"I'll do whatever it takes to make things right, Cyd. I know I've said it before, but I just can't lose you like this, baby. I need you . . . we need each other, and if we have to go to counseling or whatever you want me to do, I'll do it. Just give me one last chance. If I fuck up, then you can have your divorce. But please, please don't give up on us." I paused and took a deep breath. "I love you. No matter what, I've never stopped loving you. Your heart belongs to me, and mine belongs to you. Please stop seeing this other man and let's try to fix this."

"Then fix it, Isaac," she whispered. "Do whatever you've got to do to fix it."

"So, does that mean you're giving me another chance?"

"Just fix it," she said again.

I turned off the water and tried to kiss her. She turned her head and I kissed her cheek. I placed my hand underneath her chin and turned her face to me.

"You've given me hope. You are not going to regret this opportunity you've given me."

Cydney remained quiet, and I got out of the shower. I reached for a towel in the closet and dried off. Once she stepped out, I dried her off too. I then went into another closet to get her robe and handed it to her. She put it on, turned on the television, and sat on the bed.

Moments later, I was dressed in my faded jeans, leather sandals, and canary yellow shirt. After I brushed my waves, I was ready to go. Cydney told me to fix it, and that's what I intended to do. I told her I'd be back later, and asked if we could catch a movie. She didn't say yes, but she didn't say no. Her "we'll see" was better than nothing.

* * *

My mission started with going to see Laquinta. I knew this was going to be difficult, but I couldn't stand to lose Cydney. If the time ever came when I was forced to choose between the two of them, I always knew what the answer would be.

When I got to Laquinta's place, she was outside talking to one of her girlfriends. She was surprised to see me back so soon, and when I asked where Erica was, Laquinta said that her mother had come to get her.

"How's she feeling today?" I asked.

"She's better. A little grouchy, but other than that she'll be fine."

Laquinta said goodbye to her friend, and I followed her into her apartment. As soon as we were inside, I sat on the arm of the couch and removed my tinted glasses. I reached for her hand and wasted no time in telling her what was on my mind.

"I . . . I gotta end this with you. Things been getting hectic at home, and my life has been downright miserable. You know, lately, I've been taking my frustrations out on you, and—"

"I don't even want to hear it, Isaac. I knew you were going to do this to me, and you can take all of your promises and shove them up your ass."

She snatched her hand away and folded her arms. She was trying to be tough, but her watery eyes showed hurt.

"I never made you any promises, Laquinta. I told you I'd take care of Erica, but you've never proved to me that she was mine. Every time I asked you, you said you would, but never did."

"I don't have to prove nothing to you. I told you she was yours, and so be it. As much as you've been fucking me, how could she be someone else's? Shit, my back hurt every day from laying on it so much for you."

Even though her voice rose, I remained calm. "All I'm saying is, if Erica is mine, I will support her. I will no longer support you, and I would like a blood test that confirms she's mine."

"Whatever," she said. She placed her hand on her hip. "Well, for the record, she ain't yours, sucker. Now what, huh? Now you can take your ass back to your wife and live happily ever after. You've got all that you could get out of me, and my time is up. It's been real, and it was fun while it lasted."

She went to the door and opened it.

I sat still on the couch. I couldn't believe that she ad-mitted to Erica not being my child. "So, you put a baby off on me and you knew she wasn't mine, right?"

"Duhhh, it appears to be that way, doesn't it? Now, like I said before, get the fuck out of my house."

I slowly put my shades back on and stepped up to her. Taken aback and at the same time hurt by her words, I pointed my finger in her face. "Every last dime that I've given you for Erica, I want it back. You are so damn messed up in the head, Laquinta, and to lie to me about something like that was uncalled for. Right about now I could kick your ass, but you ain't even worth it. This fuck game was fun while it lasted, but I guess all bullshit must someday come to an end." I pushed her face, and before she reached up to hit me, I grabbed her arm and twisted it behind her back.

"Stop, Isaac. You're hurting me. Let my damn—"

I let her go and shoved her toward the living room. After I made my exit, she slammed the door behind me.

"Bastard!" she yelled.

When I got to my truck, I looked up at her window. She was looking out, gaving me the middle finger. I smiled and she closed the curtains. After that, I headed for Sprint to get a new phone. I knew she, along with some other females I'd been seeing from time to time, would call. I had to make sure none of them knew how to reach me.

Before I was even two miles away from Laquinta's place, she called. What she had to say didn't even matter. She'd used me enough, just as much as I'd used her. But when all was said and done, the reality of knowing that Erica wasn't my child stung like hell. I'd done so much for her, and I felt like a major fool for even trusting Laquinta. Certainly, she must have had a bigger effect upon me than I originally thought.

Before I went to the Sprint store, I stopped in at the jewelry store for about two hours, and I bought Cydney another ring. It was two carats and had baguettes on the sides. I was so excited about giving it to her.

When I got my new phone, I called to check on her, and she was sleeping. When I asked her about the movies again, she said, "Maybe." I told her I'd be home soon, and made my way over to Miguel's place to give him my new number and tell him about my unplanned vacation from work. I planned on taking a week off from work, just so I could cater to Cydney and Cydney only.

When I got to Miguel's place, it took a moment for him to answer the door. He opened it, and his eyes looked tired.

"Were you sleeping?" I asked.

"Naw, man. Just chilling on the couch, checking out a flick."

Miguel stepped into the living area and sat on his sofa. I sat on the arm of it and looked at the television that showed a man and two ladies fucking. Miguel reached for the remote to turn down the volume.

"You a horny motherfucker," I said, joking with him. "It's three o'clock on a Sunday, and that's all you can do is sit around watching flicks?"

"And smoking herbs," he said, placing a joint in his mouth. I'd never seen him smoke marijuana before, and it caught me off guard. He inhaled and passed it to me.

"Naw, you know I don't go out like that, man."

"And why not, Isaac?" He inhaled again. "With all of the crappy shit that's been going down wit' ya, why not?"

"Drugs ain't my solution, that's why. Anyhow, I came over here to let you know I'm taking the week off. I'm trying to work on some things with my marriage, and it's gonna require some serious effort on my part."

"Oh, really?" he said. "You and Cyd finally trying to squash all of this shit and make it work, huh?"

"Yeah, something like that. I'll call the sarg in the morning, and if you need to holla at me, here's my new cell phone number." I handed the piece of paper to Miguel and he looked down at it.

"Damn, you done got a new number already? What about Laquinta? I know you ain't turning that ass loose."

"I already did. Just a little while ago. She finally admitted to Erica not being mine, and even though I knew it, I did want to believe that she was mine."

"Hell, even I knew that she wasn't yours. She looks more like me than she does you. And had I been hitting that almost two years ago, maybe there would've been a chance. Since I just started to hit it, I know Erica couldn't be mine."

I was stunned by his words. "What did you say?"

"That night she was looking all scrumptious and shit at the club, I had to see what was up with it. When you slipped out of the front door, a few days later, I slipped through the back."

"Is that right?" I said, burning up inside. Miguel's tone and inability to look at me had me concerned. "If you were fucking Laquinta, why didn't you ever say anything to me?"

"Because she asked me not to. She was afraid you'd beat that ass, but it wasn't no biggie. She only let me hit it twice, and after that, her guilt kicked in. I tried to tell her that she owed you no explanation, but just like Cydney, she wanted to remain true to her Isaac."

"Look," I said. "Leave Cydney's name out of this. If you were fucking around with Laquinta, that's your business. She's a tramp anyway, and I expected her to do some shit like that behind my back."

Miguel inhaled the joint again, nodded, and put the rest of it out in an ashtray. He swallowed and looked at me with his red eyes. "Cydney has plenty to do with this. She's a tramp just like Laquinta is. Not only did I fuck your Cyd too, but she's been creeping behind your back with a white man. Raymond is his name, and I'm sure you've met him. I hired him to take care of her for me, and her vacation in Maui for ten days turned out to be one hell of a vacation. Thing is, ol' Raymond slipped. He slipped into your wife's pussy and can't seem to keep himself out of it. So, all this making up y'all trying to do, I hope that your mind can sustain the thoughts of her having feelings for him, and me being between those legs."

I'd heard enough. I reached for Miguel's shirt and pulled him off the couch. He smiled as I stood face to face with him.

"That marijuana better be frying your brain, and you'd better be lying to me! If you've ever, ever touched my wife, I swear to God I'm gon' kill you!"

He stared eye to eye with me and smirked. "You can fuck me up all you want, but it's not going to change a thing. This is payback for how you dissed my sister. I told you to leave her alone, but you just couldn't do it. Had you left her alone, I would have left Cydney alone. And if you don't believe that I've been hitting it, all you have to do is go home and ask her."

I shoved Miguel back on the couch and quickly made my exit. I rushed to my car, and when I reached for my cell phone to call Cydney, I put it back down. If I confronted her over the phone, she'd probably hang up on me and not let me in the house.

Instead, I drove home as quickly as I could. When I got there, I went to our bedroom, where Cydney was still sleeping. I pulled the cover off her, and she slowly opened her eyes. Still dressed in her robe, she sat up in bed and pulled her hair over to the side.

"What time is it?" she asked.

"It's time for you to get up."

"I'm up, Isaac. Why are you looking at me like that?"

"Because I just got back from *fixing* our problem. I told Laquinta it was over, and after I ended it, she even told me that Erica wasn't mine. Then I got a new phone, and I wanted to take you to the movies tonight." I reached in my pocket and laid the tiny black box on the bed. "Afterwards, I was planning to drive you to St. Louis University, where we graduated, and give you this ring like I did many years ago." My hurt was starting to show, and I took a hard swallow. "But . . . but as much as I was out there trying to 'fix it,' I found out that I couldn't, Cyd. This can't be fixed if you've allowed Miguel to have you. It's bad enough trying to put this white man behind me, but Miguel? Just tell me it's not so. Tell me he lied to me, baby, please tell me."

She sat silently for a moment. "I wish that I could tell you that he lied," she said softly, "but I can't. I regret ever—"

"Got damn you, Cydney! Here I am thinking that I'm the villain in this marriage, and you out here fucking every Tom, Dick and Harry you can get your hands on!"

"It wasn't like that, Isaac."

"Then, how was it?" I yelled. I slammed my hand

against one of the four posts on our bed and it broke in half. "Tell me, how in the hell did you manage to open up your legs so my partner could fuck you?"

"He took advantage of me. He used me to get to you. I don't know why, but I—"

"Did he rape you or force you or something? How many times did you have sex with him?"

"You're angry, and I don't want to talk about this, Isaac. When you calm down—"

"I ain't fucking calming down! I'm getting my shit and I'm getting the hell out of here! You can take your butt back to Maui and screw Raymond all you want to. And since him and Miguel planned this mess, I'll let the two of them sit around and take notes on who you screwed the best!" Cydney looked shocked. "That's right, baby. The motherfucker was P-A-I-D by Miguel to seduce you. You fell for it, and I hope like hell that your fucking feelings are hurt now that you know the man who you've been giving my pussy to is an imposter."

Cydney sat silently, and as I breathed heavily and stared at her, I could have slit her throat. I cut my eyes and quickly made my way into the closet. I laid my two suitcases on the floor and gathered all of my clothes. It didn't take me long to pack, and after gathering a few more accessories around the house, I gave her one last look and left.

CYDNEY

At this point, all I could do was stand still. I'd thought about calling Miguel and cursing him out, and I'd even thought about calling Raymond to see why he did what he did. However, something inside was telling me to stand still. No doubt, I was hurt like hell. After Isaac left, my body shut down, and I couldn't even get out of bed. I felt like a major fool, and through my own mistakes, I'd hurt no one but myself.

Foolishly, I felt bad for Isaac. He surely got a dose of his own medicine, but one thing I can say, he couldn't handle my infidelities as much as I dealt with his. The look in his eyes said he could kill me, and even though I knew he would never do that, I still intended to watch my back.

For the past two days, I hadn't heard anything from Isaac. However, his mom had been calling, and so had mine. Apparently, while I was on vacation in Maui, Isaac told my mother that we'd been having some problems. She in turn called his mother and told her the same.

Bottom line, I had some explaining to do for lying to my mother, and once I admitted to our problems, I assured her, as Isaac had done, that we'd work things out. I also told my mother-in-law the same thing, and encouraged both of them to pray for us. They promised us time to work things out, and I was so glad to get things off my chest. More than anything, I was glad that all the phone calls came to a halt.

As for any of my friends, hell, what friends did I have to consult with? I'd cut off ties with most of them many, many years ago. I got tired of them calling themselves my friends, yet judging me and criticizing my relationship with Isaac. I knew I'd put up with a lot, but what I didn't need was friends who sat around talking behind my back and calling me a fool. That obviously didn't help much, and once I found out about my backstabbers, I ended those friendships. I dealt with Isaac's and my situation as best as I could, but even I should've known better than to hang on for as long as I had.

When Darrell came into my office, I had my chair turned and was gazing out of the window. A pen was in my mouth, and when he cleared his throat, I turned to him.

"What did you say?" I asked.

"I haven't said anything yet, but now that I have your attention, I wanted to let you know that it's my time to take a vacation. I'll only be gone for a week, but while I'm away, I need you to take care of a few things."

"Sure, Darrell. Anything you'd like me to do, I'll do it."

Darrell pulled up a chair and wrote down a list of things he needed me to do. The list was awfully long, and it took us almost three hours to go over it. Since he was the boss, what could I say? Afterwards, he told me if I needed anything to call him. I told him that I would, and then he left. As soon as he walked out, Carol came in. She reached out and handed me several pink Post-it notes.

"While you were meeting with Darrell, these calls came in for you."

"Thanks, Carol," I said. "On your way out, please close the door."

She nodded and closed the door behind her.

I looked through the Post-it notes, and one in particular caught my eye. All it said was *Please call Raymond.* No number was underneath the message, so I assumed he didn't leave a number. I looked up at the bare wall in front of me and laid the Post-it note on my desk. I'd asked the maintenance man to remove the picture of the Majestic and put it in one of the closets down the hall. I wanted to forget I'd ever met Raymond, but I also wanted to find out how or why he was involved in something so cruel. I still had the card he'd given me, so I reached into my purse and pulled it out of my wallet. For a while, I held the card in my hand. Moments later, I reached for the phone and dialed out.

As soon as the phone rang, I quickly hung up. Damn him, I thought. I tossed his card in the trash and reached for my purse so I could go to lunch.

"Carol, I'll be back. Would you like anything while I'm out?"

"No, thank you. I'll go to lunch whenever you get back."

I nodded and walked off to the elevators. When I reached the lobby, I couldn't decide what I wanted to eat. So, instead of eating, I drove to the Galleria to see what new fashions they had.

While strolling around the Galleria, I felt so lost. It seemed as if everywhere I walked, there was a couple holding hands, enjoying each other's company. Of course,

I couldn't help but think about Isaac and the day we got married. It was such a beautiful and unforgettable day. Who would have thought things would turn out as they had? I took a seat on a bench and pondered our past life together. I smiled at the good thoughts . . . our honeymoon in Vegas, our first anniversary, our plans to have children. I even thought about those hectic nights he'd have at work, then he'd rush home just to hold me in his arms. I truly missed those days. Those times seemed so long ago. I wasn't sure if we'd ever be able to recover from this or if, at this point, our marriage was worth repairing.

After window shopping for at least two hours, I headed back to the office so I could get back to work. What a waste of time shopping was, as I'd left the Galleria with nothing. As soon as I got to my car, I felt a sudden need to see Isaac. Instead of going back to the office, I drove to the police station to see if I could find him. I hadn't planned on going inside to ask for him, rather my intentions were to just *see* him. I saw his truck in the parking lot, but there was no sign of him. I looked around for a few more minutes, and then I got out of my car. Rushing over to his truck, I was stopped by an officer who was apparently monitoring the parking lot.

"Ma'am, can I help you?" he asked.

"Yes . . . I mean I just need to get something out of my husband's truck. His name is Isaac, Isaac Conley."

"Do you have any ID on you?"

"Sure," I said, opening my wallet and showing him my ID.

"Okay. Go ahead, Mrs. Conley."

I went to his truck and opened the door. My purpose was to see if he had anything in his car that revealed where he was staying . . . a hotel receipt or something. The inside of his truck was neat, and there was nothing out of the ordinary. When I opened his glove compartment, I moved aside some condoms that were laid on top of a folded piece of paper. I opened the paper, and it was a receipt from the Marriot. I looked it over and saw that Isaac had been there since he walked out on me. Still, I had an urge to see him, so I decided to catch up with him later.

I put the paper back into the glove compartment and made my way back to my car. Since I'd been away from work for almost three hours, I hurried back, hoping no one would notice. When I got back to the office, Carol was at her desk doing basically nothing. When I asked if anyone had called, she said no and opened up her desk to get her purse.

"I'm going to lunch," she said. "Afterwards, I need to go to the bank. Do you mind if I take an extended lunch?"

"Feel free, Carol. I didn't mean to take as long as I did, but something came up."

She smiled and headed off for a late lunch. I went back into my office and took a seat at my desk. As soon as I sat down, the phone rang. I answered, but no one said anything.

"Cydney Conley," I said again.

"Cydney, this is Raymond. Please don't hang up. We need to talk."

"Raymond, I don't think there's anything for us to discuss. You used me, and I guess I used you too."

"No, I don't see it that way. It was a big mistake on my part, getting involved with Miguel. I've known him for a long time, and since he'd done a few favors for me in the past, I felt as if I owed him."

"Yeah, well, whatever. Miguel used a lot of people, but making me fall for you was—"

"It was the best feeling ever. Can I see you, please? I'll be in St. Louis on Friday, and I really need to see you."

"Raymond, please don't expect much from me. I feel betrayed. Don't expect for me to fall into your arms as I did in the past. Now that I know what kind of man I'm dealing with, things are going to be different."

"Fine," he said. "I'll call you Friday morning."

"Sure," I said, and then hung up.

A huge part of me wanted to walk away from my situation with Raymond, but I also wanted answers. At this point, our so-called feelings for each other didn't even matter. I was more concerned about his relationship with Miguel, and I knew there was so much more to it.

Around four o'clock, Carol called and said she caught a flat tire and couldn't make it back to work. I knew it was bullshit, but I told her I'd see her tomorrow. I stayed at the office until eight o'clock, and then gathered my belongings to go.

Since I'd left the Galleria, Isaac had been on my mind, so I made my way over to the Marriott. I'd managed to muster up a bit of hope for us, and the more I thought about his smile and the way we used to laugh together, the more I couldn't wait to see him. When I arrived at the hotel, his truck was in the parking lot. I remembered his room number, so I made my way to it. I wasn't sure what I was going to walk into, but we needed to talk.

When I reached his room, before knocking on the door, I stood for a moment. With my fingers, I teased the curls in my hair and straightened the skirt to my plaid suit. I took a deep breath and lightly knocked on the door. Getting no response, I knocked again. Finally, the door cracked and Isaac looked out.

"What is it, Cydney?"

"Do you have a minute?"

"Not right now."

"Is someone in there with you?"

He didn't say anything, but continued to look through the cracked door. I could see his bare chest, and a towel was wrapped around his waist.

"Isaac, please, just answer me. If this is a bad time, I'll come back."

"It's a bad time," he spoke in a hurry.

"I don't believe you. You just don't wish to talk about our marriage right now, do you?"

"I said it's a bad time, Cyd. I'm in the middle of something, and we can talk about our marriage some other time."

I wasn't sure if Isaac was being honest with me. He'd never been open about his affairs, and for him to appear to have no shame in his game, I challenged him.

"Open the door, Isaac."

"For what?" he asked. "I told you that it's a bad time and I'm in the middle of something. What is it that you don't understand?"

I stepped forward and pushed on the door. He freely moved back so I could see who was inside.

"I told you it wasn't a good time," he confirmed as I looked at her and she looked at me. She sat up in bed with the sheets covering her naked body. She was his usual type of woman, dark-skinned, dark hair and seductive eyes. I looked at the bottles of wine on the table, at her several outfits hanging by the door, and then back at Isaac.

"So, since you left, this is how you've been spending your time, huh?"

"What concern is it of yours?" He opened the door. "Now, goodbye, Cydney. With your own eyes, you've seen what a dog I can be, so add another notch to your shit list for me."

I wasn't about to embarrass myself, but deep down, I was hurt. Just visualizing Isaac with another woman always ate at me. I couldn't show him my hurt, so I took a hard swallow and with confidence, made my exit.

Without saying one word, he shut the door behind me. I could hear her saying something to him on the inside. Just so I didn't have to listen to him fucking her, I abruptly walked away from the door.

By the time I made it to the car, I tried to hold my head up high. We'd hurt each other so much, and I guess this was how he dealt with his hurt. I wasn't a pro at handling my situations any better, so I stuck my key in the car door and tearfully headed for home.

I pulled into the driveway, and my house was pitch black. Always afraid of entering a dark house, I quickly made my way to the front door to go inside. No sooner had I got to the door, I heard some branches crack. I turned, and once he lit a cigarette, I saw his face. It was Miguel.

"Why haven't you been calling me?" he said, blowing out his match and tossing it aside. He was dressed in all black, and if it wasn't for his light skin, I wouldn't have seen him.

I fumbled for my keys to open the door. "Miguel, I don't have time for you right now. Why don't you—"

The door opened and I rushed inside. He rushed up behind me and pressed on the door as I tried to close it. My strength was no match for his, so he forced his way inside. Once he slammed the door behind him, I ran toward the phone to call the police. He caught me by the back of my hair and placed a cold blade against my throat.

"You need to cooperate with me, or else I'm gon' hurt you."

"Please don't . . . don't hurt me, Miguel." I started to cry. "Whatever you want, just tell me."

He spoke in a sinister tone. "I want you to file for a divorce tomorrow. But not before you get on your knees and satisfy me."

I was afraid to open my mouth. "I . . . I can't—"

He pulled the back of my hair tighter, and his grip caused me to squeeze my eyes shut.

"I want some head, bitch! Turn around, get on your knees and give me some head."

My body trembled from the thought. I'd never given oral sex to any man but Isaac. Miguel knew that because I'd told him. He knew that he had me in his control, and at this point, there wasn't much else that I could do but give him what he wanted. With the blade still close to my neck, and the tight grip on my hair, I carefully turned and got on my knees.

"That's a good girl," he said while loosening his hold on my hair and rubbing it. "Take care of daddy real good. By the time you get finished, I want to call you Superhead."

I reached for the top button on his pants and unbuttoned it. Taking my time, I unzipped his pants. I could feel his hardness as he anxiously awaited my mouth. When I swallowed and hesitated, he slapped the back of his hand across my face. My head jerked to the side, and his blow almost knocked me off my knees.

"Hurry it up, bitch! Unlike your husband, my dick don't stay hard all damn day!"

He grabbed the back of my hair and positioned my head. I felt his hard dick touch my face, and then he rubbed it against my mouth.

"Open up and use your hands! And if you even think about biting or punching me, I will slit your damn throat."

Of course, I'd thought about it, but I also knew that Miguel wasn't a bullshitter. He had major issues, and I had no other choice but to cooperate.

I reached up with my right hand and held his dick. I

slowly massaged it and barely opened my mouth. As soon as he felt my tongue, he jerked my head back.

"You can do a whole lot better than that. Don't play with me, Cydney. If I have to stop this one more time, I'm gon' fuck you up!"

His voice got sterner, but I had a difficult time seeing his wishes through. Quickly, I had a change of heart, and if I had to fight with him to get myself out of this situation, I would. I opened my mouth wider, and when he jabbed his dick inside, I bit down on it as hard as I could.

"Muthafucka!" He yelled and backed up. He held his dick, and I scrambled off the floor. I ran as fast as I could down the hallway and made my way to the bedroom. I looked at the phone, but one of Isaac's guns was more appropriate right about now. As soon as I lifted the mattress, Miguel ran into the bedroom and slammed his fist into my face. I fell back on the bed, and he started to rip off my clothes.

"Miguel," I cried. "Please don't do this! I'm sorry! I'm so sorry for whatever it is that I've done to you!"

He slapped me again and grabbed at my panties. Once he ripped those off, I could barely see him lying over me in the dark. He held his dick and massaged it.

"Sssssss, damn, you fucked me up! You gon' pay for this shit!"

He backhanded me, and I covered my face. His slaps hurt so badly, but all I could do was lay there and take them. I knew if I fought again, I'd lose my life. So he would stop, I pleaded with him one last time.

"Miguel, I'm not worth it. Please stop hurting me like this. I'm so . . . sorry for playing games with you. I didn't mean to hurt you, but Isaac—"

"Fuck Isaac! All of his women play to that asshole's tune, and he could give a damn about any of you!"

"I know. That's why I've already asked him for a divorce." I was saying anything to get him off me. "My lawyer is handling everything for me. Isaac will be served his papers soon."

That news got Miguel's attention. I figured his dick wasn't in working order either, so he got off me and stood at the side of the bed. I could see the shining blade pointing in my direction.

"You'd better not mention this to anyone. I'm going to deal with your husband because the stupid-ass women in his life don't know how to deal with him."

He lifted the knife and stabbed it into the mattress. Panicking, I moved away, but it cut me on the side of my leg.

"Please, Miguel." I trembled. "Just go. I promise you that I won't say anything to anyone. Just go."

He snickered and walked toward the bedroom door. When he was out of sight, I heard the door open and then close. I lay there for a moment, until I heard his car speed off. My chest heaved in and out, and all I could do was thank God for sparing my life. Afraid to be alone, I got up and lifted the mattress again. This time, I reached for another gun Isaac had left at the house for protection, and held it close to my side. After I wiped the blood from my leg and face, I left.

When I got back to the Marriott, Isaac's truck was still there. I expected it to be, and I figured by now that he and his fling were having a funky good time. If he turned me away, I'd probably shoot him. So, instead of taking the gun inside, I left it underneath the seat.

With a swollen face and torn pieces of clothing, I made my way to his room. I'd passed by several people at the hotel, and they all stared at me as if I had mess on my face. Only one person asked if I needed help, and she was a black woman who seemed deeply concerned. I declined her help and hurtfully made my way to Isaac's room. Of course, he didn't answer his door, so I knocked harder. Soon, I called his name and pleaded with him.

"Isaac, I need your help," I whispered. "Please open the door."

I heard footsteps, but the door didn't come open. "Cydney, what do you think you're doing? Didn't I tell you that I was busy?"

"I know what you said, but I need you. Please."

He swung the door open, and his angry face turned into a puzzled one. "Wha . . . what happened to you?"

"I need you," I cried. "He hurt me."

Standing naked, Isaac pulled me inside and held my trembling body. Just being in his arms made me feel secure. "Who did this to you? Calm down and tell me who hurt you like this."

I wrapped my arms tightly around his waist and laid my head against his chest. Somewhat in shock, I couldn't say a word.

"Jazell," he said, "put on your clothes, and, uh, I'll give you a call tomorrow."

"Are you asking me to leave?" she snapped.

"No, I'm telling you," he snapped back.

"Ain't this a bitch," she said. "You've been fucking me all week, and now you want me to leave?"

Isaac let go of his embrace and stepped over to her. "You didn't even have to put my business out there in front of my wife, but since you did, get your shit on and get up out of here like I told you to!"

I couldn't help but stand by the door and watch. Angry, Jazell yanked the covers back and got out of bed. She stood up to Isaac, pointing her finger in his face.

"Nobody has ever been allowed to treat me as you have. Don't you ever, and I do mean ever, call my house again!"

"Somehow, I doubt that you haven't been treated this

way before. But if you say you haven't, then hey," Isaac replied, holding his hands out as if he didn't care.

She stepped away from him and picked up her clothes from the floor. As she slid into her jeans and tank top, she looked over at me.

"You got your hands full, lady. But you know what? You can have him."

I couldn't resist a response. "Sometimes unfortunate, but I've always had him, Jazell. He's never been yours to give to me, no matter what the conditions are. Now, I'm sorry that I interrupted your days of fame, but we have to deal with something important. Please have just a little bit of empathy for the wife, okay?"

She chuckled and walked over to me. After she removed her other clothes from the hanger, I stepped to the side and she opened the door. She gave Isaac one last look and left. I looked at Isaac, as he stood by the bed.

"Come on over here and take a seat. Tell me," he said sternly. "Who did this to you? It better not had been Miguel. But then again, it doesn't even matter."

I walked over by the bed and observed the messed up sheets. The wine and scent of sex confirmed that Isaac and Jazell had themselves a good time.

"I think I'll stand," I said. "I didn't want to come back here, but Miguel is on a rampage. He's got to be stopped, and we've got to do something about him, or else he's going to make our lives miserable."

"So, Miguel did do this to you?" he said, snatching his pants from the floor. "I told that motherfucker that if he—"

"Isaac, going after him with so much anger right now will only make matters worse. We've got to be smart about this, like he did when he used Raymond to get at me."

Isaac spoke with fire in his eyes. "Cydney, I'm going to

kill him. I can't let no fool run around here hurting my wife while plotting and scheming against me. Look at you!" His voice rose. "Look at what he's done to you!" He angrily slammed his fist on the dresser. "Did he rape you?"

"I . . . I will tell you about it once you calm—"

"I'm not going to calm down! Now, did he rape you?"

I walked up to Isaac to calm him. I held his hands together with mine. "He tried to, but I got away from him."

"How did you get away from him? That doesn't—"

"Well, I did, Isaac! I ran off to our bedroom and looked for your gun."

"And?" he said, waiting for more.

"And nothing. I just got away." I released my hands from his and turned. Isaac turned me back around to face him.

"I can see it in your eyes that there's more to it."

My eyes started to water from the thoughts. "I don't want to talk about it. Please stop pressuring me to talk about it."

"Damn it, Cyd! I want to know! Can't you understand that I want to know what he did to you?"

"And can't you understand that coming here and seeing you with another woman was painful enough for me? And to go home and . . . and—" I started to sob. Isaac pulled me to him and held me in his arms again.

"I'm sorry," he whispered. "I'm so, so sorry."

ISAAC

I was mad as hell about what Miguel had done to Cydney! After getting her back to the house and tucking her in bed, I was even mad at myself for getting her involved in my mess. I knew she'd slept with him out of spite, and even though the thoughts of the two of them together still tormented me, I couldn't worry about it right now. I told her I wouldn't do anything stupid, but my leaving the house and heading to his place said otherwise. She was sound asleep, and before I left, I kissed her cheek and left to handle my business.

When I got to Miguel's place, I took the elevators upstairs and tucked my gun behind my back. I placed my ear on the door and not hearing anything, I knocked. I had everything planned out in my mind. As soon as he opened the door, I'd rush him and beat his ass as if he'd stolen something from me, I thought. But when I knocked again, and still no one answered, I turned to my side and went full force with my shoulder up against the door. After doing it twice, the door cracked. I kicked the door. It cracked around the lock and flew open.

Miguel's loft was dark. I reached for the light switch and turned on the lights. When they came on, I could tell he wasn't there because some of his furniture was gone. When I walked over by his bedroom, his closet was partially empty, and the rest of his loft showed no sign of him. Since he'd left a few items, I knew he'd be back. When, was the question, but I didn't expect it to be anytime that night, especially after what he'd done to Cydney. He for damn sure knew I was coming for him soon.

I messed up his place before I left. As soon as I got outside, two police officers were walking toward the building. After hearing all of the commotion I made in his loft, somebody must have called the police on me. One of the officers flashed a light in my face.

"Get down on the ground," he yelled.

I did as he asked and placed my hands up high so they could see them.

"I'm a cop," I said as they moved in closer.

When they did, I saw that I knew one of the officers.

"Isaac," Smitty said. I made my way off the ground. "Man, what are you doing out here at this time of night?"

"I was at Miguel's place. We got some issues that we need to deal with, and I stopped by to see him."

"Well, somebody called in and said they heard a lot of noise. They said it sounded like somebody's door had been kicked in, and they were afraid," the other officer said.

Not trying to incriminate myself, I kept quiet. I gave Smitty a serious look, and I could tell that he knew what time it was.

"Uh, Blake," Smitty said. "This is Officer Conley. He's been with the police department for a very long time."

I reached out for Blake's hand, and even though he hesitated, he still shook my hand.

"I don't care how long he's been with the department.

If he's caused any property damage, then I intend to arrest him."

I looked at Smitty and chuckled. "He must be a rookie, right?"

"Rookie or not, I have a job to do. Now, you stay put until I go upstairs and check things out."

He walked off, and in disbelief, I looked at Smitty. "Is this joker serious? Does he really expect me to stand here and wait to be arrested? Man, I'm outta here. Tell your rookie partner that next time, he should put the cuffs on me and put me in the car."

Smitty laughed and patted my back. "Isaac, hurry and get out of here. Now, you might hear me yelling after you, but pay me no attention."

"Thanks, Smitty," I said, jogging to my truck.

"Wait!" he yelled. "Stop running!"

I hopped in my truck, and as Smitty continued to yell, I took off.

Before I went home, I stopped at Wal-Mart and bought several new locks to put on the doors. Cydney seemed paranoid, and I wanted to do everything possible to make her feel safe again.

I went to our bedroom to check on her. She wasn't in the bed, and my heart started to race.

"Isaac," I heard her call from the bathroom. "Is that you?"

"Yes," I said, making my way to the bathroom. It was dark, but she had several candles lit to lighten the bathroom. She was laid back in the tub with lots of bubbles covering her.

"I'm almost afraid to ask. Where did you go?" she asked.

I sat on the tub. "I went to Miguel's place. He wasn't there, but it looks as if he's trying to check out of here. The other day, the sarg talked to me about some previous complaints against Miguel, and he suggested hooking me up with another partner. So, until all of this mess is cleared up, it's a good thing that I'll be riding alone."

"I don't understand something, Isaac. Why is Miguel trying to hurt you so much? I thought the two of you were cool, but something must have happened that I don't know about."

I really didn't want to tell Cydney the truth, but I knew she'd continue to pry if I didn't. "He's angry with me because I messed around with . . . had sex with his sister. I only had sex with her one time, though."

"One time or ten times, Isaac, it doesn't matter," she snapped. "You have really, really put yourself out there, and for what? It's not like I couldn't give you what you wanted."

"But you didn't, baby. After I made one mistake, you said you forgave me, but you didn't. You made me pay for my mistake by not giving yourself to me, by not giving me any children, and by not showing me any love."

"I always loved you, but I just didn't trust you. You didn't give me time to heal, and less than a month later, you were already back in the sack with someone else. I figured you'd never change, so my partially forgiving you was a big mistake. I will put any amount of money on it that if I'd truly forgiven you, you still would've continued on with your affairs, wouldn't you?"

"I . . . I don't know. All I know is that I felt empty being here with you. I tried to make things work, but I just couldn't do it under the circumstances."

"Tried? I wouldn't exactly say that you tried, Isaac."

"Well, I beg to differ. You see it your way and I see it mine."

"You're right. But the only reason I put myself out there like I did was because I wanted to hurt you. I never—"

I wasn't up to discussing this anymore with Cydney, so

I reached out and touched the bruise underneath her eye. "I'm going to change all of the locks on the doors. I'll sleep downstairs tonight. I'm not leaving you in this house alone, so you can forget about asking me to leave. If you need me, I'll be downstairs."

I headed for the door.

"Isaac," she said.

"Yes."

"How well do you know Jazell? Has your relationship with her been an ongoing thing too?"

I didn't even bother to turn around. "Jazell is one of the many women who fill my voids. She's nothing. Nobody compares to what you mean to me."

"Then why did you make me leave the hotel? You knew how much that hurt me, didn't you?"

"Because I wanted you to feel the hurt I felt. I thought I could handle you being with other men, but I lied to myself. When reality kicked in, something just came over me."

"Well, no matter what happens between us, we've got to stop hurting each other, wouldn't you agree?"

"Most definitely."

It took me about an hour to change all of the locks, and I checked to make sure the keys worked. Once I finished, I took a quick shower in the basement and pulled out the sofa bed so I could get some rest. Lying naked, I put my hand behind my head and reached for my gum. I put a piece in my mouth and stared at the ceiling. I wanted to kill Miguel for what he'd done. I stayed up for another hour, trying to come up with a plan to do away with him. As I was in deep thought, I heard footsteps. I saw Cydney in her turquoise silk gown.

"Do you mind if I lay down here with you?" she asked.

"Not at all," I said, opening my arms to her. She lay close to me and crossed her leg over mine. Getting more comfortable, she hugged my chest and placed her head on it.

"Are you comfortable?" I asked.

She nodded.

I wanted to ask her if I could make love to her, but after our encounter earlier today, I was sure she'd tell me no. I wasn't up for rejection, so I accepted her just being in my arms, and rubbed her back until she fell asleep. Once she did, I did.

I slept well, but when I woke up, Cydney was gone. I went upstairs, and she was in our bedroom getting ready for work. She was dressed in a dark gray suit with a pink blouse and pink accessories. Her hair was full of loose, wavy curls that were combed back and hung on her shoulders. I was surprised that she allowed so much of her bruised face to show, but more surprised that she was getting ready for work.

"Why don't you take the day off with me?" I asked.

"Because Darrell is on vacation and I promised him that I would handle things while he's away."

"Aren't you worried about people questioning you about your face?"

"Not really. The only person who will probably question me is Carol. I'll make up something and keep my door shut."

"What about lunch? Would you like me to bring you some lunch today?"

"Yeah, that would be nice."

"What would you like to eat?"

"Surprise me," she said, grabbing her purse. She walked toward the door, and I pecked her cheek. She smiled. "Be good, Isaac. I'll see you later. Don't get yourself into any trouble."

"If I didn't know any better, I'd say you were concerned about me."

"Very concerned. Just be careful."

I nodded, and Cydney left. I guess she could tell that I was on a hunt for Miguel again, and she knew damn well that I wasn't about to let what had happened go.

As soon as Cydney left, I got dressed so I could go back to Miguel's place to see if he'd made it home. When I got there, his car wasn't outside, but I went upstairs to check things out. Still, there was no sign of him. His loft had been messed up even more, so I figured some of the other tenants must have gotten a hold of his belongings. I was glad about that, so I left and headed for the station to see if anybody had seen him around or heard from him.

No sooner than I walked through the door, Sarg yelled my name out loudly. I went into his office, and he told me to close the door. After I closed it, he tore into me.

"Tell me, how am I supposed to keep Internal Affairs out of here if I continue to get reports like this?" He dropped several folders in front of me.

"I don't know what those files contain, but if Internal Affairs have a job to do, then go ahead and let them do it. Besides, I told you before that Miguel and I aren't very well liked on the streets."

"Well, Miguel was in here earlier today. After I showed him those files, the coward turned in his badge and gun and told me to fuck off. That proved to me that some of these complaints must be true. And if they are, you'd better hand your badge over too."

I looked down at the folders and opened up the first one. There was a complaint from a woman who claimed she'd been strip searched by Miguel and me. I remembered the incident, as Miguel went overboard and I had to stop him. The second and third folders were instances where we were accused of using excessive force. In those cases, we did, and it was required because the fools resisted arrest, spit on me, and provoked me for an ass kicking. Four of the folders were simply about money that was taken from houses and vehicles. I was just as guilty as Miguel, and even though he was the one who took the money, he always gave me a healthy share. The last two folders were complaints about us planting drugs on people in order to make an arrest. Again, Miguel was the culprit, but I went right along with it.

Knowing my guilt, I closed the folders and scooted them close to the sarg. I stood up and reached in my pocket for my badge.

"You wouldn't believe me if I told you the truth. Besides, I'm sure you're not telling me everything Miguel told you. In the meantime, you have a job to do, and since I'm prepared to make it easier for you, you'll have my resignation letter by morning." I tossed my badge on his desk and walked toward the door.

"I really wanted this to work out, Isaac. I just can't allow—"

"Sure you did, Sarg. Like I said, you have a job to do, and consider it done."

I left, and my stomach turned in knots. I enjoyed my job, but I wasn't no fool either. I knew that I'd someday have to suffer the consequences for what I'd done, or I'd have to eventually walk away as I just did. For now, walking away just seemed like the right thing to do.

Finding Miguel was starting to become a difficult task. I searched for him all morning, and when I checked my watch, it was almost time for lunch. I knew Chinese was Cydney's favorite, so I stopped by China Wok to get her something to eat. To make her feel even better, I stopped at a flower shop and bought her two long stemmed red roses.

When I got to her office, Carol wasn't at her desk. Cydney's door was closed, so I knocked.

"Come in," she said.

I opened the door and stuck my head inside. "Are you busy? I bought lunch for us."

"No, I'm not busy. Come in, but close the door."

I closed the door and walked over to the sofa to take a seat. Cydney got up and came over to sit with me. Before getting to our food, I pulled the roses from the bag and gave them to her.

"I know how much you hate these, but I couldn't resist."

She grinned and took them from my hands. "Thanks," she said. "But you really didn't have to." She went over to her credenza and pulled out a crystal vase, placing the roses inside.

"They need water. Do you mind going down the hall to the kitchen and putting some water in the vase? If you look in the cabinets, you'll find some paper plates and forks for our food too."

I stood up and took the vase from her. "There should already be forks inside of the bag." I looked, but there were none. "Okay, so we need forks too."

Cydney smiled, and I left to go to the kitchen. When I came back, she was sitting on the couch waiting for me. Just as she did this morning, she looked so beautiful. Face bruised or not, my wife seriously had it going on. I couldn't help but stare at her as I wondered what in the hell I'd been thinking during all those years of cheating. Certainly, everything I needed and wanted was right there in front of me.

I placed the plates and forks on the table in front of the

couch and put the vase on her desk. Afterwards, I opened the boxes of shrimp fried rice and egg foo young.

"That smells delicious," she said. "Did you go to my favorite place?"

"You know I did. Don't you recognize the aroma?"

"I guess," she said, standing up. "Take a seat. I can handle this."

"If you say so," I said, allowing her to serve out our plates.

Cydney bent over, fixed my plate first, and then hers. I looked at her thick ass, and couldn't help but touch it. She grabbed my hand.

"Isaac, don't do that, please."

"And why not? It looked too good to resist."

"Well, contain yourself, all right? Now isn't the time."

"Then when is my time coming? Do you ever plan on making love to me again?"

She sat down and handed my plate to me. "We have other things to deal with right now. Sex isn't going to solve anything, and for you to think it is, I don't quite understand."

"Well, it's a start. I'm not saying that it's going to solve everything, but don't you think that it might help us work on our marriage?"

"Honestly, no, I really don't. And who mentioned anything about salvaging our marriage? At this point, I really don't know what I want to do, Isaac."

With that being said, I started to eat my food. Cydney noticed my demeanor and pulled my plate away from me. She placed it on the table.

"I didn't mean to rain on your parade, but the truth of the matter is, just yesterday, you were in bed with another woman. According to her, you'd been with her for several days. I don't feel as if I should have to put that behind me right now and move on. It's so very hard to swallow, as all of this has been for quite some time."

"Cydney, how do you think I feel? You act as if your infidelities don't even matter."

"But they were nothing compared to yours."

"Cheating is cheating. It doesn't matter how many times it happened. I wish like hell that you'd stop blaming me for everything and start taking responsibility for some of this mess that has happened."

"I do, Isaac. But I also know that it wouldn't have happened if you'd done what you were supposed to do in this marriage."

I was really tired of hearing it. Instead of finishing our lunch, I stood up and placed my hands in my pockets.

"I gotta go make some runs. I'll see you when you get home," I said.

"You're not going to finish your lunch?"

"I'm not hungry right now. I'll see you later."

I turned, opened the door and closed it behind me.

For the rest of the week, things between me and Cydney were quiet, but cool. We didn't disagree too often, but she couldn't help but question me about my daily runs. I hadn't told her about my job situation, but she thought I was on vacation. When I told her I stopped looking for Miguel, she didn't believe me. Actually, I'd been on a mission all week long. He must have skipped town because the brotha had seemed to have disappeared.

On Friday, Cydney seemed a bit strange. Without saying goodbye, she rushed out of the house, and I saw her dialing her cell phone as she pulled out of the driveway. When I called her, she didn't answer. I even offered to bring her lunch again, but she said no. I wasn't sure what was up, but something surely wasn't right. During my mid-day phone call to her, I could tell my suspicions were correct.

"Well, what time do you think you'll be home?" I asked.

"I'm not sure, Isaac. I told Darrell I'd keep things in order, and he'll be back on Monday. I want to make sure everything is taken care of, so I'm working rather late."

"Late as in seven o'clock late, or ten o'clock late?"

"Isaac, I don't know, but I will get there as soon as I can, okay?"

"That's cool, Cyd, I'll see you later."

She hung up, and I got dressed to go see what was up. Since Cydney still had a few hours before she got off work, I stopped at Miguel's sister's house. Since they were so close, maybe Trinity knew what he'd been up to and would be willing to shed some light on this situation.

The two-family flat that she lived in was located on the south side of St. Louis in a quiet neighborhood. Trinity was a beautician and did her customers' hair from home. She always talked about getting her ex-husband to buy her a beauty shop, but I wasn't sure if that had happened yet. Either way, my visit was worth a try.

After several knocks, she came to the door and looked out. When she saw me, she opened the door.

"What's up, Isaac?" she said with a comb in her hand and attitude in her voice. "I thought I'd never see you around here again."

She didn't offer to let me in, so I stood outside. "Have you seen your brother?"

"No, I haven't," she answered quickly. I could tell she was lying.

"When is the last time you've seen him?"

"Why?"

"Because I'm looking for him, that's why."

She walked away from the door, leaving it open. I followed her up the steps, and couldn't help but look up her short red skirt that hugged her hips and ass. Her smooth caramel skin always glowed, and her model-shaped legs were thin and pretty. No doubt, she was my type of woman, but her ass is what drew me to her.

Knowing that she had my attention, she switched from side to side and had the nerve to bend over when she reached the top step. I got a glimpse of her baby blue thong.

"Ooops, I must have dropped this on my way downstairs," she said, picking up a folded dollar on the floor. She put it inside her bra and gave me a wink. I followed Trinity into the kitchen, where she was giving a lady a perm. Another lady sat at the kitchen table, flipping through a magazine.

"Y'all, this is Isaac," Trinity said, scratching her flipped, honey blonde weave that went well with her hazel eyes.

"Nice to meet you, Isaac," said the lady with the relaxer in her hair. "We've heard a lot about you."

The other lady looked me up and down and tooted her lips.

"Trinity, you were about to tell me where I could find Miguel," I said.

"I wasn't about to tell you nothing. I invited you in because that was the appropriate thing to do. Also, I wanted to know where you've been hiding. Evidently, you must have worked things out with your wife."

"Yes . . . something like that."

"Yeah, right. I saw you running around with other women, so you and your wife didn't work out nothing."

"Okay, so maybe we didn't. But if you want the truth, the truth is I got bored with you."

"Bored? You didn't appear to be bored during—"

"Look, Trinity. For whatever reason, things didn't work out. Now, I know you don't want to sit here and tell all of your business in front of your customers, do you? All I came here to find out is if you've seen Miguel. Nothing more and nothing less."

"He's out of town, Isaac. I don't know where, and I don't know when he's coming back. If I talk to him, I'll be sure to let him know you're looking for him."

I walked toward the steps. I jogged down them and waited at the bottom for Trinity to unlock the door with her key. She came down the steps and turned to me when she reached the bottom.

"I thought you came over here to apologize for hurting me like you did. I can't believe that you have no sympathy for how you treated me. You knew how much I cared for you, Isaac."

"Okay, Trinity. I apologize for whatever hurt I caused you. But you knew I was married. I told you that I had no intentions of leaving my wife."

She leaned in to me. "That's what your mouth said. Your actions showed something different." She reached for my hand and placed it underneath her skirt. She guided my hand to her ass so I could feel the smoothness. "Nice, isn't it?"

"Very nice," I said.

"Then come back later and touch all of me. I promise not to bore you, and I doubt that I ever have."

She let go of my hand, and it remained on her ass. Actually, I reached my other hand up her skirt as well. I massaged her butt cheeks, and being nearly the same height as me, she leaned in for a kiss. I accepted it.

"I love your thick lips," she said. "I just prefer them to be somewhere else. Can you make that happen?"

"I always do, don't I?" I said, removing my hands.

She unlocked the door and opened it. "What time shall I expect you?"

"I got a few errands to run. I'll call you."

She nodded, and I left out the door. Trinity watched me until I got in my truck and drove off.

On my way to Cydney's office, I thought about Trinity being my only connection to Miguel. She was so vulnerable when it came to me, and maybe if I fucked her, she'd tell me what I wanted to know. I wasn't sure if I'd go back there, but if he knew I was still involved with her, maybe it would give Miguel some incentive to show up.

For a few hours, I waited in the parking garage and listened to some music. At 5:45 P.M., Cydney finally left the building. I followed, and when she got on Highway 40 going west, I knew she wasn't headed for home. She drove to Mariono's in Chesterfield and got out of her car. As she went inside, I parked my truck so I could see what was up.

As I walked past the door, I glanced inside and saw her waiting by the front door to be seated. Soon, the waiter escorted her to a table, but she sat alone. Knowing that her companion would arrive soon, I went back to my truck and waited. Nearly ten minutes later, he showed. He drove a black Mercedes, and as soon as he parked his car, I got out of my truck. I watched Raymond walk to the door, and when he got inside, I saw the waiter direct him to Cydney's table. She stood up and hesitantly embraced him.

No doubt, my insides burned. I knew something was up, and for her to continue to see him after all we'd been through was a stab in my back. I swallowed and headed back to my truck. If that's who she wanted, then there was nothing I could say or do about it.

Instead of going home, I stopped and picked up a gift for Erica. Yesterday was her birthday, and I wanted to let her know that I hadn't forgotten about her. I asked the clerk at the store to wrap the books, dolls, and learning tapes into one box for me. She did, and placed a huge pink bow on the top. Afterwards, I drove to Laquinta's place, and even though I had no business there, I went to the door. I knocked, and Laquinta opened it up.

"I wanted to give this to Erica for her birthday," I said, leaning against the doorway and handing the box to Laquinta.

She reached for it. "She's not here. Yesterday, we had a party for her over at her grandmother's house, and she stayed over there. Erica's been asking for you, and I'm sorry that she missed you. You can always go to my mother's house and take the gift to her."

"Naw, that's all right. You know how your mother feels about me. Just make sure Erica gets her gift."

I stepped away from the door, and Laquinta grabbed my arm. "You . . . you can come in, you know."

"Come in to listen to you gripe? No thanks."

"I promise you that I won't gripe. Just come in for a while."

I knew what going inside would lead to, but I just couldn't walk away. I also knew I was there because of the hurt I felt inside from seeing Cydney with Raymond. For now, I knew Laquinta was capable of making me forget about my frustrations with Cydney. And as much as I hated to travel down this road again, a part of me felt as if I had no choice.

I followed Laquinta inside, and she put the box on the floor beside the door. She took my hand and led me over to the couch.

"So, what have you been up to?" she said, sitting yoga style.

"Nothing much. I've been on vacation all week, and I don't go back to work until Monday."

"What did you do for your vacation?"

"Just . . . just chilled. Listen," I said, looking at her hard nipples poking through a lavender silk button-down nightie. "Can we cut the small talk? You know why I'm here."

"I do, but I just wanted to be sure."

Laquinta stretched her legs, placing one on my lap and the other around my back. She opened her legs, and I caught a clear glimpse of her good stuff. I pulled my shirt over my head, laid it on the floor, and moved my body between her legs. She wrapped them around me and rubbed her hands down the sides of my face.

"I thought you'd forgotten about me." Her eyes watered. "I've been so, so miserable without you, and no matter how hard I tried, I couldn't stop thinking about you. I called you . . . "

"Shhh," I said. "I'm here now, so that's all that matters."

I lowered my head and pulled Laquinta's silk gown away from her left breast. It popped out, and I placed my tongue on her chocolate nipple. I teased it and then sucked the entire breast into my mouth. Once I wet up the left one, I pulled the other side of her nightie back and worked on her right one.

She squirmed around and seemed so anxious to feel me. She removed her nightie and reached for my jeans to remove them. She pulled them down, and once they hung underneath my butt, I reached for my dick, put on a condom and put my goods inside of her moist and juicy pussy. The feel of it made me crazy.

"Damn, Laquinta. Why'd you give Miguel my stuff?" I pumped. "Why?"

"I didn't give Miguel anything. He came here and forced himself on me." She breathed heavily, and as I continued to work her insides, her pretty breasts jiggled up and down.

"He told me something different. After all I give to you, I would hope you didn't need sex from him."

"Never," she said, rubbing her clit. "I've never needed anything from any man but you."

My dick was finally getting the relief it needed. I fucked Laquinta well, and when I let loose inside of the condom, I sat up and she got on her knees. She removed the condom and held my dick like it was precious to her. She worked it with her lips, tongue and mouth. She knew that tightening up on my head would make me come again, so I stopped her.

"I want you from the back," I moaned in a whisper. "Let me feel my pussy from the back."

Laquinta got on the couch and got on her hands and knees. She bent down and hiked her smooth ass in the air. First, I used my fingers to tease her. I put on another condom and eased myself inside. Always, her insides were a wet mess that kept me on the verge of coming.

I tried to keep my mind on what was going on, but my mind went straight to Cydney. I visualized Raymond fucking her, and I dug deeply into Laquinta's hips.

"Damn, baby," she said, turning her head to the side. "Loosen up your grip a bit. That hurts."

"I thought you liked pain."

"I do, but you're giving it to me in the wrong place."

Knowing exactly what she wanted, I backed up a bit and scooped myself back inside of her. I continued my rhythm, and dug deeply into her to release my pain. My upper thighs slammed against her ass and caused her body to shift forward.

"Isaac, I . . . I'm about to give you something that I've never given you before," she moaned. "You are about to feel a major explosion, baby. Damn!"

"Give it to me, Quinta. Baby, give it to me good. Make me pay for walking out on you. Make me regret my decision."

She straddled even wider by dropping her right knee to

the floor. I hit her insides from every angle that I could, and we both neared our climax.

"Do . . . do you regret your decision?" She strained her words.

"Yes . . . baby, yes."

"Then beat this pussy. Tell me you'll never leave me again and beat it real good, Isaac."

I beat Laquinta's insides even more, and it was an unforgettable moment as we came together. We dropped to the floor and lay there taking deep, long breaths. Once we regrouped, Laquinta laid on top of me and gave me a kiss.

"That was . . . was worth the wait," she said.

I rubbed her sweaty backside, "You know I missed you, but I couldn't come back after you told me Erica wasn't mine. I knew she'd be asking about me, but you need to tell her the truth, Laquinta."

"Isaac, I really don't know the truth. You're the only daddy that she's known, but in the beginning of our relationship, I was seeing someone else. Erica does look more like him, but he hasn't been around for a long time."

"Is he the one I saw you in bed with?"

She nodded. "After you kicked him out, he hasn't been back since. You're the only father Erica knows, and I didn't want her having a drug dealer as a father."

"Well, you should have never slept with him then. In the long run, Erica is going to be the one hurt. You should have been honest from the beginning."

"I know," she said softly.

We got off the floor, and I lay back on the couch. Laquinta rested between my legs again.

"So, what went on between you and Miguel? He told me—"

"Whatever he told you, he lied. Miguel came over here,

tried to seduce me, and when I didn't give in, he forced himself on me. I didn't tell you because I knew you'd get mad—probably at me for letting him in here."

"You keep saying he forced himself. Do you mean he raped you?"

"Well, he didn't actually go inside of me, but he touched my private parts. When my girlfriend Lacey came by, she knocked on the door and he stopped. He left and said he'd hurt me if I told anybody about what happened. I wanted to tell you, but I was afraid to."

"Laquinta, I don't know what to believe. Miguel's been doing some messed up shit behind my back, and I've been looking for his ass. If there's something you're not telling me, I need to know."

She tightened my arms around her waist. "Baby, if I knew something else, I would tell you. I'm just glad that you're here, and I hope like hell that you aren't leaving anytime soon." She lifted her head and looked up at me. "Can you stay for a while? We have so much lost time to make up for."

"We'll see, Laquinta. I won't make you any promises, but I'm glad to be here too."

CYDNEY

When Raymond came into the door at Mariono's, I hesitated to greet him. I was so furious with him, but I craved answers. I couldn't think of anyplace else to meet him, other than in a restaurant. It was rather quiet, and besides, meeting him at a hotel, like he wanted, was out of the question. I intended to find out what I could about his and Miguel's connection, pass the information on to Isaac, and be done with it.

As for Isaac, since my incident with Miguel, he'd been nothing but wonderful to me. He was starting to show some of the ways he had in the beginning, when our marriage meant so much to me. I couldn't help but feel more love for him, but I hated to lie to him about meeting with Raymond. Isaac wouldn't have agreed with it, and I would never get the closure I needed.

Raymond took a seat across from me, barely able to look me in the eyes. He was casually dressed in blue jeans and a button-down dark blue oxford. His hair was sleek, and as gorgeous as his eyes were, they showed much shame.

"Hello, Cydney," he said, resting his hands together on the table.

"Hi, Raymond. How are you?"

"Lately, not so good. I knew that Miguel would eventually tell you about me, but I didn't think he'd do it so soon."

"So, he busted you out sooner than you thought? I'm sorry to hear that you got caught before you got another chance to seduce me."

"It wasn't like that, Cydney."

"Then, how was it, Raymond?"

"Okay, it started out like that, but I really, really started to like you. I'm not claiming to have fallen in love with you, but you're a beautiful person, Cydney. Miguel's plan backfired because I couldn't control my feelings. I had to see you again."

"Exactly what was the plan, Raymond? You seduce me, then what?"

"Then I was supposed to persuade you to come back to Maui, shower you with gifts, and eventually, hope that you'd leave Isaac."

"Please. I liked you too, Raymond, but leaving my husband, I . . . it wasn't on my agenda."

"But you told me it was. In Maui, you seemed distraught, and I thought that was the end of Isaac. And even though I've made it clear to Miguel that I don't want anything to do with his scam, I don't understand how you can still be married to such a jerk."

"Who or what I'm married to is nobody's business but my own. Why is it so important to anyone what I intend to do about my marriage? This is between Isaac and me, nobody else."

"I know, Cydney, but I was hoping that we could still be friends. "

"I don't think so, Raymond. After the lies you've told

me, I could never trust you. Besides, how did you get involved with somebody like Miguel anyway?"

"I guess I could ask you the same question. But we both know that Miguel can be quite persuasive. I've known him practically all of my life, and he and my father are business partners. I can't go into details about it, but this so-called business got me falsely imprisoned for several years. Miguel supported me the entire time I was there, and when he asked me to assist him with something that seemed rather simple to do, I figured I owed him. I never intended to hurt you, Cydney. You have to believe me."

The waiter came over to the table with my previously ordered Cobb salad and placed it in front of me. She asked Raymond if he wanted to order anything.

"No," he said. "A bottle of Chardonnay would be perfect, though."

"I'll go get that for you, sir," she said. "Will there be anything else?"

He shook his head, and so did I. She walked away.

"Once I finish my salad, Raymond, I'll be leaving. Before I go, would you mind sharing with me where I might find Miguel? I'm sure that you know where he is."

"Yes, I do, but I'm not going to tell you where he is. Miguel is dangerous, Cydney, and I don't want you to get hurt."

"Miguel has already hurt me enough. If you have my best interests at heart, then you would tell me where—"

"I do have your best interests at heart. That's why I can't tell you."

"Yeah, that's what I thought. I figured meeting you here would be a waste of time, but I also wanted you to know that it was tough being betrayed by you. I should've known that my little trip to Maui was quite the fairytale. And please do not ever contact me again."

"Regardless of whatever you think, I felt something with you that I haven't felt since my wife divorced me. There was emptiness in my life, and being with you for only a short time was a lot of fun. Will you . . . won't you at least allow our friendship to continue? I promise you that I will never lie to you again, and I will be there—"

"Raymond, let's not confuse friendship with sex. All you want is sex, and I can no longer give myself to you in such a way. I'm done making bad choices by giving myself to men who don't give two cents about me. Being with Miguel taught me a valuable lesson, and I'm not about to make the same mistake again."

Raymond stared at me with saddened eyes, and I looked down at my salad. I used my fork and played around with it. When the waiter came back with the bottle of Chardonnay, she placed it in the middle of the table.

"Thank you," Raymond said, reaching for the bottle. He filled his glass and filled a glass for me.

"Here you go, Cydney," he said, handing the glass to me. I wanted to toss the wine in his face. Raymond was so full of it, and now, I could see right through him. He held up his glass, and just because I knew I'd never see him again, I held mine up too.

"Let's drink to wishing you well, and knowing that if you ever need me, I'll be there for you," he said.

"No, let's drink to . . . it was fun while it lasted, but now our time is up."

Refusing to drink to my request, Raymond placed his glass on the table, and I gulped down my wine. I put the glass on the table and stood up.

"Well, I'd better get going. I have a million and one things to do. Thanks for taking the time out of your *busy* schedule to meet with me."

I moved forward, and Raymond grabbed my hand.

"I'm really, really sorry, Cydney. I wish that we'd met

under better conditions. Maybe things would've turned out differently."

I shrugged. "Maybe so, Raymond. Who knows?"

I eased my hand away from his and left. I thought about stopping at the cashier to pay the check, but him paying the check after the bullshit he put me through wasn't going to hurt him.

By the time I got outside, the rain was coming down. I didn't have an umbrella, so I rushed to my car and got inside. I knew Isaac was probably worried about me, so I hurried home. When I got there, his truck wasn't in the driveway, so I knew he wasn't there. I didn't have his new cell phone number to contact him, so I went inside and waited for him to return.

As it neared ten o'clock, I started to worry. In my nightgown, I paced the floor. All kinds of thoughts were roaming in my head. What if he found Miguel and they got into it? What if Isaac got hurt and couldn't contact me? As angry as Miguel and Isaac both were, what if somebody got killed? I panicked and changed into my gray jogging suit. I stepped into my white tennis shoes and grabbed my keys. It was still raining outside, so I took my time and drove around to see if I could find Isaac.

My first stop was the police station. Maybe he met up with some of his buddies and didn't tell me. After I searched the streets around the station, I drove by his parents' house to see if he'd stopped there. There was no sign of his truck, so I drove around for the next hour or so, checking out his frequent hangouts. I even drove by his brother's house to see if he'd stopped by there. I had no luck, so I pulled my car over to the side of the road and called home. The phone rang four times, and then the answering machine picked up. I closed my phone and went in deep thought. Laquinta's place was on my mind, but after making some progress with Isaac, I didn't think he'd go to her place. For what? Especially when he told me everything about her this week. She'd lied to him about Erica, and he was so adamant that he never wanted to see her again.

I pulled my car away from the curb and headed for home. He'd eventually show up tonight, and I was tired of driving around. Not only that, but the gas prices were killing me. I stopped at the gas station to fill my tank, then, instead of heading home, I turned my car around and headed for Laquinta's place.

No sooner than I pulled into the parking lot at her apartment complex, I spotted Isaac's truck. Immediately, my heart dropped into my stomach and I placed my hand on my forehead. I took a hard and deep swallow, as my throat ached so badly. What kind of hold did this . . . this ghettofied whore have on my husband? I couldn't quite understand it, but whatever it was, I couldn't continue on with this bullshit. I kept telling myself that maybe he stopped by to get something that he left, but I sat for a couple of hours and watched the lights in her apartment. When they all went out, I started my car and left.

By morning, I was in a different world. I hadn't gotten any sleep, and thank God that I didn't have to get up and go to work. If I had to, I never would have made it. I took a deep breath and opened the drawer next to me. Today, it was simply time to get ugly. I reached for the large white envelope that contained my divorce papers. I'd had them drawn up a little more than a month ago, but I could never find the appropriate time to give them to Isaac. Now was the perfect time. I kissed the envelope and laid it on my bed. After that, I got dressed and reached for my keys. When I stepped outside, the sun was shining and the rain had cleared. I checked the trunk to make sure my bat was still there. I got in the car and headed back to Laquinta's place.

Sure enough, when I pulled up, Isaac's truck was still there. He must have had himself a good time and couldn't pull himself away. Before climbing the steps to her apartment, I opened my trunk and removed the bat. I dragged it on the ground with my right hand, and tucked my divorce papers underneath my arm. Taking my time, I strolled by Isaac's truck and used my key to scratch along the side of it. The metal made a screeching sound that surely put just a tiny smile on my face. I made my way up the steps and lightly knocked on the door. I didn't know what to expect, but without asking who I was, Laquinta opened the door.

"Is Isaac here?" I asked.

She looked into my eyes, and then down at the bat. She gathered her robe in front of her and shook her head from side to side.

"No, he's not," she lied.

"I know it's the norm for the other woman to lie in an effort to protect her lover, but I really need to see him this morning." I pulled the envelope from underneath my arm. "Besides, I have our divorce papers right here. I'm sure that my giving them to him will brighten your day."

Not saying another word, she stood behind the door and pulled it open. I stepped inside and couldn't see much because I was in a hallway. I could, however, smell bacon. I figured she was cooking breakfast for the two of them, and when I looked over to the right, the busy kitchen confirmed it.

She pointed down the hall and spoke softly. It was obvious that she didn't want this bat to go upside her head. "He's in there on the couch."

I walked down the short hallway, and once I saw my

husband sleeping peacefully on Laquinta's plaid sofa, I could've thrown up. The back of his arm was resting on his forehead, one leg was on the floor, and only a sheet covered him. I knew he was naked, and it wasn't quite the room for Isaac if the smell of sex wasn't in the air.

I walked over to him and stood over him. Just to check on Laquinta, I turned. She stood quietly in the kitchen's doorway and watched with her arms folded. I rolled my eyes at her and turned back to Isaac. Slowly, I lifted the bat and placed it on his chest. Lightly scraping the bottom of the bat across his chest, I soon added pressure to wake him. He turned his head to the side and slowly opened his eyes. Once he saw who I was, his eyes widened and he abruptly sat up.

"Cyd?" he said, shocked.

"Yes, honey. You're not dreaming, so wake up."

"Wha . . . what's going on?"

I lowered the bat to my side, still holding it in my hand. I put the envelope against his chest, and he looked down at it, appearing to still be in shock.

"What's this?"

"Something I should've given to you a long, long time ago. Your divorce papers, Isaac. Now you can stop feeding me your bullshit, and we both can get on with our lives."

He looked at me angrily and snatched the envelope off his chest. He jumped up and tore the envelope in half. "How dare you come over here with this bullshit? If you think I'm gon' let you go be with another motherfucker, then you are sadly mistaken! It ain't going down like that, Cydney!"

"Oh, you'd better believe it is! And to hell with Raymond! Raymond doesn't have a damn thing to do with you over here constantly fucking this bitch!"

"The only reason I'm here is because you were with

that motherfucker yesterday! You lied to me, Cydney! When I asked you—"

"You are so fucking full of lies. Yesterday, I met with Raymond to find out his connection with Miguel! Basically, I put closure to the bullshit, but you damn sure didn't put closure to yours, nor did you ever intend to! You ran to this bitch, like you've always done in the past, and I hope you're satisfied with the end result. You can tear up those papers all you want, but there's more where those came from."

I turned to walk away, and Isaac came up behind me. Feeling my frustrations, when he grabbed for my arm, I powerfully swung the bat around and hit him in the leg.

"Damn," he yelled and squeezed his eyes together. He lowered his hand to hold his leg. I looked up, and Laquinta made a move toward me.

I held up the bat. "Come on, bitch! Make my day. I'd love to break your fucking neck for interfering with my marriage."

She saw the look in my eyes and backed up. I hurried toward the door and made my way down the steps. Isaac came limping after me with the sheet wrapped around him.

"Damn it, Cydney! Would you stop running and listen to me for a minute?"

I continued down the steps, and injured leg or not, Isaac was on my tail. By the time I reached the bottom step, he was close to me. I stopped and turned around. I held the bat up high, in a swinging position.

"Back off, Isaac. Just let me leave in peace and stay the hell away from me."

He wasn't foolish enough to step forward. "Listen, calm down and let's go home and talk about this. You're the one who lied to me about Raymond, so I was left to assume that something was going on between y'all when I saw you at the restaurant."

I chuckled. "You're such a fool. You didn't give me a chance to explain, but you couldn't wait to come over here and jump in the bed with Laquinta. When are you going to face it, Isaac? She has something that I simply can't give you. Hell, every woman does, don't they?"

"No, no, she . . . they don't. I was hurt and I—"

He stepped forward, and still not in my right mind, I swung the bat again and gave him a blow to his muscular arm. He frowned, and raging anger covered his face. I knew I had to stop him from getting at me, but when I went up with the bat again, he blocked it with his lower arm. The bat broke in half, and that was my cue to jet. Of course, I could never run faster than Isaac. As soon as I got to the parking lot, he caught up with me. He tripped me to the ground, and I fell hard. I turned over on my back and took deep breaths as he bent down and looked over me. His left arm had blood dripping from it, and he held it with his right hand.

"You see, I could hurt you, Cyd, but I'm not going to. I don't know what kind of devil took over you, but I've never seen you act so ridiculously childish. You'd better rethink some shit and do it fast. As for the divorce you want," he reached for the torn envelope and tore it into tiny pieces. They trickled down on top of me. "I'll never agree to it, and I'll fight you to the end. You know why," he said, kneeling down next to me. "Because I love no other woman but you. My hurt is what brought me here, and I didn't know how to handle seeing you with Raymond. I'm sorry, but it was my only solution. You were right. We've got to stop hurting each other, and when matters have resulted in this, somebody is liable to get physically hurt. Now, I'm going back inside to get my clothes, and then I'm leaving. If you wouldn't mind waiting just a few minutes for me, we can leave together. I'd appreciate it."

He stood up and made his way to the stairs. As he neared Laquinta's door, I sped away, listening to him yell my name.

ISAAC

My arm was in serious pain, and I didn't know if it was broken. I asked Laquinta to get me a wet towel so I could wipe the blood from my arm. When she came back, she handed the towel to me and she sat on the kitchen chair while I leaned against the counter.

"Does it hurt?" she asked.

"Damn right it does," I said, wiping my arm. A small chunk of wood went into my arm, so I squeezed my eyes and pulled it out. I tossed it in the trashcan and looked at Laquinta. "Why'd you let her in here? Before you opened the door, didn't you ask who it was?"

"No. And when I did, I wasn't about to challenge her with that bat in her hand. Besides, you brought that on yourself. You only came here because you thought she was with somebody else, not because you missed me like you said you did last night."

I knew Laquinta was about to get started, and I wasn't in the mood. My purpose for being with her from the beginning was to get away from all the bullshit. Now that the bullshit seemed to find its way to her every time we got together, it was time to go. I ignored Laquinta's comment and went into the bedroom to get my clothes. She stood in the doorway and watched me put them on.

"I thought you were staying for a couple of days."

"I never told you that, Laquinta. There you go assuming things again."

"You're a piece of work, Isaac. When will all of this back and forth shit stop? I wish you'd just leave me the hell alone. I swear I do."

"Be careful what you wish for. The solution to your problem is simple, as long as you stop making yourself available. There's no need to wish when you're in command. I might keep on being the man who I am, but if I keep on hurting you that much, just be woman enough to end this."

"So, now I'm not woman enough? You didn't say that last night, or any of the nights and days before that. My pussy—"

"Your pussy is the bomb. So what? It controls the hell out of me, and I think we already know that. But there's an exception. My heart, baby. My heart belongs to my wife. I don't know what else it is that you want from me."

Fully clothed, I made my way to the door. Laquinta held up her arm to stop me. "I want you to show me some love in return. You can't tell me that you never loved me, Isaac. Many times, I felt it. If you didn't love me, I want to hear you say it."

"All . . . all you felt was my dick inside of you, giving you much pleasure. That's all you wanted, Laquinta, and up until recently, you haven't required anything else. For two and a half years, my dick satisfied you, and now you want something more?"

She gritted her teeth. "I said, do you love me? I want the truth and I want it now!"

She just wasn't reading between the lines. I ignored her

and removed her arm from the bedroom doorway. Attempting to make this less painful for both of us, I made my way to the front door. I reached for the knob, and Laquinta held her hand over mine. She gave me a stern look. "Do you?" she yelled.

I shook my head. "No. Never."

She lifted her hand and allowed me to freely walk out of the door.

On the drive home, my arm was in enormous pain. I didn't think it was broken because I could move it. It had swelled a bit, and I could kill Cydney for coming at me like that. I'd never expected a woman of her caliber to get down like she did, but I guess she'd reached her boiling point. If only she'd been honest with me about Raymond, then maybe things would've turned out differently. Then again, why did she expect me to believe her? For all I knew, they could still be seeing each other behind my back. Everybody in my life was playing games, so why should I think any differently about her?

When I got home, I surely wasn't up for more arguing. Hopefully, Cydney had gotten off her chest what she wanted to get off. I knew damn well that if she hit me with a bat again, I was going to make her pay.

I opened the door, and having a slight cramp in my leg, I squeezed my calf muscle. I went to our bedroom and looked at Cydney, sitting on the bed, eating ice cream.

"You know my arm broke, don't you?"

"Good."

"My leg might be too."

"Spectacular."

"You were seriously trying to hurt me, weren't you?"

"It's obvious, isn't it? And if your leg was broke, you wouldn't be walking or standing on it. Now, get over it and please go somewhere so I don't have to look at you. I'm still very upset with you, Isaac."

"And I'm upset with you too," I said, walking farther in the room so I could go to the bathroom.

Cydney licked the ice cream from the spoon and mumbled something.

I stopped. "What did you say?"

She held the spoon in her hand, looking as if she was in deep thought. "I . . . I was wondering about something, Isaac."

"And what's that?"

"Does your dick ever get tired? I mean, just about every time I see you, you're always giving it a workout. After getting so much usage, I don't see how that poor thing can function properly."

"Why don't you see for yourself how well it can function? And hell no, it don't get tired. It got tired of your rejection. Don't be mad because it found itself a new home."

"An ashy, ugly, tacky and contagious new home, you might want to add."

"Whatever," I said, going into the bathroom and closing the door. I took off my clothes and took a lengthy shower. Once I finished, I dried off and put on my cotton robe. I slid into my house shoes. Early afternoon or not, I was going back to bed. When I opened the bathroom door, Cydney had gotten into bed and was watching TV. Knowing that she didn't want my company, I headed downstairs to the sofa bed.

"Isaac?"

"What?" I turned.

She held the container of ice cream in her hand. "Take this to the kitchen and throw it away for me. And bring me a glass of Kool-Aid when you come back."

"What? Do you think I'm going to cater to you after you damn near broke my arm and leg with a bat? Woman, please. I ain't that big of a fool, and if the shoe was on the other foot, this shit wouldn't even be going down like this and you know it."

"No, it wouldn't. But you can be a forgiving husband just as much as I've been a forgiving wife. Now, you said that you loved me. Would you mind taking this container, throwing it in the trash and bringing me some Kool-Aid, please?"

"Loving someone means sometimes compromising. I'll throw away the container, but you can get up and get the Kool-Aid yourself. Besides, I'm not coming back. I'm going downstairs so I can sleep peacefully."

"I'm sure that after all the *work* you put in last night, it probably drained you. Isn't it amazing that some men are so fortunate to be able to come home after a night like yours and sleep peacefully?"

I walked over and snatched the container from her hand. "You'd better not come fuck with me, Cydney. And if you throw any hot grease or water on me, I'm seriously going to hurt you."

"Now, do I look like the type of woman who would do something like that? Isaac, please. Don't you know me any better than that?" She smiled.

"Yeah, whatever. I thought I knew you, up until today."

I left the room and shortly came back with Cydney's Kool-Aid. She gave me a sinister grin and took the glass from my hand.

"Thank you," she said.

"You're not welcome, and you'd better stop looking at me like that. You're making me nervous, Cydney."

"If I make you that nervous, then leave. You shouldn't want to be in a house with a woman who frightens you."

I cut my eyes at Cydney and headed downstairs to the basement. Just in case, I took my pistol with me for protection.

For at least three hours, I tossed and turned and kept

listening for Cydney. There seemed to be something in her eyes that had me kind of worried. I didn't think she'd go to the extreme of doing something she would regret, but who knows? While lying on the sofa bed, I looked up at the ceiling and placed my hand on my chest. I glanced over at the wide screen television and watched a few minutes of ESPN. Soon, my eyelids started to flutter, and then I was out.

The sound of two sportscasters going at it on TV awakened me. I sat up to turn down the volume and noticed a white envelope on my chest. After using the remote to turn down the TV, I opened the envelope and saw my divorce papers inside. There was a sticky note on top that said *Please Sign*. I tore the papers in half, and on my way upstairs to Cydney, I tore more of the paper into tiny pieces.

When I got to the bedroom, she was asleep. I looked at the clock. It was after one o'clock in the morning. Being very quiet, I sprinkled the torn papers over her and went back downstairs to get some rest.

By morning, I could hear Cydney walking around upstairs. I figured she was getting ready for work, and when she yelled downstairs for me to wake up, I headed upstairs.

She was leaning against the kitchen counter, drinking coffee. Her thick hair was full of long, loose curls, her silky skin looked smooth as butter, and her black suit fit every curve in her body. She'd definitely lost some more weight and looked fabulous.

"You must have another date with Raymond." I couldn't resist.

"No, actually, I'm going to a funeral after work today. Don't worry, it's not yours. Not yet anyway."

"I know damn well it ain't mine. And it better not be mine."

Cydney smirked. She turned to put her cup in the sink

and turned on the water to rinse it. Instantly, my dick shot up as I glanced at her shapely ass. She turned off the water and reached beside her for a towel to dry the cup. Afterwards, she hiked up on her heels and opened the cabinet above her. She put the cup inside, and that's when I made my move. I stepped up behind her, wrapped my right arm around her waist, and pressed my hard dick against her butt.

"Wha . . . what are you doing?" she said, trying to remove my tight embrace.

With my lips, I moved her hair away from her ears and whispered. "See what you do to me? Don't you know how you make me feel? You look awesome this morning, and I want you to have a spectacular day."

I backed away, and as soon as Cydney turned around, she looked down at my goods. My dick was aimed in her direction, and I removed my robe so she could get a better look. I tossed the robe over my shoulder and held out my hands.

"We can't help how we feel about you," I said.

She rolled her eyes and walked past me. I knew Cydney wanted me too, but there was a time and place for everything. Now wasn't my time, so I chuckled and put my robe back on. When the doorbell rang, I yelled down the hallway to Cydney and told her I'd get it.

"Who is it?" I asked. I got no answer, so I looked through the peephole. What I saw, I hoped like hell I didn't see. I quickly opened the door, and sure enough, Erica was strapped to a car seat on the porch. The gift I'd bought her was next to her, and a folded piece of paper was on top. I quickly stepped outside and looked up and down the street. There was no sign of Laquinta, so I loosened Erica from the car seat and picked her up. She was asleep, and I laid her head on my shoulder. I went inside as Cydney was coming down the hallway.

"Who was at—" she paused and looked at Erica. "What the hell is going on?" she said. "That hoochie didn't have the nerve to show up at my house, did she?"

"She left, Cydney. I didn't see her, but she left Erica in her car seat on the porch."

A look of disgust was on Cydney's face. "You've got to be kidding me."

Cydney stepped outside and walked to the end of the driveway. She looked around and came back toward the door. She lifted the box.

"What's this?" she asked.

"It's a present I gave Erica for her birthday. Yesterday, I gave it to Laquinta."

Cydney pointed her finger at me. "You need to get this mess under control! Before I get home today, I want that child out of my house, and it wouldn't hurt if you'd be gone too."

Not saying another word, she stepped inside and went to our bedroom to get her keys and purse. Still a bit in shock, I stood by the door, still holding Erica in my arms. Cydney walked past us and slammed the door on her way out.

I went to the bedroom and laid Erica on the bed. Then I stepped outside to get her car seat and gift to bring them inside. I unfolded the attached paper.

Since you're not man enough to love me, maybe you can find some love for your child. Maybe she is yours or maybe she isn't, but you running in and out of our lives made her believe that you were. You failed to do the right thing by me, so now is your chance to do right by her. See you later, SUCKER!

This bitch was out of her damn mind. How in the hell was she going to stick me with a child that wasn't even mine? She knew darn well Erica wasn't mine, and to leave her on my doorstep like this proved to me that I'd been dealing with one stupid, non-caring and ignorant woman.

I heard Erica crying, so I rushed down the hallway to my bedroom. She was sitting up in bed, wiping the tears from her eyes.

I ran up and held her in my arms. "What you crying for?" I said, lifting her over my head. I jiggled her around in the air and she laughed. "I got you. Your da . . . daddy's got you, okay?"

Erica squeezed her eyes, and spit drizzled down from her mouth. It caught me in the face, and I lowered her to my chest. She put her arm around my shoulder.

"Did you boo-boo?" I asked because I smelled something.

She smiled and nodded.

I knew Laquinta had been trying to potty train Erica, but I wasn't sure if she'd been successful. I placed her on the bed and removed her pants. She had on a Pull Up, and it was filled with mess. I frowned and she smiled. She placed her hands over her big brown eyes and scrunched her nose.

"You are too cute, but Daddy don't have nothing for you to change into." I took a deep breath and looked around the room. I didn't see anything that I could use, so I took her to the bathroom so I could clean her up. After I washed her up, I held her up over the toilet and looked down into it.

"If you have to boo-boo again, do it in here, okay?"

She nodded and we left the bathroom.

Once I cut up a white sheet and wrapped it around Erica's bottom, I found some safety pins and clipped them to the sides. I reached for the phone and called Laquinta's place. Of course, she didn't answer, and I didn't expect her to.

"Listen, I don't know what kind of game it is that you're playing, but you'd better come and get Erica by the end of the day. If not, I will contact DFS and have her permanently taken away from you. I'm sure your mother wouldn't like that, so you'd better rethink some shit and get your butt over here soon."

I hung up and thought hard about Laquinta's mother's last name. I knew her first name was Virginia, but I also knew she'd been married at least four times. I didn't have a phone number, an address or nothing. "Damn." I sat thinking and overloading my brain for answers.

By mid-day, Erica had taken another nap, and we both lay in my bed. She was a good two-year-old and wasn't much of a problem at all. When she woke up, it was almost three o'clock. I knew she was hungry, so I went to the kitchen to find her something to eat. As I searched through the fridge, I saw a chicken nugget TV dinner that might be good for her. It had a side of mash potatoes and corn to go with it.

As soon as I stuck the TV dinner in the microwave, Erica started to cry. I looked at her sitting on the floor. The wrapped sheet around her had drooped to her knees. She sat in urine and reached out her arms to me. Just as I picked her up, I heard a car door shut outside. I rushed to the window, hoping it was Laquinta. Instead, it was Cydney. First, she went to the mailbox and then she came inside. She came through the kitchen's entrance, and I stood with a soaking Erica in my arms.

"Why are you back this early? I thought you had a funeral to go to."

"And I thought that I told you to work out this situation. I see you haven't done anything as of yet."

"I called Laquinta several times, but she won't answer her phone. I've also tried to figure out where her mother lives, but it's just not coming to me. Trust me, I'm working on it, Cyd, but I can't just throw Erica outside and send her on her merry way, can I?"

Cydney looked at Erica, and Erica reached out for her.

"Hiiiiii," Erica said, waving her hands. Cydney took a swallow and stepped up to me. She took Erica from my arms and looked at me.

"Why is a torn sheet in the middle of the floor? And I'm afraid to ask what it's sitting in."

"I didn't get a chance to go to the store because I didn't want to miss Laquinta if she came back for Erica. Do you mind if I go to the store to get Erica a few items? She needs some Pull Ups and some food. I'm not worried about clothes because I know Laquinta ain't stupid enough to leave Erica here overnight."

Cydney handed Erica back to me. "I'll go to the store. You clean up this mess and see about her."

"No, I don't mind going to the store. Besides, I want to stop at Laquinta's house to see if she's there and just not answering her phone. Maybe some of her neighbors might know where she is too."

"And I guess you want me to watch Erica? I don't think so, Isaac."

"Please. Only for a little while. All I'm doing is going to the store and over to Laquinta's. I'll be right back."

I handed Erica over to her again.

"Why didn't you go to work today? I thought your vacation was over."

"It is, but I don't have time to explain it to you. I'll explain it to you once I get back." I snatched my keys from the table. "We need to talk about that long scratch down the side of my truck too. You wouldn't happen to know anything about it, would you?"

"I haven't a clue what you're talking about. What scratch?"

"Yeah, that's what I thought you'd say."

When I got several blocks away from my house, I could've sworn that I saw Miguel in a blue Navigator. I quickly turned my truck around and followed behind the Navigator. It was driving in the direction of Trinity's house, and as soon as it made it on her street, I passed it by. I pulled over to the curb, and from a distance, I watched Miguel get out. He jogged up the steps and unlocked the door to let himself in. I made a mental note to call Trinity later, apologize to her for not stopping by, and make it my business to stop by soon. Now I had to deal with this situation with Erica, so I hurried to the store so Cydney wouldn't trip.

I left the store with Pull Ups, fruit cups, ice cream, spaghetti and chili mac in a can. I knew Erica would enjoy something sweet, so I picked up a bag of suckers and some chocolate chip cookies.

After I left the grocery store, I stopped at Laquinta's place and parked my truck. I went to her door and knocked several times, but no one was there. If she was, then she was ignoring me.

"Laquinta," I yelled. "Open the door!"

I continued to knock, but nothing came of it until her neighbor across the hall opened her door.

"Sorry for the noise," I said. "Ms. Ruthie, have you seen Laquinta today?"

"Earlier. She and Erica were going somewhere, but I don't think she's been back since then."

"Ms. Ruthie, do you know her mother Virginia? I'm trying to find out where she lives."

"I don't know exactly where she lives, but I know it's over there by Forest Park."

"Forest Park is a huge park, Ms. Ruthie. Do you have any idea what street by Forest Park?"

"I think somewhere on Skinker Ave. That's all I know is somewhere on Skinker near Washington University."

Ms. Ruthie really wasn't much help at all. She was an elderly lady, and since she was known for being nosy, I was surprised that she couldn't tell me more. I reached in my pocket for a pen and piece of paper. I wrote my name, number and address down and gave it to her.

"If Virginia happens to stop by, please give this to her for me."

She nodded and closed the door. I left and made my way back home.

CYDNEY

Erica had been with us for four days. Laquinta hadn't shown up, and I was damn mad about it. I even tried to reach her myself, but the tramp had disappeared. Isaac wasn't too happy about it either, but we both had to make the best out of a bad situation. Either way, we enjoyed Erica. She was adorable and was very much attached to Isaac. She called him Da-Da, and whenever he'd leave the room, she'd follow after him. I was surprised to see what a good father he could be, and he was the one who fed her, bathed and cleaned up after her.

After Erica's first night with us, I'd given up our bed and slept in the guestroom. Isaac and Erica slept in our bed, and it was the only way I could get some sleep. Erica was a night owl. She wanted to play all night long and sleep during the day. Basically, Isaac was worn out.

He'd told me about resigning from work, but I knew there was much more to it. He loved his job, and if he was innocent of all the things his boss accused him of, then Internal Affairs couldn't have kept him away. Actually, I wasn't too surprised to hear about some of the things

Miguel had done. I knew what kind of man Miguel was. But even though Isaac wasn't always a self-righteous individual, I was a bit stunned by the accusations against him. I wasn't sure what he was going to do, but I knew that the burden of taking care of everything wasn't going to fall on me. And even though things didn't seem to be getting any better, I continued to ask for his signature on our divorce papers. I laid them in bed with him every single night. By morning, either the torn papers were spread out over me, or they were clearly in the trashcan where I could see them.

On Thursday, I was sitting at my desk, busy with work. Again, Carol was absent, which caused me to have to do more work. Darrell was back, but he was so busy trying to play catch-up that I didn't want to bother him about wanting to fire Carol and find a replacement. I made myself a mental note to chat with him later. As I was typing up my own letters to two customers about their denied claims, Isaac entered my office with Erica. Earlier, he'd left me a message, but I hadn't had a chance to call him back.

"We brought you lunch," he said, sticking his head in the door. He put Erica on the floor and handed a brown paper bag to her. "Go give it to her, honey," he said.

Erica held the bag and trotted over to me. She was moving so fast that she tripped and fell. My heart dropped, and I jumped up to see if she was okay. She started crying, and I picked her up from the floor. I held her close to my chest and told her that it would be okay. She stopped crying, so I sat her up on my desk and bent down to check her knees.

"Did that carpet burn your knees?" I said, looking at them. I rubbed her knees and she smiled. She reached out for me, and I picked her up. Isaac grabbed the bag from the floor and set it on my desk.

"It was just a toasted tuna sandwich and some chips," he said.

"Yucky," I said, looking at Erica. "Did your Daddy . . . Isaac make me a yucky lunch?"

Erica nodded. "Yep," She clapped her hands.

"Then let's go get something good to eat. Would you like something good to eat?"

She nodded. "McDonald's," she screamed and clapped again.

I tossed the paper bag in the trash. "Then McDonald's it is."

"Hey," Isaac said. "I spent a lot of time in the kitchen making that sandwich. You could have at least eaten it."

He reached for Erica and I pulled back. "I got her. Sorry about the sandwich, but it was smashed anyway."

He cut his eyes at me, and we made our way to the elevator. As soon as we got on, still in my arms, Erica reached for the buttons to push them.

"No, no," I said, moving her hands away from the buttons. She kept trying to reach for them, and when I moved away from them, she started to cry. I kissed her hands and tickled her. She loved to be tickled.

"You can't play with those, sweetie. I'll buy you something to play with later, okay?"

She nodded, and Isaac looked at me from across the elevator. He cleared his throat. "I knew you'd make a good mother. I wish—"

"Don't even think about it, Isaac," I said, stepping off the elevator. "You need to hurry up and find Laquinta."

We left my office building and went down the street to McDonald's. I got Erica a Happy Meal, Isaac wanted a chicken sandwich, and I got a salad. Once we got our food, we went outside so Erica could play on the playground. She couldn't really do much, but watching the other kids seemed to bring her much enjoyment. One of the other little girls on the playground took Erica's hand and tried to show her around. Erica's eyes watered, so the little girl brought her over to us.

"I don't think she wants to play," the little girl said, giving Erica's hand to me. "What's her name?"

I reached for Erica and put her on my lap. "Her name is Erica."

"She's really pretty. How old is she?"

Isaac spoke up. "Two. She just turned two."

Erica held up two fingers and put them in my mouth. "That's right. You're two," I said, removing her fingers from my mouth and showing them to her.

"Two," she said.

I smiled and rubbed my nose against hers. As for the little girl, she stood next to us and stared. "Is everything okay?" I asked her. "Thanks for bringing her over to me."

"She has a tear in her pants." The little girl pointed to it. I looked at the tear. It had been there since Laquinta brought her over. I'd washed Erica's pants, but we hadn't gotten her any clothes because we didn't know how long she was going to stay. Besides, since she'd been with us, all she wore was Pull Ups around the house. I looked at the little girl.

"Thanks for pointing that out."

She shrugged, and after saying goodbye to Erica, she left to go play with the other kids. We quickly finished up lunch and made our way back to my building.

"Isaac, meet me in the parking garage by my car."

"Why?"

"Because I want to take Erica somewhere."

"What?"

"Would you just do as I asked you to do?"

"Take her somewhere like where?"

"She needs a few things. While we go shopping, you can go home and get some rest."

"What makes you think that I don't want to go shopping?"

"Do you? I thought you might want to take this opportunity to catch up on some rest."

"Now, that doesn't sound like a bad idea."

"Well, bring your truck to the parking garage so I can get her car seat."

"What about your job? Don't you have to go back to work?"

"I'm cool. I'll play catch-up tomorrow."

Isaac left, and Erica and I went to my car. He soon came to the parking garage and put her car seat in my car. He tightened Erica in and closed the door.

"Be careful," he said to me. "And I appreciate you doing all of this." He reached into his pocket for his wallet.

"I don't need any money. Just make some calls and see if you can find Erica's mother, grandmother or somebody, okay?"

"I'll do what I can," he said, walking back to his truck. After he drove off, I drove off behind him.

Erica and I stayed gone until nine o'clock that night. After I picked out several outfits for her at six different stores, I stopped and got her some toys to play with too. After that, I took her to the grocery store with me, and before we left the store, she wanted to ride on the tiny carousel. I let her ride, but she threw a tantrum when it was time to get off. I thought another ride would save me the embarrassment, but when the ride was over, she got angry with the horse. She hit it and cried as if it had done her some serious harm. I picked her up and carried her out to the car. A bagger saw that I needed help, and strolled my cart to the car to assist me.

"Thank you," I said. He placed the bags in my trunk

while I tightened Erica in her car seat. I closed the door and offered to tip the bagger.

"No, thank you, ma'am. It's my job."

I thanked him again and left. Just that fast, Erica was asleep. I smiled and kept watching her in my rearview mirror. She moved around a few times, but for the most part, she was out.

As I neared home, I called Isaac on the phone and asked him to meet me outside with my things. He was asleep, but when I pulled up, he was outside waiting for me. I got out of the car and removed Erica from the back seat.

"Isaac, there are some things in the trunk and on the back seat. Would you mind getting them for me?"

He opened the trunk, and I went into the house to lay Erica down. I put her in the bed, and when she sat up, I climbed in bed with her. She put her arm around my neck and lay back down.

"Go back to sleep," I whispered. She closed her eyes.

Isaac came in and placed the bags on the floor. He looked up at me and shook his head. He left again, and came back in with more bags.

"This is ridiculous," he whispered. "You shouldn't have bought all of this."

I ignored him, and when Erica was in a deep sleep, I eased out of bed to go put up the groceries. Isaac followed behind me and helped me in the kitchen.

"Baby, if you don't mind me saying it, I think you're getting too attached. You know Erica—"

"Look Isaac, I know what I'm doing. She's been around here for four days and didn't have any clothes or nothing to play with. This has nothing to do with being attached. I'm just trying to make the best out of a horrible situation. Have you had any luck with Laquinta or her mother?"

"None. But I'm sure that one of them will show up soon, especially Virginia. She spent a lot of time with Erica, and I'm sure she's wondering what the hell is going on."

Once the groceries were put up, Isaac and I headed back to the bedroom. I got ready for bed, and he said that since he'd gotten so much rest, he was going downstairs to watch TV. I told him I'd see him in the morning, and I sat on the floor and went through all of the things I'd bought for Erica. I held the cute outfits in front of me and counted fourteen of them as I laid them on the floor. I then reached for the bags of toys, and when I found the receipt, I looked at it. The total came to four hundred dollars and some change. I knew better than to go all out like this, especially for a child that belonged to my husband's lover. What was wrong with me? Was I crazy? Some women would've thrown their husband out with his so-called baby. Why didn't I have the heart or the courage to end this?

In deeper thought, I got off the floor and hung Erica's clothes in the closet. I put her toys back in the bags and put them aside. I opened up the drawer and pulled out another white envelope with my divorce papers inside. After I got in bed, I placed the envelope close by my side and tucked myself in with Erica. Before going to bed, I rubbed the fine baby hair on her forehead, touched her soft afro balls, and then I kissed her cheek.

ISAAC

Three whole weeks had gone by, and I still hadn't heard anything from Laquinta or from her mother. I called Smitty at the police station to see if he could find an address for Virginia. He came up empty, and as I'd gone back to Laquinta's place several times, I came up empty on that end too. I didn't know where the fuck she'd gone, and apparently, no one else did either. I did know, however, that Cydney had gotten too attached. She spent a lot of time with Erica, and the funny thing about it is that Erica took well to her too. Not once did she cry for Laquinta, and if Erica even appeared to be uncomfortable with her surroundings, Cydney surely made her feel better. Since she'd bought Erica a potty, Erica learned how to use the toilet. Cydney had taken a few days off work so we could take Erica to the zoo, and had been teaching her three-letter words. At night, she put her to sleep on time with bedtime stories.

As for us—to me, things were getting better. During the night, Cydney continued to drop the envelope on my chest, and I continued to tear it up. How many of these damn papers did she have? She was seriously wasting printing paper because there wasn't a chance in hell that I'd sign them.

The other day, I called Trinity to apologize to her for not showing up. I told her something important came up, and I promised her that I'd make it up to her soon. When I asked her about Miguel, at first she said she hadn't seen him. I pleaded for the truth, and then she said he'd stopped by. I knew I could get more information from her, and since I was so anxious to get back at Miguel for what he'd done to Cydney, I was willing to do whatever I had to do to make sure he paid for what he'd done.

Cydney and Erica had gone to the movies. She asked if I wanted to go, but this was the perfect opportunity for me to go see Trinity. I shaved my face clean, gave my waves a shine and brushed them to perfection. I put on a maroon velour sweat suit with a black wife beater underneath. For safety precautions, I slid my gun down inside my sweat pants.

Before heading over to Trinity's house, I called to make sure the coast was clear. She said that she was alone, and I told her I was on my way over. She seemed thrilled, and I quickly ended our call.

When I arrived at Trinity's place, I drove up and down the street before parking my truck close to the curb. I went to the door and knocked. Moments later, she opened the door with a glass of iced tea in her hand. She had on a flowered silk robe, with a Victoria's Secret two-piece lace ensemble underneath. It was white, and showed all of her supposed to be hidden good parts. Her sexiness turned me on, and I wasn't too mad that my visit might lead to something unexpected.

"Close your mouth," she said, moving away from the door to let me in. I stepped in, and after she locked the door, she walked up the steps. I followed behind her, and then touched her ass.

"Girl, you know you should be on the runway. Tyra Banks better watch out."

"Tyra Banks isn't on the runway anymore. She's getting paid doing other things like I'm going to do someday."

When we reached the top step, instead of turning to the right, Trinity turned to the left to go into her bedroom. She placed the glass of iced tea on her dresser and leaned against it.

"Have a seat," she said.

I sat on the bed and put my keys in my pocket. "Listen, before we travel back down memory lane, you got to promise me that you won't tell your brother I was over here. In addition to that, you have to confirm that he's not going to walk through that door while we're doing our thing."

"You can't tell me what not to talk to my brother about, but I assure you that he won't come through that door. He's out of town and won't be back until tomorrow."

"What time tomorrow? I'm sure you know that we had some beef, but I quit my job and so did he. An investigation will be going on soon, and I need to talk to him so we can get our stories straight."

"He'll be here tomorrow around noon. I don't know if he'll talk to you because he's been angry with you for a long time."

"I know, but I don't understand why. I'm just trying to make peace with him, especially if I'll be coming over here to see you, I don't want any trouble. As soon as he gets here tomorrow, will you call and let me know?"

"I don't have your number anymore."

I reached in my pocket for my wallet and pulled out a

piece of paper. I asked her for a pen, and she handed it to me. I wrote my number and handed the paper and pen to her.

"Don't forget. Call me, okay?"

"Sure."

My eyes searched her body, and while observing it, I reached in my pocket for some gum. While Trinity reached in her drawer for a condom, I blew a tiny bubble and it popped on my lips. Trinity turned, dropped her robe and moved toward me. She straddled my lap and remained on her knees. Since she was rather tall, I leaned back on my hands, and she leaned forward to kiss me. She pulled the gum from my mouth and put it in hers. She chewed and then swallowed. As she kissed me again, she rubbed the lower part of her body against mine. My dick had already given her some attention, and my hands roamed around her entire body. As I sunk my fingers into her wetness from behind, she got excited. She let out moans and folded her bottom lip.

"Hurry up and take off your clothes," she said. "And . . . remove the gun, please."

I knew she could feel my gun while she pressed her body against mine. I removed my fingers and started to undress. Trinity did the same, and once we were both naked, she got back into position on my lap. I lay back on the bed, put on the condom, and placed the gun underneath the pillow.

"You really don't trust me, do you?" she said.

"Baby, I don't trust nobody. Now, don't worry about my gun. Show the doctor what you're working with."

Trinity let out a chuckle and lowered herself. She soaked my dick with her mouth and massaged it well. Her tongue worked wonders, and when she tightened her jaws, I wanted to bust one in her mouth. Instead, I put her on her back and placed her long legs on my shoulders. I pressed her

legs close to her chest and grabbed my dick to put it inside of her. She flinched and dug her nails into my ass.

"Ohhh, Isaac. Don't hurt me, baby. Please don't hurt
me."

"I'll do my best," I said, taking my time with Trinity.
Her pussy was tight, and it had a serious choke on my
goods. The feeling made me want to come quickly, but I
was able to maintain my composure. Every time I backed
out and went in, Trinity let out a hurtful moan. Sometimes, she wouldn't even move, and that shit just drove
me crazy. No matter what, I desired a sista who knew
how to work well with a man inside of her. Her sex was
always a let-down, and that was one of my reasons for
ending it between us before.

"Isaac, I . . . I'm about to come. You don't care if I
come, do you?"

I sped up the pace. "Baby, that's what I want you to do.
But once you do, you gotta turn around so I can get mine
too, okay?"

She nodded, tightened her eyes and screamed out
loudly. Her body jerked backwards and she dropped her
legs from my shoulders. She quickly lay on her stomach,
and I pulled her ass cheeks apart. I inserted myself, and I
knew that my time was soon to come. Just as I started to
pump inside of her, I heard a gun click. My head snapped
to the right, and Raymond and I stared at each other.

"Get your dick out of my wife," he said. "Don't think
that I won't shoot you, Isaac, because I have plenty of reasons to do it."

As I backed out of Trinity, my dick instantly went limp.
She pulled the cover over her and looked angrily at Raymond. "I'm not your wife anymore, and you can't walk in
here whenever you get good and ready to! Now, put the
damn gun down!"

"Hell no," he said. "You might not be my wife anymore, but I told you that I didn't want you fucking with him, didn't I?"

As they went back and forth, all I could think about was my gun underneath the pillow. Not only that, but Trinity being married to Raymond just fucked me up. I guess since he'd known Miguel for so long, anything was possible.

Trinity continued to cover herself with the sheet and got off the bed. She tried to ignore Raymond, until he shot a bullet into the wall behind her. She squatted down and nervously placed her hand on her forehead. "Raymond, please don't do this." She sounded panicked. "Just go, and leave me alone, please!"

"Put some fucking clothes on and go in the living room. If I can't stop you from giving yourself to Isaac, maybe Miguel can."

Trinity snatched up her robe and ran past him. He held his gun steady. I knew that one move from me would cause him to open fire. To play it safe, I remained kneeling on the bed and waited for him to direct me further.

"Miguel," Raymond said with the phone up to his ear. "I just got to Trinity's house and there was a surprise waiting here for me. You might be interested in who was here when I got here." He paused. "Yeah, that's right." He paused again. "No, he's still here. I have a gun covering him, but I don't believe in this cops and robbers bullshit. If you want him, you'd better get here fast."

After that, Raymond hung up and looked at me.

"You disgust me, Isaac. Cydney deserves so much better than you, and I hope like hell that she leaves you high and dry. Now, put on your clothes so you can join me and Trinity in the living room!"

I slowly reached for my clothes and tried hard to get my gun. Raymond's eyes were stuck to me like glue until Trinity yelled his name. He turned his head slightly to the side, and I took that opportunity to reach for the gun and slide it into my sweat pants.

"What is it?" he yelled at Trinity.

"Would you please come here?"

"Sit down and shut up until I get there," he said.

I put on my clothes and was very cooperative as I made my way past him. He shoved me in the back, and we both made our way to the living room.

"Would you please just go?" Trinity begged. "This is my life, and I'll do whatever it is that I want to do. I'm tired of you and Miguel trying to run my life. I'm sick of it!"

Raymond stood over her, his back facing me. I saw the perfect opportunity to shoot him in the back, but he wasn't at all who I was looking for. I intended to wait until the real deal got here.

"Trinity, don't make me hurt you. Now, sit still and be quiet until Miguel gets here."

"I'm going to tell him that you shot at me too," she pushed. Raymond was aggravated and backhanded Trinity with the gun. She fell back on the couch and held her face.

"I don't give a fuck what you tell Miguel! He's a piece of shit, just like you are. I shouldn't have never got involved with such a fucked-up family."

Trinity cried, and just as she was going through her sobbing phase, I heard the front door open. I could hear hard footsteps coming up the stairs, and my eyes were glued to the doorway. Soon, Miguel appeared, and surprisingly, behind him was Laquinta. She stood by the doorway and turned her head to the side.

I couldn't help but show my anger. "You need to come get your child, bitch!"

She ignored me and kept her head turned.

Miguel removed his silver-framed glasses and shot daggers at me with his eyes. "What the fuck are you doing over here?"

"Nigga, I was fucking your sister, that's what!"

"Miguel," Trinity yelled, halting his steps toward me. "Stop this, please!"

He looked angrily at her. "Did you fuck him? After all the hurt he caused you, you let him screw you?"

"No, I didn't."

Raymond instigated. "You're a fucking liar. I caught the two of them in bed."

Miguel walked up to Trinity and pulled the back of her hair. "Did you lie to me? After all I've done for you, you have the nerve to lie to me about fucking this bastard!" He zoned in on the red spot and swelling underneath her eye. "Did he hit you? What the fuck is wrong with your eye?"

Trinity reached up and pulled Miguel's hand from her hair. "You might want to talk to my ex-husband about that."

Miguel looked at Raymond. "Did you hit my sister?"

"Your sister has a smart mouth, and both of you are lucky that I didn't do more than that after seeing her in bed with Isaac."

Miguel threw a punch that landed on Raymond's jaw. It dropped him back onto the floor, and Raymond didn't hesitate to raise his gun and pull the trigger. Screams rang out from both Laquinta and Trinity. Laquinta headed toward the back door to leave, and Trinity dropped to her knees on top of Miguel. I pulled out my gun and rushed toward Laquinta to stop her. I held her in a chokehold so she wouldn't get away.

"Naw, naw. Don't you go anywhere just yet," I said. "Stay your ass right here."

Since I had the gun in my hand, Raymond aimed his

gun at me. I turned mine his way and used Laquinta as a shield.

"I don't have no fucking beef with you, Raymond, so let this shit go! If you don't want to get arrested for shooting an ex-cop, get the fuck up and get the hell out of here!"

Raymond thought about it and slowly got off the floor. He watched his back and made his way toward the back door. Trinity looked up at him and charged at him. As she stepped away from Miguel, I watched as he held his side in pain and squirmed around on the floor. I let loose of Laquinta and shoved her on the couch.

"Don't you move!" I yelled and tucked my gun inside my pants. I squatted down next to Miguel and leaned over him. I moved his gun away from his hand and pulled him up by the collar.

"You're a sorry motherfucker," I said, spitting in his face. "Before you get out of here, this ass kicking I'm about to give you is for Cydney."

I punched him hard, and his head snapped to the side. He fell backwards, and I punched the other side of his face. My continuous blows forced his head from side to side, and I didn't stop until I heard police sirens from a distance. I knew the chaos outside between Raymond and Trinity and the sound of a gunshot would prompt someone to call the police. As soon as I stood up, I kicked Miguel several times in his wounded side. He cried out in pain, and his face was a bloody mess.

I looked at Laquinta. "I promise to save your ass kicking for another day. But you got one damn day to come get your child, or else I promise you that you will never see her again."

On my way out, I couldn't help but smack her ass as hard as I could. She dropped to the floor and crawled over to get Miguel's gun. Once it was in her hands, I rushed down the stairs and pulled on the doorknob. The key was in it, but the door was locked.

"Isaac," Laquinta said. Even though my back was to her, I knew she was at the top of the stairs with the gun in her hands.

"Shoot him." I heard Miguel strain his words.

I stood in front of the door and spoke calmly.

"Shoot me," I said without turning around. "If shooting me gives you pleasure, then pull the fucking trigger!"

She didn't say a word, so I slowly reached for the gun inside of my pants. I pulled it out and quickly turned to her.

"So, we're going out like this, huh? You shoot me and I shoot you. I guarantee you that my aim is a lot better than yours. If your gun goes off before mine, you better make sure you hit your target."

Laquinta stood nervously at the top of the stairs. The gun shook in her hands, and a mean-ass mug was on her face.

"Shoot him," Miguel strained out again.

I looked at Laquinta and could tell she didn't want to do it. "If you listen to him, you're going to lose your life." I turned back around and turned the key in the lock. The door opened, and I looked up at her.

"I hate you," she sobbed, and dropped the gun. "I swear to God that I hate you!"

"If you did, you would have pulled the trigger."

Not saying another word, I left and hurried to my truck. I drove off, and slowed my pace as I passed six police cars and an ambulance on my way down the street.

I rushed home to tell Cydney what had happened. Well, not everything that happened, but mostly everything. However, when I got home, it was late and she was sitting on the bed with a furious look on her face. Erica was asleep next to her.

My heart raced, as I feared for the worst.

"Baby, what's wrong?" I said, sitting on the bed. "I'm sorry I'm late, but—"

"Erica's grandmother called today," she snapped. "She's coming to get her in the morning."

My frustrations showed too. To comfort Cydney, I reached out and hugged her.

"Baby, don't be mad, especially since I told you not to get too attached. We both knew that Erica couldn't stay here with us forever."

She pulled away from me. "I never said she could. But with you being her father, you have some rights, don't you?"

"She's not my child, Cydney. You know that."

"But nobody else knows, except for me, you and Laquinta, right? Erica's grandmother doesn't know, does she?"

"I really don't know. I've only met her a few times, but there's no telling what Laquinta told her."

Cydney painfully held her forehead and closed her eyes. "Can't you do something . . . anything, Isaac? Don't you even care?"

"Yes . . . yes, I care. And I'll talk to Virginia tomorrow and see what she says about letting Erica spend time with us. I'm warning you, she's a bitch, and if it doesn't involve money, she ain't trying to hear it."

Cydney lay back down next to Erica and kissed her cheek. She closed her eyes and took a deep breath. "Where have you been all day?"

"Please don't be mad at me, but I was out looking for Miguel. I caught up with him at his sister Trinity's house and we got into a scuffle. Raymond was there too, and things got pretty ugly. He wound up shooting Miguel, and before the police got there, I left."

"Is . . . is he dead?"

"I really don't know, but his injuries looked pretty serious."

"What made you go to his sister's house? Have you been keeping in touch with her?"

"Only to find out if Miguel was there. I just happened to call, and she told me he was on his way there."

Cydney took a deep breath, and I could tell she wanted to know more. "Why did Raymond shoot Miguel? I thought they were buddies."

"Can you believe that Raymond is Trinity's ex-husband? When Miguel arrived, he saw that Raymond had hit his sister, and Miguel got angry. He tried to attack Raymond, and that's when he pulled the trigger."

"Why did Raymond hit Trinity? Was he upset about something?"

"Baby, I don't know. By the time I got there, Trinity gave me the scoop. She let me inside, and Miguel and Raymond were arguing."

"But you said that you and Miguel had a scuffle. How did he scuffle with you and he'd been shot?"

I knew exactly where Cydney was going with this, and since I was lying my ass off, I had to cut our conversation. "Actually, we didn't scuffle at all. After he'd been shot, I roughed him up and left before the police got there. My kicks weren't nearly enough punishment for what he'd done to you, but I guess you can say that Raymond took care of my business for me."

Cydney swallowed and looked away.

"Get some rest," I said. "We'll continue to talk about this tomorrow."

As usual, I went downstairs to calm myself. It had been a busy and crazy-ass day. I didn't know what was going to happen to Miguel, but I hoped like hell that he somehow got what he deserved. To me, being shot and a good ass kicking wasn't enough. As for Laquinta . . . what a joke. She'd lied to me about seeing him, and I didn't want anything else to do with her. I knew that if I kept in contact with Erica, that would put me in contact with Laquinta. It was time to put final closure to it all.

By morning, I'd gotten only a few hours of sleep. I heard Cydney upstairs walking around, so I got up to check on her. When I got upstairs, she was fully clothed, and so was Erica. Cydney had her beautifully dressed in a pink-and-yellow polka dot dress. Her hair was in one perfectly combed afro ball with a pink-and-yellow ribbon around it. Cydney said that Virginia was coming at seven o'clock, and it was already a quarter 'til.

"Let me hold her," I said, reaching out for Erica. Cydney hesitated to give her to me, but she turned her over. "Hello, precious. Don't you look beautiful this morning."

My thoughts quickly turned to yesterday. Had Laquinta shot at me, I would've very well taken her life. Erica was on my mind the entire time I stood by the door. And even though she had a bullshit-ass mother, I hoped like hell that Laquinta was capable of bringing happiness to her little girl's life.

I kissed Erica and held her up in the air like I'd always done before.

"Be careful with her," Cydney said, biting her nails. "You're wrinkling her dress, baby. Put her down."

Seeing how tense Cydney was, I put Erica down. I even handed her back to Cydney and allowed her a little more time.

Moments later, the doorbell rang. She looked at me and quickly handed Erica over to me. Cydney opened the door, smiled at Virginia and invited her in.

Virginia quickly acknowledged Cydney and held her arms out for Erica.

"There goes Ganty's baby." She took Erica from my arms and kissed all over her. "Your Ganty missed you. Look at how pretty you look. Who made you look so pretty?"

Erica smiled and clapped her hands. "Da-Da," she said.

Virginia looked at me. "Did you buy her this pretty dress and doll her up like this?"

"No. My wife, Cydney, did. She's been taking care of Erica a lot more than I have."

Virginia turned to Cydney and looked her up and down. "Thank you," Virginia said. "I don't know what's wrong with that damn daughter of mine, but I'm going to set her straight. She will not get Erica back until she gets her mess together."

Cydney nodded, and Erica reached out to her. Virginia acted as if she didn't want to turn her loose, but Erica put up a little fuss. Virginia released her to Cydney, and she took a deep breath.

"You be good for your grandmother, and don't forget everything that I taught you, okay?" As Cydney spoke, Erica nodded. "Don't nod. What's the word?"

"Yes," Erica whispered softly.

"Good girl," Cydney said, giving her a hug.

Virginia got really jealous and took Erica from Cydney's arms.

"We'd better get going," she said.

Cydney quickly spoke up. "Do you mind . . . can she visit us sometimes? Isaac is her father, and we'd like to spend some time with her too."

"I . . . I don't think so. Laquinta told me that Isaac wasn't Erica's biological father, and I don't want her growing up confused."

"Confused?" Cydney said, raising her voice. "Your daughter is the one confused. Now, Isaac and I have both attached ourselves to Erica, and we can't help it that we were lied to."

"I'm sorry, but I'm in control of things now. Erica already has a family, and she's not about to be tossed from one home to another."

Rage covered Cydney's face. I knew she was about to lose it, so I stepped up to her and placed my arm around her waist. "It's okay, baby. Calm down. "

She snatched away from me, "Do something about this, Isaac! Are you going to stand there and do nothing?"

"Baby, there's not much—"

She begged Virginia. "If only once a week, please let her come and visit with us."

Virginia had no sympathy for Cydney. She turned toward the door and opened it. "Thanks, again, but—"

"Please," Cydney snapped.

Virginia walked out and left Cydney in anger.

"Do something!" she yelled at me. "I can't believe you're just standing there after all you've done for that little girl!"

I had my reasons for not stopping Virginia, but once I grabbed Erica's bags of toys and clothes, I went after Virginia to please Cydney. Virginia had put Erica into the car, and I put the bags in the trunk. She had a change of heart, and looked up at Cydney biting her nails while looking out of the window.

"Only one day, Isaac. You and your wife choose one day, and not on the weekend."

"Thanks, Virginia, but that won't be necessary. My wife just lost a child, and she got extremely attached to Erica. We'll get through it. Just make sure Erica is taken care of, and make sure that her biological father knows that he's her daddy. I don't want to confuse her, because in the long run, if she continues to see me and my wife, she'll really be confused."

"I agree," Virginia said, looking at Cydney. "That's what I was trying to tell her. I hope she understands."

"Eventually she will."

I kissed Erica and waved goodbye. She waved back. Shortly after, Virginia got in her car and drove off. When I went back inside, Cydney stood with her arms folded and waited for a response.

"I . . . I'm sorry, baby. She just wouldn't agree to it."

I held Cydney in my arms again, and it was a bad-ass feeling to see her look so hurt. I felt for her, but there was no way possible for us to move on if I kept in contact with Laquinta or her family.

CYDNEY

My heart was crushed. Never in my wildest dream did I think I'd get so attached to my husband's lover's child. Thing is, I knew Erica would someday leave us, but the way Virginia just came in and took her was devastating. She gave no thought to my feelings, and her decision was based on pure jealousy.

Once Isaac told me what had happened at Trinity's place, I didn't expect to see Erica ever again. This time, I'd really set myself up for a downfall, and I couldn't stop myself from being so angry inside.

Isaac was doing any and everything possible to make me forget about what had happened. He'd taken me shopping, to the movies and to the park. One night, we went dancing and had ourselves a blast. It was as if we were falling in love all over again. A serious plus was that he cooked dinner for us every day. He'd even talked about taking a trip together, but I just wasn't up for it. I told him maybe some other time, and for the next several weeks, I was in and out of my slumps. That was, until I got a call from Virginia. I was excited to hear her voice. She called to thank me for teaching Erica so many things.

"I'm sorry for bugging you," she said. "But I'm amazed at all of the things Erica has learned. These games you bought her have been really helpful."

"Yeah, we had fun learning things. Erica's a good girl, and you should be proud of her."

"I am. But I just wanted to say thanks. I kind of rushed out of your house without showing you my appreciation for what you and your husband did."

"I guess you had your reasons. All I wanted to do was see her from time to time. She seemed really close to Isaac, and I didn't think—"

"Well, Isaac and I agreed that it wasn't in Erica's best interest to be running back and forth. And I'm sorry for your loss, but a loss like that can never be replaced."

I was puzzled. "What loss? What are you talking about?"

"Isaac said you'd lost a child. I offered to let the two of you see Erica, but he said it wasn't in your best interests."

"You what?" I yelled. "Virginia, don't play games with me, please. I'm seriously hurt by—"

"Mrs. Conley, I'm too old for games. Now, I offered, and I'm not going to make the offer again. I just wanted to say thanks and—"

I hung up on her and made my way to the kitchen where Isaac was. He had on an apron and some stone washed jeans. His chest was bare. He stirred a spoon around in a pot. When he turned around, he held a spoon with spaghetti sauce on it.

"Baby, you've got to taste this. It's the bomb."

"How could you do that to me?" I whispered.

"Do what? What is it now? I haven't even been any-where to do nothing."

My voice rose. "Why did you tell Virginia that we didn't

want Erica to visit us? You knew how much I wanted to see her. Damn it, Isaac, you knew it!"

He was at a loss for words. "I, we . . . when did you talk to Virginia?"

"It doesn't matter!" I screamed. "Why do you keep on hurting me? Don't you ever get tired of hurting me?"

"Look," he said, stepping up to me. "You've got to stop all of this crazy talk and get yourself together. Erica was here for a purpose, and as soon as you realize what it was, then you'll be able to see things better."

I covered my mouth, feeling like I wanted to throw up. Instead, I pounded Isaac's chest. I could've killed him for the hurt he'd cost me. He reached for my hand and held it.

"We can always have a baby, Cydney. Why can't we have our own child?"

I reached up and slapped his face hard. He tugged at my arm and yelled at me.

"You'd better get your shit together! Now, I'm sick and tired of being your damn punching bag! The only reason I didn't accept Virginia's offer is so that you or I wouldn't have to deal with Laquinta again. If we'd kept Erica in our lives, you know damn well Laquinta would've continued to do more harm to our marriage. I want to save my marriage, baby. I . . . I want a child with you, and I saw what a good mother you could be. I can be a good father too. Just give us a chance, okay?"

I was so disgusted with Isaac that I just walked away. I went back into our bedroom and lay across the bed. Shortly after, he came in and tossed the white envelope on the bed. The divorce papers inside were hanging half-way out, staring me right in the face.

"Finally," Isaac said, darting his finger at me. "You got what you wanted. Take those to your lawyer and let's be done with it."

Isaac went into the closet and pulled out several pieces of his clothing. He laid them on the bed and went back in the closet for his suitcase. He laid it on the floor and put the clothes inside. He then went back into the closet, and as he spent more time in there gathering his things, I pulled the papers from the envelope and saw that he'd signed on the bottom line. I gasped. My heart dropped, and I took a hard and hurtful swallow. Seeing his signature on the papers made me realize how badly I didn't want this to happen. Maybe I overreacted. Now I understood why he wanted to cut ties between me and Erica. Being with her showed me what a good mother I could be. Isaac was a good father too, and the love we showed Erica, even knowing that she wasn't his, could be given to our own child.

I laid the envelope on the bed and made my way toward the closet. Isaac was squatted down, throwing his shoes in a pile. I walked in and touched his sweaty back. He turned his head slightly to the side.

"I . . . I'm sorry." I paused. "I do want a baby, Isaac. Please give me a baby."

Frustration was written on his face. "You don't want a baby, Cydney. You want a man that you can boss around and hit on, and—"

As Isaac continued to rant, I dropped my cotton robe to the floor. I stood naked and held out my arms for him to embrace me. He didn't budge.

"Make love to me," I asked while rubbing the waves in his hair. "Please just take me in your arms and comfort me."

While still on his knees, Isaac turned and gazed at my body. No doubt, he was shocked by my words and could barely move. I lifted my right leg and placed it on his strong shoulder.

"What's the matter? You forgot how to make love to me?" I asked.

Isaac looked up at me and then looked between my legs. He put his hands on my waistline and squeezed it. Feeling more of me, his hands lowered to my ass and softly touched my cheeks. He was gentle, and once he positioned my leg on his shoulder, I wasn't prepared for what happened next. Isaac's curled tongue went inside of me and separated my neatly shaven wet slit. He swiped his tongue against my clit, and his fingers went into me from my backside.

As he rotated his fingers inside of me, there was no way possible for me to keep my balance. I stretched out on the floor and opened my legs wide to welcome him inside. Isaac got back to business, and I squirmed around like a slithering snake. My legs trembled from the tingling sensation inside, and I was so, so ready to come. One thing I knew, though, was Isaac hated to put in all of the work. He wanted to be pleased too, and as he was in the midst of loving my insides, I sat up and scooted backwards. All I had to do was look at him, and he knew what I wanted. He stepped out of his jeans and lay on his back. I straddled my legs across his face, laid my body on top of his, and lowered my head. His dick was thick, hard and scrumptious-looking. With pleasure, I put it into my hungry mouth. I gave Isaac much pleasure, so much that he took a moment away from my insides and took tiny bites on my inner thighs.

"Ah, baby, that feels good," he complimented. "I love the way you make me feel. Damn!"

I kept at it, and I could feel his body getting tense. He never liked to come like this, so I lifted myself and ceased the action. I remained straddled across his face, and he held my thighs tightly down on his face. He vibrated my insides, and seconds later, I felt my juices starting to flow in his mouth. I pulled my hair and tightened my thighs on the sides of his face. The feeling was so good that a tear rolled from my eye.

"Isaac, I love you," I whispered. "My pussy . . . we love you so, so much."

Isaac moved my legs back and snickered. "I love you too, but it's time for this foreplay bullshit to come to an end. Can we please get the hell out of this closet?"

Having it my way, I lay on my back and positioned Isaac between my legs. "Sometimes," I said, putting his dick inside of me, "you have to work with what space you've got. Now, you don't want to stop and go somewhere else, do you?"

"Hell . . . naw," he moaned. My insides must have felt good. He stroked in and out of me and shook his head. "Damn, Cyd. Why you make me wait so long for this? Baby, I don't think I can hold it. I feel like a kid in a candy store."

"Then don't hold it. Remember, I want all that you got and then some."

"All of it," he said, loving my insides harder.

"Yes, baby, all of it."

Isaac and I went from lovemaking to pure, deep fucking. He fucked me from the closet floor to our bedroom floor. After that, we crawled our way to the bathroom floor and he dug deeply into me while holding me up on the bathroom counter. We ended up against the wall in the shower, and the water hadn't been turned on yet. Major sweat dripped from both of us, and we stood body to body, taking deep, heavy breaths. We sucked each other's wet lips, as if kissing was going out of style.

"Baby, I can do this all night long. What about you?" he said while grinding inside of me.

"All night," I moaned. "I don't know how much more of this my pussy can take."

Isaac snickered again. "You know you be talking shit. But I love the way your words roll off your tongue."

I smiled and licked around Isaac's ear. I whispered, "Fuck me as long as you want to fuck me. When you're done fucking me, I want you to gather yourself and fuck me some more. My pussy craves for you. Don't you feel how wet my insides are for you? My breasts . . . damn, look at my breasts, Isaac. They need you."

Isaac laughed out loudly and cupped my breasts in his hands.

"Mmmm," he said, sucking them like a baby drinking some milk. He hiked me up, and I placed my legs around his back. "Hold on," he said.

"Where are we going now?" I laughed.

"To the bed. We haven't done it on the bed yet."

"But we need a shower first. Look at how much we're sweating."

Isaac ignored me and carried me to the bed. He laid me back on it and crawled between my legs.

"Do you have any idea as to how many shots I've given you tonight?" he asked.

"I lost count. Why?"

"I'm just wondering. But you know what?"

"What?"

"I heard that if I come inside of you while you're lying back on your head, that instantly makes a baby."

"Bullshit, Isaac. I ain't trying to get a headache. Why don't we just stick to the basics?"

"Aww, that's no fun," he said, standing up. He went to the bottom of the bed and kneeled down on the floor. I knew the routine, and while on my knees in bed, I backed up to him. When I reached him, I lay flat on my stomach and stretched my legs out on his shoulders. My pussy met up with his lips, and he held my legs in place on his shoulders. He then gave me a slow, yet soft lick between my legs.

"You were drying up a bit, weren't you?" he asked.

"I couldn't tell, but I know for a fact that you have what it takes to spice things up again."

"Ah, you betcha I do."

Isaac loved my insides again, and once he finished, he got in bed with me. I sat up on him and looked at the white envelope beside me. I picked it up and held it in my hand. He tried to snatch it away, but I pulled it back.

"No, no. I can't believe you signed this."

"You damn right I did. You wasn't gon' keep on treating me like shit and get away with it." He smiled and snatched the envelope from me. He was getting ready to tear it up, but I took it from his hands.

"The pleasure is all mine," I said.

I tore the envelope and paper into tiny pieces and let them fall on top of Isaac. He looked at me and grabbed me into his arms.

"I love you," he said while holding my face. He rubbed my messy hair back and brought my face to his. He ran his fingers through my hair and squeezed it tightly as he aggressively kissed me. "God knows I love you, and I hope that you know how—"

"I do," I said. "Baby, I do."

After our kiss, Isaac lay back and smacked my ass. "Then saddle up. I'm ready for a rough ride."

I smiled, and of course, proceeded to give my husband just that.

That night, we couldn't seem to get enough of each other, and by morning, we were passed out on our backs. Isaac's loud snoring awakened me, but my body was too sore to move. I felt like I'd been in a fight that lasted all night as I inched my way out of bed. When I stepped on the floor, my body wanted to collapse. I held my sore back and stepped slowly to the bathroom.

Needing to relax in the tub, I ran my bath water and dropped some dissolvable fragrance balls in the water. I even poured in some bubble bath. I couldn't wait to sink myself deep inside. Before I did, I looked in the mirror and pulled back my thick and curly, but nappy hair into a ponytail. I thought about my amazing night with Isaac and hoped this would be a turning point for us. Things were surely looking up, and the feeling that I had today, other than my soreness, was a feeling that I wanted to feel forever. I got in the tub and slid down. My thighs were in pain, so I rubbed them. When I heard Isaac clear his throat, I looked up at him.

"Good morning," I said.

He stretched his back and held it. "And a good morning it is. Move up so I can get in."

"Isaac, my body is too sore. I know you couldn't possibly—"

"Baby, trust me. I've had enough of your sweet stuff. My dick cussing me out for putting it into overdrive."

We both laughed, and I scooted up to let Isaac in behind me. He groaned from body aches, and when I leaned back on him, he told me to take it easy.

"Aw, come on," I said. "You're the one who got us into this mess. Remember?"

"Woman, please. That was your hot ass. Oh, baby, fuck me . . . fuck this pussy all night long. Remember?"

"Please, I didn't say nothing like that. I did say fuck me, but you were the one who insisted that I saddle up."

"Yeah, I was the one who initiated it, but you didn't have to follow my lead."

"If I knew I'd feel like this, I surely wouldn't have." I wrapped Isaac's arms around me. "Either way, it was good, and I wouldn't take it back for nothing in the world."

"Same here," he said, kissing the back of my head. "Same here."

ISAAC

Well, what can I say? Simply put, I was deeply in love with my wife, and it wasn't as if I'd ever not been. Now, she'd pissed me off, but I always knew our marriage was worth saving. I just had to get her to see it.

For months, things had been going smoothly. We'd taken a vacation to Jamaica, and even though Cydney's boss, Darrell, wasn't happy about it, he was pleased to see us work things out.

As for Miguel, while he was in the hospital, his shit caught up with him. Raymond went to the Feds and snitched. Miguel had been a police officer by day and a major drug dealer by night. Raymond and his father had been dealing too, however Raymond cut a deal and was let off scot free. As for Miguel, the news reported that he was looking at twenty-five years in the slammer. I could only imagine what was going to happen to him in prison, and my thoughts made me smile.

Cydney met me at the counselor's office. We both figured counseling could only help our marriage more, so we agreed to make an appointment. I didn't know what to expect, but I was a bit nervous. As Cydney walked toward me, she seemed to be fidgeting as well. She clenched her hands in front of her, and when she stepped up to me, she took my hands.

"Are you ready?" she asked.

"As ready as I'm going to get." I kissed her cheek and we stepped into the counselor's office.

The counselor was an attractive older black woman with gray-and-black hair neatly pulled back into a bun. Her eyes were covered with dark-blue framed glasses, and her tailored blue suit looked as if it cost a fortune. For two hundred bucks an hour, I sure in the hell knew how she could afford to look so classy. She introduced herself as Mrs. Tillman.

"Mr. and Mrs. Conley, please have a seat." She smiled as Cyd and I took seats in the leather and wood chairs in front of her desk.

At first, honestly, she bored me. She went on and on about procedures, confidentiality, and of course, payment. After she asked us to sign some papers, she got down to business.

"Isaac, I want you to tell me some things that you love about Cydney."

She caught me off guard, and I looked at Cydney. She was waiting for a response too, so I swallowed. I knew one thing that I wanted to say, but I didn't feel comfortable saying it. "I . . . I love her sexiness." I paused. "Her, uh, smile and, uh—"

Mrs. Tillman stared deeply at me. She cut me off, "Cydney, let's hear it for Isaac."

I turned and waited for her response.

"I love his smile too, and, uh, the way he takes care of his body." She paused, and soon, Cydney was cut off too.

"Listen," Mrs. Tillman said. "We have some work to

do. When the two of you get home tonight, jot down at least ten things that you love about each other. Then, share those things. I'm sure if I asked both of you what things you dislike about each other, the words would've flowed from your mouths. Let's not focus on those things. Let's focus on your inner qualities and on appreciating each other more, okay?"

We both nodded.

"Now," she said, handing us both a mirror. "Cydney, you first this time. I want you to look in the mirror, and tell us what you see."

Cydney lifted the mirror and looked at it. "I see a beautiful, smart, witty, admirable woman with a bright future." She put the mirror back down.

"Okay," Mrs. Tillman said. "Now, look harder. Tell me some things about you that your husband might not have liked about you. Who was the woman in his life several months ago? Describe her to me. Take your time and tell me who you saw."

"I saw a woman who loved her husband, but hated him for the pain he'd caused. Then I saw a scorned woman who wanted nothing but revenge. The only way she felt she could get it was by sleeping with other men and depriving him of the things that he wanted in our marriage. When he looks at me, I think that, at times, he sees a fat and non-healthy woman. A bossy woman who wants to have her way, and a stupid woman that has no courage to leave him no matter what."

I touched Cydney's hand. "Baby, I never felt like that. Why would you—"

Mrs. Tillman interrupted. "But that's how she thought you felt about her. Now, Isaac, pick up your mirror and tell me, what do you see? If you'd like, you can refer to the past as well."

I looked in the mirror and turned my head to the side.

"I see an awesomely handsome man who's smart, funny, loving and irresistible," I said. Mrs. Tillman laughed. "In addition to that, I see a man who betrayed his wife many times. A liar, a cheat, a manipulator, and a man that I'm not proud of. I'm ashamed of who I am, and my parents didn't raise me to be this way."

Mrs. Tillman slammed her hands together. "That's what I wanted to hear!" she yelled. "Sometimes we have a hard time accepting and hearing the bad things that people see in us, and when we see those things too, that's a good thing. It means we can possibly make some changes. Isaac brought out more than good things about himself, and shared the bad things as well. I want both of you to recognize your faults, and put forth every effort to change those things. Remember, though, resolving means recognition."

"But I also mentioned some bad things too," Cydney said in her defense.

"Yes, you did. But let's not point the finger at each other and make excuses for our own actions. Realistically, you made some serious mistakes too. I want the two of you to look at each other and admit that you've both made some mistakes."

"Now?" Cydney said.

"I can't think of a better time."

Cydney and I turned to each other. She spoke first, but her voice was kind of . . . dry. "I . . . I made some mistakes too and I'm sorry."

"Now," Mrs. Tillman said, "look him in his eyes and say it like you mean it. It's obvious that Isaac has caused you a lot of pain, Cydney, so this might be a bit harder for you to grasp. But if the two of you want this to work, you must show some effort. Isaac, I want your input as well."

Cydney held my hands. "I made some mistakes too,

and I'm sorry. I can't take them back, but I hope that you can forgive me, and that we can now move on."

"I made some mistakes too, baby, and I will never make them again. I'm asking for your forgiveness, and no matter what anybody says, you and I have made a decision to leave the past in the past. Let's keep it there. Nobody has walked in our shoes but us. I love you, and I'm excited about what the future holds for us."

A tear rolled down Cydney's cheek. She leaned in for a kiss. "I love you too."

Mrs. Tillman smiled. "Isn't it amazing what a little communication can do? If the two of you replay the last several years of your marriage in your mind, you will see that the breakdown happened because of the lack of communication. At times, you might have assumed the other person knew what you were feeling, but unless you've shared your feelings with them, I assure you that the other person had no clue what was on your mind. Learn to express yourself and discuss any and everything that you can. Talk about your careers, your future endeavors, your plans to have children . . . whatever they may be. Lean on each other. That way you don't have to go out and find other people to lean on. Always be willing to listen, and even if you don't have a comment on what the subject at hand may be, just listen to your spouse. Know what they are thinking and understand what they are feeling. Communication is the key to a long-lasting, healthy and secure marriage." She took a deep breath and smiled as we looked at each other and nodded in agreement. We'd failed terribly at communicating, and for so long, our way of communicating consisted of arguing and saying negative things to each other. I felt horrible, and as I thought about all of the hurtful things I'd said to my wife, I felt even worse.

"This wraps up our session for the day, but don't forget to make your list tonight. If you can come up with more than ten things you love about each other, that's great. And you should, after so many years of marriage. Tomorrow, bring your responses back to me, and we'll discuss them. In the meantime, start thinking about how you can give one hundred percent of yourself to the marriage. It's been proven that 50/50 doesn't work anymore, and it actually never did. But with giving 100/100, you're bound to work things out."

We thanked Mrs. Tillman, and Cydney and I left her office holding hands. She had to get back to work, and I had an appointment with the sarg about getting my job back.

Later that night, Cydney and I sat in bed, writing our lists. We laughed about today's session, and couldn't wait to see what else was in store for us. I'm sure Mrs. Tillman had more tests and I knew it would be for the best.

"So, when do you start work?" Cydney asked while jotting something down on paper.

"Next week. I can't wait to get back either."

"You and Miguel should've never taken that money. We are going to spend a lifetime paying it back."

"Not really. I only took responsibility for some of it, not all of it."

"Hmmm . . ." Cydney said in deep thought.

I took a peek at her paper, and she folded it down so I wouldn't see it.

"Let me see what you got so far. Mrs. Tillman told us to share it anyway."

"Let me see what you got," she said.

"You first," I said, snatching her paper from her.

I looked down at the paper. It read:

I love Isaac's succulent lips, muscular body, squeezable ass, overly satisfying dick, and I'm delighted that he got his job back so that he can help me pay some bills.

I laughed and rolled on top of Cydney. My list was similar to hers, so I balled up both list and tossed them on the floor.

"I wanted to see yours too. You are so, so unfair," she griped.

"I just want to quickly show off some of the things you love about me, and in return, get into some of the things I love about you. Some things like," I lowered myself to her breasts and licked around her nipples, "your breasts." I pecked down her stomach and kissed the top of her pussy. "Your pussy." I went down further and lifted her leg. I kissed it. "Your pretty legs." I kissed each one of her toes. "Your toes." I laughed and dropped her leg. "Turn around," I asked. Cydney turned and lay on her stomach. "And your ass," I said, massaging it. "Damn, your ass." I licked my tongue down her crack and tasted her from the back. How Cydney and I would ever be able to explain this to Mrs. Tillman tomorrow, I simply didn't know.

As usual, we were right on time. We walked into Mrs. Tillman's office holding hands and sat in the chairs in front of her. She wasted no time in reaching her hand out for the lists.

"Where are my lists?" she said, putting on her glasses.

Cydney and I looked at each other. "We started on them," I said, "but we kind of got sidetracked."

"Oh, really. Sidetracked as in sexually sidetracked?"

We looked at each other, smiled and nodded.

"That's fine and dandy," Mrs. Tillman said. "Sex in the marriage is good, but let's take this thing to a higher level. The lists are supposed to encourage sex, as well as encourage you to want to do other things. Basically, Isaac tells you, Cydney, what he likes about you and vice versa. After that, explore your likes about each other."

"Oh, we explored it," I said.

"Every bit of it," Cydney added.

Mrs. Tillman smiled. "You two are going to be just fine. Remember to keep on loving and respecting each other, and always keep God first. There's no doubt that you love each other, but when times get hard and decisions have to be made, I want you to turn to God. Say 'God, I love you more than I love myself. I love you more than I love my spouse.' Repeat it to yourself and mean it."

"Mrs. Tillman, do you believe that every marriage can be saved?" Cydney asked.

"With all my heart. But for some people, it might be easier to let go. Every situation has to be dealt with on an individual basis. Some couples aren't willing to put forth the effort, and it has to be a joint effort. The woman, she can't do it alone, and a man can't either. When you took your vows, you joined *together* in holy matrimony. Until death do you part. Your vows are a serious promise to God, and we must do our best to honor them. If you can't, God knows your situation. He knows if you're responsible for destroying your marriage. My advice would be to fix it while you can. If your spouse isn't cooperating and you know that you've done all that you can do, just move aside. Don't afflict yourself with pain, but just move aside. Turn it over to Him, and I assure you that He will do His work."

Cydney and I sat quietly, as we'd definitely afflicted ourselves with pain. For whatever reason, there seemed to be a new light, and I was anxious to see what the future had in store for us. Almost an hour later, Mrs. Tillman wrapped up our session, and we thanked her again and left.

I was back on the job, and things were going pretty darn smoothly. Since we'd been in counseling, Cydney and I had our first disagreement. She wanted me to go to the doctor with her, but I couldn't because I'd already taken so much time off work. I wanted to make a good impression and show the sarg that I was serious about keeping my job. Eventually, Cydney said that she understood. We'd learned that disagreements were always going to take place. We had to work through them and never, ever go to bed angry with one another.

Compromising, I told Cydney that I'd take my lunch break to check in on her at the doctor's office. When I pulled into the parking lot, there were no spaces close by the entrance. I parked in another parking lot and got out of the car.

As I walked toward the entrance, I saw Cydney walk out. She was dressed in an off-white pants suit that perfectly fit her waistline. Her hair was full of teased curls, and the sight of her just brightened my rough day. I removed my police hat from my head and tucked it underneath my arm. As I unwrapped a stick of gum, I made my way to her. She saw me, and headed my way. Her eyes looked sad, and when I saw her wipe her eyes, I knew something was wrong. I walked faster toward her, and she seemed to walk at a slower pace. When I reached her, she slid her arms around my waist.

"What's the matter, baby?" I asked.

"Are you listening good?" she whispered in my ear.

I nodded. "Yes."

"We're going to have a baby!" she screamed and slammed her tiny handheld purse against my back. I wanted to scream too, but my enthusiasm didn't compare to Cydney's.

"Calm down," I said. "Give me a kiss and tell me what the doctor said."

She trembled as she spoke. "He said . . . we're going to have a baby!" she shouted again and did the cabbage patch.

I laughed and smiled. "A baby, huh? All my hard work has finally paid off."

"Our hard work," she said, placing her arms on my shoulders. We kissed, and I hugged her tightly. I wanted to cry because things had turned out so sweet for us. I'm glad that I never gave up on Cydney, and that she never gave up on me.

"How much more time do you have for lunch?" I asked her.

"Not much. I gotta get back to the office, and I'm already late."

"Well, we can celebrate later, okay? As soon as I get off work, I'll be home and I'll bring you some ice cream."

Cydney kissed me again, and I walked her to her car. Once inside, she blew me a kiss and drove off. I felt like a new man as I made my way to my police car and drove off. I'd soon have a son or a daughter that was really and truly mine. In my mind, I visualized all sorts of things, from the delivery to bringing the baby home. I'd even thought about what college I wanted my child to go to.

As I was in deep thought, I pulled over at a nearby McDonald's to get something to eat. I went through the drive-through and then parked my police vehicle. As soon as I turned off the engine to eat my food, I heard a horn blow. I looked over to my right, and saw one gorgeous, brown-skinned tender beside me. She resembled Lauryn Hill, and with her glossy lips, she mouthed for me to lower my window.

"Officer, I'm having some trouble with my rear right tire. I was wondering if you could assist me with it."

"You don't have Triple A, or no other type of vehicle insurance to assist you?"

"No, I don't. If I did, I wouldn't have asked." She spoke softly yet seductively.

I hesitated, but exited my car. She got out of hers too, and we walked around to the right side of her vehicle. I looked down at the tire, but not before glancing at her smooth legs that showed because of the thigh-high skirt she wore. I bent down and rubbed the tire. I felt and saw a nail.

"It looks like you have a nail in there. Do you have a spare tire in the trunk?"

She walked around me and switched her hips from side to side. I glanced at her ass and turned my head. She opened the trunk and confirmed that a spare was in there.

I stood up and removed the spare, tiny jack and 4-way from her trunk. I laid everything on the ground, and she watched as I got busy changing her tire. Once I was finished, my hands were black, and sweat dripped from my forehead.

"Thank you so much," she said. "Is there any way that I can repay you? Whatever you want, it's yours."

I stepped to the back of her car and put the damaged tire in the trunk. I then reached for a towel in the trunk and wiped my hands on it. After putting everything else in the trunk, I closed it.

"You didn't answer my question," she said, being persistent. "Can you talk?"

I looked up and then looked down and closed my eyes. "I love you, God," I mumbled quietly. "I love my wife, but I love You more than her and more than I love myself."

I opened my eyes. "Thanking me is more than enough. If you'd like, you can always call the police station and throw in a good word for me. My name is Isaac Conley."

"Officer Conley, my name is Sabrina. I think you're awfully sexy, and I wouldn't mind kicking it with you sometimes."

"Sorry, but I'm married," I said. She gave me the "so what" look that I'd seen many times before.

"Married? Ummm, that's a shame. I'm married too, but—"

"But I have to get back to work now. I hope that spare tire works out for you. Have a nice day."

I went inside McDonald's to wash my hands, and then headed back to my police car. As soon as I drove off, I looked across the street. I could've sworn that I saw Cydney in another car. When the woman in the car winked at me, I turned on my sirens and quickly turned around. I drove up next to the car and put my car in park. Sure enough, it was Cydney.

I lowered my window and she lowered hers. "You set that up, didn't you?" I said.

"What are you talking about?" She smiled.

"I'm talking about the woman whose tire I changed at McDonald's."

"What woman?"

"Cyd, don't lie to me." I smiled. "Remember what Mrs. Tillman—"

"Okay, so I couldn't resist. I saw that she was having trouble with her tire, and I directed her to you. I paid her to flirt with you, so don't flatter yourself thinking you're that handsome. She gave me thumbs up, and told me you passed the test. So, sorry for the trouble, but you know I had to see for myself how you'd conduct yourself under those circumstances."

"First of all, you were wrong for that, and secondly, I am as fine as they come, baby, and I always feel flattered. Next time, though, find a woman with a little more curves in her hips, darker skin, thicker thighs, and more ass. You know I gotta have more ass than that. Then I might not be able to resist."

Cydney rolled her eyes. "You're not mad at me, are you?"

"No, because I have nothing to hide. I wish you'd trust me, though. We've got to trust each other, okay?"

She nodded, and I looked at the car she drove.

"Whose car are you driving? I know damn well it's not yours."

"No, it's not. And trust me when I say that it's not a man's car either. It's Carol's car. She let me use it."

"Uh-huh," I said, joking. "Sounds like some bullshit to me."

She laughed, and my radio came on. Someone reported a car accident and an intense argument only a few blocks away.

"I gotta go," I said, blowing her a kiss. "I'll see you later on this evening."

"Be careful," Cydney said.

I turned on my sirens and sped off. As I made my way to the scene of the accident, there were so many people outside and on the street. In particular, there were some females outside with major skin showing. The one who rushed up to my vehicle, she insisted that the Asian man in the car purposely hit her.

"He just slammed right into me, officer," she yelled as I got out of my car.

"Calm down and tell me what happened."

"My cousin can tell you too. He called us names and—"

I looked at the Asian man standing by his BMW with his arms folded. He looked disgusted.

"Where's your cousin?"

"Over there." She pointed to her. "Andrea, come here!" she yelled.

Andrea slowly made her way across the street and displayed a tiny gap between her legs. She wore a pair of blue jean shorts that met up with the cheeks of her ass. Her striped half shirt showed her flat midriff and the belly ring clipped to her navel. No doubt, the temptation was there. I couldn't do anything about it, but I knew I had to work hard at focusing on what was important: my child, my wife and our marriage. When Andrea smiled at me, all I could do was smile back. No doubt, some women were always going to be out for one thing, and some out for another. I just had to make sure I was man enough to deal with any setbacks in my marriage that could occur when dealing with another woman. I wasn't up to having anymore setbacks, and that decision in itself was man enough for me. For a bit more confidence, I looked up then looked down and closed my eyes. I repeated the words Mrs. Tillman had taught me and opened my eyes. I then laughed and smiled at the thought of, like so many couples, how much Cydney and I deserved each other. After that thought, I got back to work.

"All right, ladies. From the beginning, tell me what happened," I said. I pulled my notepad from my pocket and started to take notes.